THE BIG MELT

NED TILLMAN

SOUTH BRANCH PRESS

The Big Melt

Copyright ©2018 Ned Tillman

ISBN 978-1-7324841-0-8 (print)

ISBN 978-1-7324841-0-8 (eBook)

South Branch Press, Columbia, MD

Publisher's Cataloging-In-Publication Data (Prepared by The Donohue Group, Inc.)

Names: Tillman, Ned.

Title: The big melt / Ned Tillman.

Description: Columbia, MD : South Branch Press, [2018] | Interest age level: 013-018. | Summary: "Marley and Brianne woke up on the day after their high school graduation to find their lives turned upside down as a series of climate catastrophes descended on their town. As basic living conditions become more affected, Marley and Brianne team up with scientists and political leaders to understand and address the changes in their environment. They find their voices and their purpose for living while struggling to save their family and friends, their town, and civilization as we know it."--Provided by publisher.

Identifiers: ISBN 9781732484108 | ISBN 9781732484115 (ebook)

Subjects: LCSH: Climatic changes--Juvenile fiction. | High school gradu-ates--Juvenile fiction. | Environmental degradation--Juvenile fiction. | Natural disasters--Juvenile fiction. | Speculative fiction, American. | CYAC: Climatic changes--Fiction. | High school graduates--Fiction. | Environmental degrada-tion--Fiction. | Natural disasters--Fiction.

Classification: LCC PZ7.1.T5467 Bi 2018 (print) | LCC PZ7.1.T5467 (ebook) | DDC [Fic]--dc23

Book design by StoriesToTellBooks.com

THE BIG MELT

ACKNOWLEDGMENTS

The manuscript improved from the author's discussions with Jodi Duff's biology class at Long Reach High School, Rita Allan's environmental science class at Howard High School, and Stephanie Doodigian's biology and environmental classes at Reservoir High School.

I would like to thank the following for reviewing the book: Tim Lattimer, Bob Bell, Tom Keech, Becky Reese, Jo McLaughlin, Kathleen Duble, Susan Branting, Ken Crandall, Gavin Kohn, Catherine Strawley, Mark Southerland, Elsa Barnes, Sophie Bell, Jill Lee, Maggie Smith, Sam McGuire, Tracey Manning, Elaine Pardoe, Nat Williams, James Borrelli, Debby Stathes, and Stefan Apse. I would like to thank my editors, Ruth Katcher and Jenny Margotta, for their insights and for editing the manuscript. I would also like to thank Nan and Biff Barnes of Stories To Tell for their assistance in publishing this book.

I would like to thank Kathy Tillman, Anna Roth, and Leigh Tillman for continuous feedback in the formulation of the concept of the story through editing of the final manuscript. Kathy's years as a high school teacher and mentor to numerous young adults was invaluable in this process.

I would like to thank the following people for their ongoing support of all of my books: Ellen Giles, Ann Strozyk, Julie Dunlop, Lisa Wingate, Caleb Gould, Wanda MacLachlan, Tim Singleton, Bob Marietta, Laura O'Donnell, Jeff Agnor, Anne Curry, Lynn Coleman, Audrey Suhr, Marianne Pettis, Marianne Alexander, and Marsha and Rod Lemley.

PART ONE

THE CHANGES

CHAPTER ONE

THE LAST DAY OF SCHOOL

M arley slouched at his desk, eyes half shut, his whole body struggling to stay awake. It was his very last class, on his very last day of high school, and he was ready to get on with his life.

He smiled. In less than an hour the public school system would finally release him, and he would be free. His whole life lay ahead of him; he could do whatever he wanted. He would work with Ranger Max at the park again this summer and then off to college in the fall. No more petty rules and responsibilities, no more high school social pressures, and no more small-town prejudices.

Making the situation even worse on this late afternoon was the heat inside the classroom. It was unbearable—everyone was sweating. The electrical grid had failed again, so the AC was not working. Marley's teacher, Doc, kept wiping the sweat off his forehead with a handkerchief. But by this late in the day, it was drenched and did little good.

Marley pushed his bleached, unraveling dreadlocks back on his head and turned to look out the windows. Every living thing outside was seeking shelter from the sizzling rays of the sun. Marley watched as three large black buzzards landed on the split-rail fence. They hopped, side-stepping along the top-rail toward the shade of a large oak tree. As far as he could see, the skies and the fields were now empty of all living creatures. This historic warming trend was affecting everything. It felt to him like life on Earth was becoming unbearable just as he was getting ready to graduate.

The stifling heat slowed Marley's mind into a placid, dream-like state. He tried to imagine his future, seeing images of college life mixed with dystopian scenarios he had seen in movies. He then fell asleep, his body slumping forward onto his desk.

He felt his hands grip the top edge of the desk as if he were lying on a boogie board—he imagined floating in cool water at the beach. Next, he pictured himself at the controls of a plane, piloting the desk and the whole classroom somewhere off into the future. It was exciting—he had always wanted to fly, and now he was doing it. For a moment he felt that he just might be in control of his own destiny.

Marley imagined flying high above the busy little town of Sleepy Valley where he had lived his entire life. The town was just off the interstate, an easy on/easy off for the residents, but like most small towns in America, most travelers just passed it by.

He glanced out his plane window and surveyed the town. From his elevated vantage point, he saw Blue Lake over on the east side of town and the park to the north. He passed over the suburban west side of town, where he lived, and the Hilltop Observatory to the south.

Marley watched as little people drove their cars around in circles, shopped in the same old stores, commuted to the same offices, and walked to the same churches. He waved goodbye to all of that and eagerly steered his imaginary plane to places unknown.

When he looked out the side window of the cockpit, he noticed three large black buzzards—he wondered if they were the same ones he had seen earlier—flying in formation along with the plane. *That's weird. I never thought birds could fly this fast.* One of birds came up close to his window, and Marley could swear it winked at him. *Now I know I'm dreaming.*

The buzzards banked to the left and the plane automatically followed, leading him in a completely new direction. He had no idea where they were headed, but he didn't try to fight it. He realized he was no longer in control; he was just along for the ride.

A loud sneeze from the front of the room brought him back to reality. Marley opened his eyes, released his grip on the desk, leaned back in his chair, and tried to catch up on what Doc was saying. But it was so hot he was only able to listen half-heartedly. *The dream. What did it mean?* He had no idea. He wasn't sure dreams meant anything.

Marley's brain moved on to the upcoming weekend. Friday night was graduation, with a party to follow. Then on Saturday morning he had invited a group of old friends to skateboard around town with him. It would probably be their last gathering, since most of them would soon be off to jobs, college, and a world of cars.

On Saturday night the whole group would camp out at the park. It was one of the best places to hang out during the heat wave because of the cooling effect of the trees and the refreshing waters of the river.

His friend Brianne had agreed to drive her mom's old Jeep out to the park with food and camping supplies. She had invited her girlfriends to come along too. She wasn't really his girlfriend, but who knew? It promised to be a good time.

Marley's phone lit up. It was on his lap, so he bent over to read the message: "record high temperatures set all across the country." He shook his head and looked out the window. How hot can it get? It seemed like everything in town was drying up and blowing away.

A text came in from Colin, one of his skateboarding friends. "Hey, man, let's get out of here."

At the front of the room, Doc rambled on about the vicious

cycle of a changing climate. Marley, fighting sleep, yawned—a little too loudly—and thought, *Yeah, yeah, yeah, it's happening, and we need to do something about it. Everybody knows that already. When's the bell going to ring?*

"Mr. Jones!"

Marley jumped at the sound of his name. His phone fell to the floor, and several students in the room laughed.

Doc stared at Marley. His head was tilted down. His glasses had slid down on his sweaty nose, and he addressed Marley over the rims. "Mr. Jones, why is there so much apathy in your generation about the most significant threat to our civilization . . . and to your future?"

Marley looked down at his desk and tried to collect his thoughts. "Ahhhhh . . . I don't know . . . I guess it just doesn't seem like there's anything we can do . . . It's way too big a problem for any of us to fix." He paused a minute, looking around the room to see if anyone else cared about this topic any more than he did. "It's also a problem that's way off in the future, so it's easy to ignore," he continued. He noted that everyone in the class seemed numbed by the heat, the topic, and the late afternoon discussion.

"That is the great conundrum of your generation. In order to prevent human suffering in the future, in *your* future, you have to act now. So let me ask the question . . . What are *you* going to do to slow down the warming?" Doc stopped speaking, leaving the question hanging in the hot afternoon air. Letting it soak into any mind in the class that was still open this late in the day. He just stood there, looking from one person to the next.

Moments later, the bell rang, and all the students started cheering. They jumped up out of their sweaty seats, high-fived each other with sweaty hands, and headed for the door.

Marley was the last to leave, as always, still contemplating Doc's question. *What am I going to do about it?*

Doc waited for him, and when they shook hands, Doc said, "Your generation is facing a big challenge. It'll take people like you to fix it. Good luck."

As he left the classroom, Marley said, "Thanks a lot," not sure if he was thanking Doc for being a good teacher or for dumping the weight of the world on him on the last day of school. The comment was probably a little of both. As Marley walked down the hall, Doc's words settled on his shoulders with a profound sense of responsibility. *What did Doc mean by "people like me?"*

Just then, Brianne came bouncing up to him and waved her hands in front of his face. "Hey, graduate, you look like you're in a daze. What's up?"

"I've just got to wake up. Doc lectured right up to the bell."

"Sounds like Doc. You still up for the campout?"

"Sure. The guys are psyched."

"Great. The girls are too. Let's go load your stuff into Mom's Jeep."

"You have time?"

"Yeah. I've got all the time in the world," she said with a big smile.

Marley had to laugh at her excitement. It was infectious. That's what he liked about her; she was always fun to be with.

They waved to their friends and took off to get the Jeep.

CHAPTER TWO

A RIVER OF OIL

On Saturday morning following graduation, Marley, his skateboard in hand, was the first to leave the house. He was excited. He had graduated, and now he was going to spend the whole day exploring the town with his friends. He barely heard his mother ask, "Will I see you for lunch?" He left the question floating in the air as the door slammed shut behind him.

As he took his first steps across the porch, an overwhelming blast of hot air hit him in his face. It felt like a furnace with the doors wide open or a dragon challenging him to come outside and be scorched by its fiery breath. But the wall of heat didn't stop Marley. In fact he felt a surge of freedom vibrating through his body. He knew the sweat on his forehead would cool and refresh his body as soon as he got moving on his board.

How fast can I make it downtown today? he wondered. He knew he was rusty, but even now, at 18, he welcomed the challenge of trying to beat his old record. He checked the time on his phone as he started down the steps.

* * *

As Marley stepped out from under the front porch roof, something quite hot hit his face—on both cheeks. "Ouch, what's that?" As he reached up to touch his face with his hands, he also stepped in a small puddle of black goo, and his foot slipped out from under him. "Whoa," he yelled as he struggled to get his balance. It was a good thing he was short and coordinated.

Marley gingerly made his way down the stairs to the concrete sidewalk leading to the street. The rest of the steps were clear, but his right shoe left black footprints all the way to the street. *What's with the oil?*

Taken aback at these changes right in his front yard, Marley stopped a moment and glanced back at the roof of his house. Oil dripped from the black asphalt shingles on the southeast-facing roof. Looking around, he now saw oil dripping off every roof in his neighborhood. *What's with the shingles? How can they be melting? It's sure hot, but can it be that hot? I doubt it. It's kind of . . . unreal.*

After wiping the oil off his face, Marley tried cleaning the black goo from his hands by drying them on his faded, Led Zeppelin T-shirt. He then smoothed back his unruly hair, realizing too late that he did this with oil-scented hands. *Great, now I smell like oil and sweat.*

When Marley reached the end of the sidewalk, he dropped his board on the street like he had done a thousand times before. He was glad to be away from the oil dripping from the roof. He then stepped up onto the deck of his board and leaned forward to launch himself on his way downtown.

But the board didn't move. It was as if it had a mind of its own. Losing his balance for the second time in a matter of minutes, he screamed again. He didn't fall, but he did wobble. He flailed his arms, trying to find his center of gravity. He leaned and twisted, and with great effort the board started to move.

Pushing off with his right foot, he nearly lost his black hightop as the sole stuck to sticky asphalt. It felt like he was engaged in a tug of war with the street as if the street was intentionally trying to slow him down. *What's going on?*

Looking around, he noticed that the black asphalt road had begun to melt; it was covered with black bubbles. He had read in one of his newsfeeds how roads had melted in India and

Australia last year. *But this isn't India or the outback of Australia! This is Sleepy Valley.* Or at least, it *was.* He wasn't quite so sure anymore.

As Marley wavered back and forth, trying to balance on his board, he saw—or thought he saw—the street in front of his house moving ever so slowly downhill. It appeared to be flowing like water after a storm, except much, much slower—more like mud or maybe even lava. At first he wondered if he was hallucinating.

This can't be happening. He felt like he was transitioning into a new and unpredictable world. A world much more surreal and challenging than anything he had pictured in his daydreaming back in school. He struggled to make sense of it all.

Marley stood there dazed for a few minutes. *I was hoping to get on with my life now that I've graduated. But the extreme heat and the melting oil might just change all that.*

With sweat oozing from all his pores, Marley scanned the tree-lined streets to see who else might be up and outside. Where were his friends? He wanted to find someone to talk with about what was happening. Someone to share his concerns with, someone who could help answer the questions bouncing around inside his head.

Surprisingly, he hardly saw a soul on the streets, on the sidewalks, or even in their yards. He felt so alone. He did see Mr. Gitt trying to get to his car, which was parked on the street. The older man kept slipping and falling on the oil-covered road. He eventually gave up and crawled back to his house. There were also two cars that had evidently slid off the road earlier that morning. One was in a ditch, and the other had collided with a tree. It was not a day to be driving or walking. *I wonder how far I'll make it on my board.*

Marley took off, moving very slowly down the hill. Surprisingly, it proved to be a decent way to get around, and the board was high enough to keep his shoes from getting totally coated in oil. He kept going, hoping to meet up with his friends. Maybe even Doc, who lived in the neighborhood, would be up, or Brianne, who lived downtown. He wanted someone to explain to him what was happening.

Marley's phone dinged. He looked at it: a text from Colin, one of his skater friends who had agreed to meet up with him this morning. "Hey, dude. Can't make it this morning. Too hot to go outside. Am tied up in video game with grant. Catch ya later. Tonight."

Well, that's too bad. Two of the guys already checking out. But he understood. It was too hot, and the oil would probably mess up their boards. *I bet nobody will show.* But he wasn't about to give up. He wanted to know how the asphalt could be melting and what else might be happening in his town.

Usually, Marley headed downtown as fast as he could, weaving in and out around people, pigeons, and cars. Sometimes, he'd let loose with a long, primal call to warn innocent bystanders that he was coming. But today, he wasn't setting any speed records or scaring people on the streets—there were no people, pigeons, or cars on the streets to scare. Sweat dripped down his brow. He was thinking about his board. The oil might degrade the bearings in his wheels and destroy his grip tape, but he decided he wasn't going to let the oil stop him. He set his mind to relearning his sport. He needed to be mobile, and skating looked like the best option. These new oily conditions presented just another set of hurdles he would have to overcome.

CHAPTER THREE

THE KUDZU INVASION

Doc lived alone in a small house a few blocks down the hill from Marley. He was a small man with wire-rim glasses and usually sported a few days' growth of hair on his face. Doc hadn't taken the time to get to know his neighbors, and that seemed to be fine with them. The neighbors just accepted the fact that he was a bit eccentric and liked to keep to himself.

Marley, however, did stop by occasionally, ever since he had signed up for one of Doc's classes the previous fall. They got along well because Marley was curious and full of questions, and Doc always took the time to answer questions from one of his students.

One of Doc's habits his neighbors really didn't like was that he never mowed his lawn; he seemed to be happy just letting nature take over. Marley offered to mow the grass once, but Doc just shrugged the offer away with the question, "Why?" Marley hadn't known how to respond to that. He came to realize this was consistent with Doc's philosophy of reducing his use of gasoline because of the greenhouse gases it produced. Doc was a man of strong principles. As a result, Doc's yard looked like a jungle.

Then a few months ago, an extensive network of kudzu vines with leaves the size of baseball mitts discovered his unattended lawn and invaded it. Tentacles of green kudzu hungrily reached up and grasped the red bricks in a strategic effort to scale the walls and reach Doc's roof. It seemed to Marley that the long, green vines had come to support Doc's self-imposed exile and were hell-bent on completely covering the house.

"Kudzu's an Asian vine that's been moving north—another not-too-subtle manifestation of the warming climate that everyone ignores," Doc told Marley.

In fact, Marley had noticed that, over the last few months, kudzu, with its big leaves and aggressive, climbing stems, had taken over vast expanses of the town. Marley had watched the citizens of Sleepy Valley try to manage this invasion by cutting their lawns daily—a costly, polluting, and time-consuming adaptation. But on vacant lots, unattended yards, and open spaces, the vines aggressively invaded their town, street by street and yard by yard.

The townsfolk assumed it was *someone's* job to fight the kudzu. But the town did nothing to stop it, because fighting kudzu wasn't in anyone's job description. The council was not about to add additional staff; most of the council members thought that the town was too big already.

They told the kudzu-removal advocates, "Just wait and see what happens. There's no reason to over-react to a new plant in town. Kudzu is just part of the natural world. There's nothing to worry about." But by not taking action early on, when action would have been easier, this unfortunate, short-sighted decision doomed the town to a future living with kudzu.

The creeping kudzu camouflage did reinforce everyone's opinion that Doc lived a monk-like existence. Only Marley knew that every night when Doc returned home from school, he went straight inside his house, locked his door, and sat down to focus on his writing, his first and only love.

No one in town had ever been inside Doc's house except Marley. Marley realized this was probably a good thing since disturbing, dystopian drawings of future worlds—which might upset others—covered Doc's walls. The images accurately reflected Doc's views of the future, and these pictures had inspired his science-fiction writing.

On the day that the streets started to melt, Doc walked along the only path left open in his waist-high, kudzu-covered lawn. The track looked more like a dent, a small cleavage in the lush green, rolling surf of his yard. Marley spied him from the street as Doc flowed toward the mailbox, looking like an old sea captain wading through the marshes at the edge of a vast ocean.

Marley waved and shouted as he slowly slid to a stop by the fence in front of the house. "Doc, your roof, is it melting?"

Doc looked startled by the inquiry and froze in his tracks. "Wh-what?" he stuttered and then turned to look where Marley was pointing.

All Marley and Doc could see at first were broad kudzu leaves. But when they looked closer to the house, they noticed leaves splattered with oil. "I guess it is," replied Doc. He looked confused, probably due to the abrupt interruption and to the very strange occurrence of melting shingles. "Now that's something I hadn't expected. How come I never thought of melting asphalt in my books?"

"The roads are melting too, Doc. There's so much oil that the streets are flowing." Marley took a few minutes to relay what he had seen in the neighborhood. As he described the oily streets, a green vine stretched up and entangled Doc's long, graying locks. Doc had been standing in one place for too long and had attracted the attention of the kudzu. His yard was a dangerous place to stand still.

Doc pulled the vine off, and Marley watched as the puzzled look on Doc's face became one of real concern. "These changes you describe may be significant, Marley. They are unprecedented. You need to write down all the crazy things you see. I wonder if we've reached a tipping point of some sort? This could be the start of the End Times."

Marley shook his head. He wasn't sure he'd heard correctly. "What're you talking about, Doc? The End Times sound scary. The End Times of what?"

Doc continued, slowly and thoughtfully. "I always wondered how it would happen—a deadly virus, maybe a flood or famine, the eruption of a super volcano, a close encounter with a meteorite, or even an alien invasion. I guess I was wrong; it has nothing to do with random natural events or extraterrestrials. It's much sadder than that. It looks like it's going to be The Big Melt, a totally manmade collapse. We're doing ourselves in . . . very, very slowly. I've always wondered when our actions would catch up with us."

Marley was pacing back and forth along the fence. "Are you saying that we caused all this melting?"

"Of course we did. We've been emitting greenhouse gases for decades."

Marley shook his head. "Yeah, I guess that's true. This year's hotter than last, which was hotter than the year before. But I've always just felt like a spectator watching the extreme events happen elsewhere. It never seemed real to me. Now all of a sudden it's very real, right here in Sleepy Valley, and it's messing up our lives."

"It's real alright," Doc replied. "Ice caps are melting. Forests are drying out and catching fire. We're seeing larger storms. We call the big flooding events 'extreme weather' and love watching it all play out on our newsfeeds in real time. But we rarely talk about the steps we need to take—*now*—to prevent these events from happening again and again, all over the Earth."

"So why don't we stop it?"

Doc snorted. "Good question. Unfortunately, most of us focus on what we think are more pressing, short-term needs and ignore all the warnings. We're like a frog in a pot of water warming up on the stove that doesn't move until it's too late."

"Is it too late?"

Doc paused for a minute, stroking his chin. "In this case, it may be. Especially if we *have* passed a tipping point. Then we would be in uncharted territory. We can probably slow down the warming so it reduces the suffering. We might also be able to stop it. But it will have to become one of our top priorities—like the space program was in the 1960s.

"You youngsters do have options. Do nothing and watch our civilization self-destruct, or take steps now to slow down the warming. I'm afraid we're launching you and your generation into a future of change, and you'll never be coming back to the way things were. We all have to realize that *summer's coming,* with all of its heat waves, hurricanes, droughts, and fires."

Marley mumbled something about feeling powerless; after all, he was only one person. But this sort of whining attitude just caused Doc's attention to drift back to the mailbox. "Sorry, Marley, can't talk anymore right now. I've got to check the mail. I'm expecting a royalty payment from my books. As critical as these changing conditions may be, I guess I'm just like everyone else. I have several pressing, short-term matters to deal with, like paying my overdue mortgage." He turned, slowly fighting his way through the maze of vines to the road.

Marley was shocked. He tried to get Doc's full attention again, but it was too late. Doc was back in his own private world. *How can people just turn off their attention to such important matters?* He shouted as Doc walked away, "But, Doc, what can I do?"

Doc stopped and turned back around. "Collect data. Discover all that's happening around town. Find out as much as you can over the next day or two, and then let's decide what you and I and maybe even the whole town should do. We have to know more before we can respond effectively." He waved and resumed his trip to the mailbox.

"Thanks. I will." Marley appreciated the perspective Doc had given him. Yes, he would be Doc's eyes and ears, finding out the full extent of what was happening. Then they could assess what to do next. It sounded like a good plan.

As he was preparing to leave, Marley heard Doc whistle for his dog, Dante. There was no answer. But this was no surprise because Doc had not seen his hound for months, ever since the kudzu took over the yard. This was unfortunate; Dante had always been more than just a close companion to Doc. He had served as his "muse." It was a severe, double loss to Doc, and he was still struggling with how to deal with life without Dante.

Marley watched as Doc turned toward the house and made his way back along the narrowing path. Marley heard him mutter, "It's hard to believe it's happening so fast. What's next?"

CHAPTER FOUR

THE SUPER THERMAL

He waved goodbye to Doc, but Doc wasn't looking; he was totally engaged by the immediate challenge of fighting his way through the kudzu thicket back to the house. So Marley just stood there on the street, feeling alone, totally perplexed, and contemplating what Doc had said. He wasn't quite sure what it meant or what to do with the information Doc had given him, but it gave him a lot to think about. The talk about the End Times shook him up quite a bit. *If this is the beginning of the end, that's a big deal.* But he recalled Doc had told him to collect data, so he decided to explore the entire town. Of course there must be other things happening. He would survey the town and then go back to Doc to see what his teacher recommended next.

Marley also wasn't sure how to react to what he had already seen. It certainly looked like there was going to be a big change in his life. It was all a bit shocking, to say the least. Yet he was far from feeling hysterical. *Should I be more alarmed?*

He did have a growing desire down deep in his gut to know everything that was happening. Maybe it was just a distraction. But this desire to explore and understand what was occurring in his valley helped him calm his fears about what might be coming next. He also realized that the more he knew, the better he could adapt to any future changes.

Marley wanted to find one of his friends to explore the town with him, to talk about the changes, and to discuss Doc's prophecy. He had received two more texts while talking to Doc, and he had been right—none of the guys were coming out to join him today. He sent a text back to Colin: "have you looked outside?"

"I know, i know." Colin replied. "Dad crashed the car this morning. He's really scared of what might happen next. He's locked the front door and even has his guns out and loaded. He's teaching me how to use them. It's all a bit scary."

What? That certainly sounds like an over-the-top response. But maybe that's what we all should be doing – protecting our homes and families.

Marley stepped back onto his board and continued his snail's-pace trip down the hill. He found he made better time on the edges of the road where the asphalt was thinner.

Despite the fear and concern about the End Times, Marley found that his attention quickly returned to the immediate challenge of riding on the oily streets. It caused him to forget the bigger issue and focus all his efforts on not falling off his board into the oil. So far he had managed to keep his clothes clean, but all it would take would be one fall. He soon realized that, just like everyone else, his attention was refocused back on the near-term demands of life.

After a while Marley's legs started to cramp up. *Gosh, this is tough. But at least I haven't crashed into a tree yet. I have more control than the cars do.*

He was concerned for his board, though. He hoped all this oil wouldn't damage it too severely. After all, every dent, every mark, every gash spurred a proud memory for him. Much like an application for a job, the board boasted a record of his accomplishments. The board represented who he was . . . or at least who he thought he was up to this point. But recently, he had started to think about his future. He would probably have to buy a used car and get a part-time job. He wondered if the board would continue to be a part of his life.

On the way to town, Marley experimented with how to control his board, leaning way to the right and then to the left. He felt that his usual moves no longer worked well, so he had to recalibrate every motion. Making matters worse was the varying viscosity of the oil, depending on whether he was in the sun or shade. Sometimes it was slippery, and other times it was sticky. He was excited about these new challenges. They gave him something he could get better at. He was starting to get a real feel for riding in these new conditions.

The only benefit he could see to skateboarding on a flowing mass of oil was the stability of the board; the oil held the wheels like sticky fingers keeping the board from flipping over. This was a big help when doing power slides around corners, but the stickiness prevented him from jumping or doing his normal tricks. That was disappointing; he loved to jump and spin in midair. But today he felt a heaviness settling in his legs.

Once Marley re-established a sense of comfort on the board, his thoughts came back to the bigger challenge of the day: the melting oil. He had plenty of time to think while moving along at a glacial pace.

He shouted to the trees, "What's happening?" His voice disappeared into the green canopy stretching over the road. Silence. There were no people or even any birds to hear or respond to the question. He was alone.

As he left the green suburbs and approached the downtown, Marley noticed that the river of oil was deepening on the streets. The beautiful, old, downtown square, lined with 19th-century brick and wood buildings, was now a sea of black oil. A young man who owned the shoe store was the only person out on the sidewalks. He was using a snow shovel to push the oil into the streets and down the storm drains, making his shop look open and a little more welcoming. He was a lonely figure among the bricks and mortar. As Marley watched, the man stopped shoveling long enough to glance up and down the barren streets as if desperately searching for customers.

The heat radiating off the old brick and newer concrete buildings made the downtown much hotter than the tree-shaded suburbs. As a result, the melting was even more severe. As the sun rose higher, more and more melting occurred on the hot roofs, and oil continued to drip. Marley saw what appeared to be black icicles of tar and oil hanging from rain gutters on the asphalt-covered rooftops. They looked like stalactites. Many of the black stalactites had already reached from the overflowing gutters to the ground. It looked as if the buildings, as well as the earth, were bleeding black blood.

"It feels like a war zone," Marley mumbled as he scanned the streets. All the buildings had vertical bars around them as if to keep the residents in or burglars out. Marley smiled, feeling lucky he was outside and not trapped behind bars.

The town was so quiet that Marley found it unsettling. No other adults or teenagers had come out of their homes. Marley had severe misgivings about what was happening. He passed storefront after storefront. No one was inside the stores. The only other sign of life he could see was the two elderly Hall sisters baking scones in their tea room. Bertha and Gertrude Hall lived above their store, so they didn't have to leave their home, except to shop. He doubted anyone would be visiting them today.

Marley checked the time. *It took forever to get here. The heat's going to affect everything I do from here on out. I can't imagine what life will be like if the temperatures get hotter and hotter.*

* * *

"Hellooooo?" Marley called as he slalomed his way to a stop in front of Brianne's white townhouse, which was at the bottom of the hill. She was standing on her porch, looking bewildered, apparently trying to find a way through the dripping oil that blocked her exit. He watched from the street as Brianne grabbed a red umbrella and stepped through the black curtain of oil. She made it safely, left the umbrella for her mom, and then slid her way to the curb.

Looking up, she smiled and said, "It's like sliding through mud after the river floods, except it smells a lot worse." Marley could tell she was attempting to make light of their circumstances, but she clearly looked concerned about what was going on. Her footing appeared a little uncertain as she tried to keep her balance on the slick oil.

"Watch out, Brianne. It's tricky."

She looked up at him with a smirk. "Can't be that bad. Looks like you made it down the hill on that old piece of plywood without falling." Marley chuckled. He was used to her poking fun at him and his skateboard. "What's with the tough-guy look?" she added. "You should see yourself. You've got black smudge marks below both eyes. I always took you for a nice guy."

"Must be the oil. I tried to wipe it off when it dripped off our porch roof and hit my cheeks. You like this new look? I could start doing it all the time."

Now it was Brianne's turn to laugh. "No, just stay the way you are."

Brianne, her brother, and mother lived in a row house built on a floodplain. It had repeatedly suffered from storms in the past. The current dry spell had been a blessing for her neighborhood because there had been less flooding, less repair costs, and fewer headaches with insurance claims. But now they were being flooded with oil, which was sure to produce a whole new set of problems.

Brianne wasn't a skateboarder—she biked or roller bladed everywhere. But Marley liked her anyway because she loved getting outside and exploring as much as he did. She always had great ideas for crazy weekend adventures. Marley was excited that the oil hadn't stopped her from getting out. She would be the best partner for exploring the town.

As she pulled back her wild, black hair with a colorful headband, she gave him a quizzical look. "I can't believe the asphalt's melting. Is it this bad in your neighborhood?"

"Not quite this bad, but the whole town's melting," Marley replied. "It's dangerous. No one's on the streets."

"Everyone must be scared to go outside. My mom sure is. She's mad at me for leaving the house. What do you make of the melting?"

"It's hard to explain, but it's real. Something really big is happening. Doc says it might be the end of life as we know it!"

"What? Doc said that? That sounds pretty extreme, even for Doc. What do you think he meant?"

"I don't know, but Doc suggested we get a better handle on everything that's happening, so we can figure out what to do next. Let's go find out what else is going on around here." Marley waited while Brianne grabbed her bike. It sounded just like another adventure for the two of them. It was what they did when they had free time together.

Brianne jumped on her bike and tried pedaling in the thickening oil that now covered all the low-lying areas near the streets, but the bike slid all over the road. She tried to stay on the driest parts, but that didn't help much. She just wasn't able to master the physics of riding in thick oil.

Marley noticed that her wheels sent a spray of oil out behind the bike, and drops quickly dotted her long, dark legs and shoes. There was also a Milky Way of oil splatters running up the back of her shorts and her yellow shirt. He smiled. As usual she was game to try anything and wasn't about to let the heat and the melting oil slow her down.

Marley realized that the oil in the streets had deepened to the point that the deck of his board was floating, and he no longer had any traction. "Let's just walk," he suggested. "I think we can keep to the higher ground and still make it down to the river." They left the bike and the board in her garage and set off on foot.

By this time the oil had overflowed the roadbed and filled the ditches on both sides. It carried away everything in its path, anything left outside by the people of the town. Beer bottles, soda cans, Styrofoam, plastic bags, and paper flowed downstream. The trash from Coca-Cola, McDonald's, and Pizza Hut products continued to advertise their brands in the aftermarket debris that floated on the oil.

The oil also picked up plastic toys, lawn furniture, bird's nests, diapers, and even a cardboard box of kittens. This random collection of human residue flowed into storm drains or directly into the local streams.

"I've got to see what happens to all this stuff when it hits the river," Marley said. "We might even get a chance to rescue those kittens if they get close to shore."

Brianne smiled, and Marley smiled back. He knew she liked his softer side and that he wasn't hesitant to show he cared about a wide range of things. Although he was considered kind of an outsider at school, he was the kind of guy who always wanted to set things right.

"Sure, let's do it," Brianne agreed. As they headed toward the river, she pointed out, "Hey, take a look at the oil flowing down into the fox and woodchuck holes."

Marley pictured the creatures of these underground worlds, huddled together, hiding in cavities with snags of roots hanging from ceilings, clusters of rocks decorating the walls, and dry twigs and old bones carpeting the floors. He imagined the oil flowing down into all the subterranean tunnels. It would fill up the side rooms and the abandoned chambers, chasing the inhabitants out the back doors. These refugees would then join mice, skunks, ants, snakes, earthworms, and beetles–all the underground species—in trying to find dry ground. The ones lucky enough to escape their homes would be ushered further downhill by the oil flowing on the surface. Some animals, like foxes, would be able to outrun the oncoming flood, at least for a while. Smaller ones might be lucky enough to hitch a ride on a floating branch, a dry leaf, or a Cocoa Puff box. There was plenty of trash to go around.

Marley realized that many of the animals would perish—entombed in oil for posterity. Much like the animals that had fallen into the La Brea Tar Pits thousands of years ago in what was now Los Angeles. Doc had described the animals that had been found there in one of their classes.

Brianne and Marley slid their way past buildings, oil-flooded parks, and escaping animals down to the river that ran through the center of town.

Brianne pointed and said, "Look at the river, it's running black with oil. It's overflowing its banks." They both stared at the once fast-flowing Sleepy Valley River, which had been full of aquatic grasses, turtles, insects, and fish. It was now a sluggish black highway, devoid of all life but full of trash.

They also noticed that in addition to many small items, the viscous oil that filled the river transported much larger items as well, everything that fell into its sticky grasp. It carried an assortment of livestock, a bright blue port-a-pot, and a vintage Volkswagen van—stuff collected from towns, farms, and businesses upstream.

"What a mess."

"Brianne, I'm trying to picture what happens downriver as the oil floods the next town—it's all built on the floodplain. They'll have to evacuate. Where will the people go? They'll be refugees looking for a place to live."

"I guess they'll come here, seeking our help," Brianne replied. "I hope we'll welcome them. I've got friends and cousins in that town. Mom was trying to reach them this morning, but she couldn't get through. She was fretting so much that I didn't know what to do. It's good to be out of the house. . . as long as I have one to go back to."

Marley and Brianne plopped down on a log by the river bank, exhausted from navigating the melting streets. "It's a total mess," Marley said as he examined the river, its banks, and his oil-coated shoes. "And a total disaster."

"This was my favorite swimming hole," Brianne whispered, gazing across the river. "Dad brought us here on weekends to fish and have cookouts, up until the month he died. He taught me how to swim right over there in the large pool below the dam. I still remember how scared I was the first time he threw me into the water. It was cold, and the water was flowing fast. But he always caught me before I washed away. I can't believe it's all covered with oil. It's hard to realize those days are gone forever."

Marley remembered this was the spot where he had organized a birthday party for her, with a campfire right here on the banks of the river. He had known this place was special to her, but he hadn't heard her talk about her father like this before. Just the fact that she was sharing these personal memories with him made him feel closer to her. He leaned over and tried to wipe some of the oil off her cheek. She smiled and rested her head on his shoulder.

Thinking back to her birthday party, he remembered that all their friends had come and they'd had a blast. It had been so hot that they had all ended up in the refreshing water. Brianne had looked great in her dripping-wet clothes. For him the party had been the highlight of their senior year. He knew Brianne appreciated that he'd planned it for her. She had given him a big hug at the end of the evening.

But that was weeks ago. Marley now stared at what had been a beautiful river. His mouth opened as if he were about to say something, but he had no words to describe what they were witnessing. The valley stank, oily splotches covered their clothes and skin, and the black, opaque river with its diverse cargo looked as if the stopper had been pulled out, and the entire town was flowing down the drain.

Marley sat there on the log, reflecting on how his first day after graduation was going. He couldn't get a handle on all of it. All morning he had been in a state of total disbelief. *This can't be happening.* But it was. It was real and he had to get used to it.

Sure, he had read about how the planet was warming, but he never thought something like this could happen, especially not in Sleepy Valley. He had always thought the problems and the impacts were happening somewhere else, to someone else. He always pictured coastal cities flooding and droughts across the Southwest, but not something so drastic that it would disrupt his life.

Marley fidgeted with a couple of sticks he had picked up and wondered if the melting was also occurring in other towns and cities around the country and the world. "Do you think the Mississippi and Susquehanna rivers, and maybe even the Nile and the Ganges are all flowing black with oil today?"

"Wow, I hadn't thought of that," said Brianne. "How about the oceans? What will they look like tomorrow or next week? What will happen to all the sea life? Can anything live in these polluted environments? There certainly can't be much life, if any, left in this river."

As he absorbed this, his words came very slowly. "I think this heat is going to change everything . . . our lives will never be the same." They sat in silence, taking it all in.

Brianne tried to wipe the oil off her fluorescent green sneakers with one of Marley's sticks—but to no avail. "I'm suffocating from this smell," she said. "My nose is itching. My eyes are tearing. I can even taste it on my tongue. Just think, everything in the river and along its banks is dying. I can't believe this is happening to us."

Marley continued to sit there, lost in his thoughts, just staring at the river for several minutes. He then heard someone say, "So what are you going to do about this?"

The question came across so clearly that Marley turned around to see who might have asked it. Seeing nobody, he turned to Brianne, "Did you just ask me a question?"

"No. Why?"

Marley was a little embarrassed. "I must have just thought it," he said, assuming it was some inner voice speaking to him. "Do you ever have conversations with yourself where you ask yourself a question?"

"Oh, sure. All the time. What's the question?"

"I was just asking myself what I'm going to do about all this melting," Marley said.

"That's a great question. I want to do something to clean it all up too. But there's so much oil. I don't know where to start."

"Yeah," Marley agreed, happy to be moving on with the discussion but still puzzled about the voice he'd heard. "I doubt there's anything we can do about such a gigantic mess," he continued. "It's not like the trash brigades you like to organize where a handful of us pick up bottles along the river on a Saturday morning. This is way too big a challenge for any small group to tackle."

"It would take the whole town coming together to clean up this amount of oil, and even if we could organize the whole town, I doubt we could even make a difference." Brianne's tone was thoughtful.

"It's a big challenge," Marley said. "Doc once told me it took fifty years to clean up this river after the unregulated stage of the industrial age polluted it with gasoline. Now, in just one day, it's much worse."

Marley could tell Brianne was getting angry; her voice dropped and sounded a bit threatening. "Whoever's in charge has got to get busy fixing this mess. And soon. What if it catches fire? The whole town would go up in a blaze."

"It may be too late," replied Marley. "It's so overwhelming. Maybe we'll just have to adapt to a new world—one with melting streets and many more things to contend with. Doc says it's bound to get worse—the warming isn't going to stop anytime soon."

"There must be things we can do," Brianne replied. "We need to find out what actions might be of some help."

After a moment or two, Marley said, "I also wonder what we did wrong that caused this to happen. It's always far cheaper to prevent things than try to fix or adapt to them later."

"Or maybe it was something we *didn't* do," Brianne offered. "We certainly didn't care enough to stop the warming."

They sat for a long time. The silence there along the slow-moving river of oil was deafening. But the voice in Marley's head kept asking the same question over and over again. "What are you going to do about it?"

✳ ✳ ✳

After a while Brianne pointed out to Marley that the wind was picking up speed. They watched as it carried dry leaves in a broad, circular path over the town. The swirling updraft of hot air lifted the leaves higher and higher, following an inverted funnel that extended as far as their eyes could see.

They were intrigued by the funnel; it helped them escape the fear and anger that had been simmering in their guts. Brianne had grown up interested in these types of natural occurrences. She had liked watching the weather channel ever since she was a kid. Then last summer Jim Quartz, the town's meteorologist, had offered her, on Doc's recommendation, an internship at the observatory. She jumped at the opportunity and had learned a lot. It had inspired her to take an even greater interest in the things happening all around her.

Now, as she looked at the skies, she said, "It appears that a gigantic thermal cell has developed right over the town. You normally can't see them, but this one's pretty clear."

They were both mesmerized as they watched leaves, insects, birds, and plastic bags climbing higher on the hot, rising air. The thermal cell sucked everything it could lift off the ground up into its belly. It was like an enormous vacuum cleaner or a slow-moving tornado.

"I've never seen such a big thermal. Look at all the leaves and trash—there must be a million leaves flying up to the clouds," Brianne said.

"I wonder when and where all that stuff will come crashing back down to Earth?" Marley replied.

"I don't know. I would guess after the sun sets. When the land cools down a bit, the thermal will weaken. I bet tomorrow morning we'll see a blanket of leaves on everything."

"I'm really getting concerned, Brianne, about what's happening, how extreme the weather events have become, and where it will all lead."

As they sat there next to each other on the log, the hot, dry wind blew its sultry breath directly into their faces as if it were trying to chase them indoors. It evaporated the moisture in their eyes, noses, and mouths. Even their ears dried out. Marley felt as if his whole body was shrinking as it dehydrated. Along with everything around him, he felt that he was drying up like a raisin. He watched Brianne intently, not wanting her to dry up and blow away. Today was the wildest adventure they had ever been on together, and he was glad she was with him. Her presence there on the log gave him a lot of comfort. He could not picture trying to get a handle on all these changes alone.

Brianne brought his attention back to the area where they were sitting. Pointing up into the tree canopy, she cried, "Marley . . . the trees. They're not just blowing in the wind. They're drying out, losing their leaves and their branches. These hot winds can't be good for them. As difficult as it may be to understand, I think they're dying from the extreme heat."

With a look of total disbelief, Marley responded, "That's pretty spooky. It's happening so fast. I was wondering why we were seeing so many dry leaves this early in the year."

"Yeah," Brianne said. "Watch out—the branches are starting to fall. We better get out of here fast. It's getting dangerous sitting next to all these dying trees."

They rushed back into town as fast as they could, trying to find cover from the hot winds. The winds howled and threw branches at them, chasing them away from the river. They could see each tree they passed changing right before their eyes. Marley was concerned for himself, Brianne, and everyone else in town. He realized that houses, businesses, cars, and people would suffer a lot of damage from the high winds and falling trees.

When they got back to town, they took shelter in the Tea Room, the only place that was open. Brianne was shaking; they were both totally undone by the turmoil and the fury of the wind. "Marley, what's happening to us, to our town? I'm scared to go back outside."

"I don't know, but I'm starting to feel scared too. This isn't the way I'd envisioned the future."

"First the heat and the oil . . . and now the wind and the trees," Brianne replied. "What else could happen?"

"I don't know, but I'm worried what might be going on at my cousins' farm. They've got all those animals and buildings. That's a lot to protect in this extreme weather."

"Why don't you call Ranger Max at the park to see what he knows?" Brianne suggested.

"Good idea. Better yet, you know Jim Quartz up at the observatory. If anyone has the answers, it should be him. He's the weather expert. We need to tell them both about the changes we're seeing. They should know what's causing the chaos."

Marley tried calling on his cell, and Brianne sent texts and emails. There was no response from either of their mentors. When Brianne looked at Marley, he could sense she was feeling desperate.

"That's really strange," she said. "They both always have their phones on them. They should be answering."

They tried again and again but to no avail. A feeling of isolation and tragedy settled over them. They hugged each other, more out of fear than anything else. Some strange force was playing with their lives. They wondered what else might be happening to their town and their friends. They kept asking themselves, "Why aren't Max and Jim answering?"

CHAPTER FIVE

THE GREATER SAPPHIRE BEETLE

C haos crept into the Sleepy Valley park on Friday night while Marley and Brianne and many others were celebrating graduation, so no one was available to witness what happened, except for the animals and Max Bunyan, the park ranger. He witnessed it all—and Max barely lived to tell the tale.

Max was the quintessential park ranger. He treated the forest as a grand, green cathedral, a cathedral full of life. To him the park was a very special place, a safe harbor for thousands of species, a diverse habitat he wanted to preserve for posterity. A place anyone could visit to find peace and comfort among the millipedes, mosses, and mushrooms. A place to recharge your immune system just by breathing in the essential oils exuded by the trees.

When the previous, retiring Ranger had handed the park keys over to Max, the old man had looked deeply into Max's soul and said quite solemnly, "You're on duty now, Bunyan. The future of the park and all living creatures in the park depends on you."

Max was momentarily taken aback at the enormity of the responsibility. But at precisely that moment, a warm feeling of something like maternal love flowed from the old man and flooded into Max's body. He could sense the warmth from head to toe, and a smile grew on his face. He was a bachelor, yet he felt as if he were adopting a large family. He looked around to thank the old ranger, but the man had disappeared.

From that point on, Max was often seen down on his knees, pulling invasive plants, tending new growth, or nurturing a motherless crow. Max grew to love every square inch of ground, every tree in the forest, and all species of life, from the mighty oaks to the tiniest butterfly. The forest thrived under his care.

To the people of Sleepy Valley, the park served as a beautiful escape, and Max was well known and respected as its faithful guardian. No matter where he went, they always associated him with the park and with nature because he looked like something that belonged in the forest: a big, gentle man in work boots, a full beard, and rustic clothes.

* * *

The park was also one of Marley's and Brianne's favorite places to explore on weekends. It encompassed hundreds of acres of trees and paths, cascading streams, and wildflower meadows. They loved getting lost in the tall trees and in the thick understory of shrubs. Every visit was different and offered up new discoveries.

Marley was so taken by the park that he had been working there during the past few summers. He had worked his way up to assistant ranger, having learned a great deal from Max and developing a deep love for nature. Marley, like most people, assumed the trees and the park had always been there—after all, the trees were huge.

Then one day Max told him, "Eighty years ago, back before I was born, the park was a lifeless wasteland, an over-worked Depression Era farm."

"No way," Marley said. "How could that be? It looks like an old growth forest to me." Later that night he repeated to his father what Max had said about the trees.

"I think Max is right," his father replied. "As I understand it, the land was restored by Roosevelt's Tree Army in the thirties. General MacArthur himself was right here in town at the dedication of the park. It was one of the programs put in place that helped pull the country out of the Great Depression."

Marley had heard of these famous men but still found it difficult to comprehend that this mature forest with thousands of hundred-foot-tall trees had all been planted by humans—and not that long ago.

His father also told him, "Young men, about your age, were employed by the Civilian Conservation Corps to plant billions of twelve-inch saplings all across the country in an effort to restore our soils, rivers, and forests from overuse and extreme weather. I've seen pictures from that period. Sleepy Valley, like much of our country, looked a lot different back then."

Marley nodded. "Max called it a wonderful gift from the people of that desperate era to all of us today."

* * *

On the evening of graduation, Max was not in his office. But then again, he never sat down at his desk for long. He often said, "Rangers are most effective at their jobs when they spend their time out among the trees, the animals, and the visitors, in that order." His office paperwork would pile up on his desk until it slid to the floor. It then flowed out the door, where it was read and recycled by a family of fungi living in the soil just beneath the wooden steps.

On this particular Friday night, Max had quietly slipped away after a long day outside in the heat with elementary school children, Rotary work teams, and casual visitors. At sunset he walked out to an overgrown meadow. It was a young, emerging forest of shrubs, grasses, and small trees. He sat there at its edge, watching the clearing. He was hoping to see the mating dance ritual and mythical flight of the mighty woodcock—one of nature's most dramatic displays of love and longing.

Fully covered in camouflage, Max sat as still as a rock, waiting for the romantic interlude to begin. After twenty minutes his legs cramped up and his back ached, but he knew not to move. He had trained himself over 20 years for moments like this. The only movements he could not control were the droplets of sweat that formed on his forehead. They rolled down from his brow and drip, drip, dripped off his nose and onto the thirsty ground. Even this late in the day, it was still unbearably hot.

He sat so still that birds and insects landed on him, mistaking him for a decaying stump. Several small white moths chewed on his graying beard. At one point a chipmunk scurried up his back and hid a seed in his left ear. Max didn't flinch but made a mental note to clean his ears when he got home.

Just as dusk settled onto the meadow, his heartbeat sped up a notch and his left ear twitched. A male woodcock entered the clearing a few yards in front of him. The bird looked around and then called out in all directions with a distinctive "PEENT, PEENT."

Max could smell the bird's musky presence and sense the bird's excitement. The ground was dry, the vegetation drier. Max's nose itched, but he didn't move. Moments later, a female woodcock appeared, and after a few preliminary courtship rituals and amorous sounds, the male woodcock started the long, spiral climb to the heavens.

Without moving his head, Max's trained eyes followed the woodcock's flight skyward as he waited patiently for the dive. The male always returned to the exact spot just above where he took off. The dive was followed by a high-risk maneuver only a few feet above his intended partner and the hard ground. It was one of the more dangerous mating rituals of birds in the whole country. Max wondered how precisely the male would execute this risky move, considering the stiff breeze that was bending the treetops. He sat there frozen, awaiting the finale of the flight, and silently counting the seconds: 1, 2, 3.

At three Max stopped counting. He had noticed, out of the corner of his eye, a brilliant blue beetle climbing up and over his left hiking boot. He recognized it immediately as the hated and feared Greater Sapphire Beetle. Its pungent aroma pierced his nose, creating a metallic flavor in his mouth. He also felt its unique vibratory motion—the beetle's abdomen keeping time as it marched forward, invading his forest.

Breaking his silent and motionless vigil, Max immediately and instinctively smashed the beetle into a gooey mess with his right hand. This violent behavior was definitely out of character for him. Max never killed anything in the park or anywhere else for that matter. In fact, Max regularly lectured visitors on the importance of all life—including snakes, mosquitoes, and bats—to the forest ecosystem.

But the sight of a highly invasive Greater Sapphire Beetle here in *his* park unnerved him so much that his reptilian brain took over. He acted totally in self-defense—realizing he was forced to do this to protect himself, his woodland family, and the forest he cared about so much.

Max sat there, shaking and horrified, as one after another member of this forest-destroying species crossed his boot. They were aggressive—the kudzu of the insect world. He had known that someday, as the climate warmed, they would get to his forest. But he had hoped that scientists would have found an antidote before the beetles arrived or that he would have discovered some other way to keep them out of his park. But to have them here, *now*, and in such vast numbers could only mean that a threshold had been breached, and his forest was doomed.

He screamed a curse, condemning all Greater Sapphire Beetles to hell. He then jumped up and did a foot-stomping dance, the likes of which he had not done in public since high school, as he tried to kill each and every one of the Greater Sapphire Beetles he could see. His wild antics chased the woodcocks off in opposite directions, the woodcock mating ritual interrupted and spoiled, the romantic moment lost.

Over the next several minutes, Max's physical response became manic as the number of beetles increased geometrically with every passing moment, his big, size-14 boots killing eight to ten beetles with a single stomp. But all too soon he realized that he was fighting a losing battle against overwhelming odds. Max finally collapsed onto the forest floor, totally exhausted. He fell into a shock-induced coma—his eyes tightly shut, hiding back in the recesses of their sockets, not wanting to witness the complete destruction of his forest.

Thousands of the conquering beetles surrounded his body and secreted an intoxicating elixir into his pores. His body stiffened as if rigor mortis had set in. The beetles picked him up and carried him off—deep into the forest. They wanted to keep him out of commission until they had completed the invasion and total destruction of his park.

* * *

As Max knew all too well, the Greater Sapphire Beetle, an infamous recent immigrant from the other side of the world, killed trees rapidly. With the much hotter temperatures now occurring across the globe, this species had mutated into an extremely aggressive variety. They behaved like the old beetles on steroids.

The mutants attacked with such voraciousness and in such vast numbers that, once they arrived in a forest, the trees were doomed. The beetles invaded every nook and cranny in the ground and penetrated the trees' defenses at their weak spots, the base of their trunks. These hungry insects ate right through the bark and cut off the food supply lines. Any heat-stressed tree attacked by this more aggressive and toxic species died immediately.

Nobody had ever seen anything as damaging as these beetles before. Once a forest was infested, there was no hope. The sap immediately drained out from the leaves, branches, and trunk, forming a sticky pool of tasty, toxic syrup in the soil. Many animal and insect species were attracted to the syrup, and as a result all life in the forest succumbed.

With the searing temperatures and dry conditions being fanned by the mounting winds in Sleepy Valley, the trees became brittle in a matter of hours. When the hurricane-force downdrafts—occurring on the edges of the town's powerful super thermal—began to blow the following day, trees splintered like toothpicks. Every large tree that crashed to the ground took out a dozen smaller trees; they fell like dominos. The park would not be a safe place until this forest-decimation process was complete. But by then it would be uninhabitable and inaccessible for years.

The Greater Sapphire Beetle invasion devastated the forest in the blink of an eye. Eighty years of forest restoration gone in a flash, another result of a rogue climate igniting a series of unpredictable catastrophic events. Not satisfied in just trashing the park's trees, the binging beetles moved on the next day to the trees along the river and every street in town.

On Saturday morning, Max awoke briefly from his coma to the sound of his cell phone ringing. It rang and rang, but he ignored it. He looked around and found himself entombed by the corpses of trees from his beloved forest. They had all blown down, and the park was in shambles. Max just lay there, expressionless, his whole world in tatters. His hair was a mess, his ranger uniform torn, and he had scratches on his arms and legs. He had lost the battle. He had also lost the will to move. Most importantly, he had lost the desire to live. He closed his eyes and fell back into the coma.

CHAPTER SIX

LAKE EFFECTS

Sleepy Valley's East Side, the older part of town, bordered a rather large lake teeming with fish. It also boasted a beautiful, white sandy beach and excellent swimming. Blue Lake attracted kids and families from all across town. The lake was the best, if not the only, attraction on the East Side.

However, every time Marley and his friends went to the lake to swim, they were treated as outsiders. The old-timers on the East Side didn't think much of the riff-raff from the West Side coming over and using *their* lake. The residents here were older and set in their ways. They didn't like the hairstyles, music, or the fancy clothing the teenagers from the West Side wore. They also didn't want their daughters hanging out with West Side boys.

"I don't get it," Marley said to his friends on one excursion. "Why don't they like us? It's as if everyone on the East Side belongs to a different tribe." As a result, Marley and his friends didn't go there very often and didn't know many of the residents.

* * *

When the sun rose on the East Side on the morning after graduation, life began to percolate with a different set of challenges than those occurring on the West Side. Ed Perkins, the oldest man on the East Side, woke up and started gathering strength to venture out for his "daily constitutional." He relied on this morning walk first thing every day to get his body going—it took some doing. On this particular morning he woke up well after the sun was shining. He stretched for several minutes, and then, still lying in bed, he wondered, *What the heck did I do yesterday to make my body ache so much today?*

Ed grunted to break the silence of his solitude and then shouted at himself, "Time to get up, you old goat. You can't sleep the whole day away."

He stood up with a fair bit of grumbling and dressed in pretty much the same clothes he had worn the day before. Ed then walked right out the front door of his house, all set to amble down to the Blue Lake Diner for coffee. His daily routine involved sipping coffee while sitting under the open-air pavilion and pontificating with his buddies for most of the morning.

This daily pattern rarely changed. It centered him. Ed judged all things in his life based on how they would impact his morning routine. He didn't like change, and if something different ever did happen in Sleepy Valley, he could instantly sense it.

On this particular morning, Ed didn't get ten feet from the front door of his house before he stopped short, looked around, and mumbled, "It's hot. Damn hot. I've never felt it so bad before." He wet his forefinger and raised it into the breeze. "The wind's stronger than normal this morning. Coming from the West Side. Something's different. Something's wrong—very wrong."

Old Ed sniffed the air and listened carefully. He heard nothing except the blood coursing through the veins of his withered ears and his heart still pumping loudly from the exertion of getting out of bed. He shook his head; he was puzzled. Then he adjusted his faded John Deere visor, tilting the brim lower to keep the bright rays of the hot summer sun out of his eyes. His hat played a key role in his wardrobe; he never wore anything brighter than John Deere green. The hat also kept his few white hairs orderly and kept the sun from peeling the last remaining layer of translucent skin from his scalp.

Ed peered across the valley, searching for answers. The lake rested at the bottom of the hill as always, nothing funny going on there. But he sensed something peculiar about the West Side of town. He squinted and stared. He removed his hat with one hand and scratched his head with the other. Something was different. The West Side seemed a bit darker today, as if a layer of smoke or smog hovered over it. He had never noticed that before. He also noticed a massive cloud of dust over the park. He thought it must be an early release of pollen from the pine trees due to the intense heat.

Ed wanted to know what was going on—he had a habit of making all town-related matters *his* business. He took note that the day was starting out very hot and sunny. It was cloudless, so clouds weren't the cause of the shadow on the West Side. He then spoke aloud again, a habit he had acquired after 30 years of living alone following the passing of his wife. "Never seen anything like this before. It's odd. Must be those darn newcomers on the West Side. What're they up to now?"

Old Ed proceeded to hobble up the gravel road to Maple Street. He was still very stiff-legged this morning and was thinking he should have ridden his Harley. As his stride loosened up, he gained a bit of steam and sauntered down Pine Street. His pace increased with time, especially on the flat stretches, but he still didn't move too fast. Everything passed him: squirrels, stray dogs, and the hot morning breeze. Even the soapy yellow water from the guy in the blue house washing his red Camaro outpaced him as it flowed down the gutter. But he didn't care about something as insubstantial as speed. After all, he was a town elder and was preoccupied with trying to figure out what had gone wrong with his town.

When he reached Lake Avenue, he took a left and walked down the concrete road to the pavilion, across the street from the Blue Lake Diner, to join his friends, or more accurately, his lifelong acquaintances. This group of old men never planned to do anything together, as friends might. They just hung out at the pavilion by the lake each morning and judged people and things that happened elsewhere. This morning they were all there, having coffee and watching the swallows flying low over the waters of the lake.

Ed got a medium coffee—black, as always—at the diner and then walked over to the pavilion to find Ben, his oldest acquaintance. Ed didn't particularly like anybody much who lived in Sleepy Valley except for Ben, and sometimes, he didn't even like Ben. But Ben was the best of the lot. He could usually be trusted to have similar opinions to Ed. But of course that never stopped them from arguing the finer points.

Ed noticed that Ben was sitting quite still, sipping coffee and staring across the lake. Ed eased his boney butt down on the seat next to him and said, "What's going on over there?"

After a few moments Ben said, "Can't be sure, but it certainly can't be good. What do you make of it?"

Ed didn't know, of course. That's precisely why he had asked the damn question. He frowned, perturbed that Ben had not only copped out but had volleyed the question back to him. Now he would have to hazard a guess or lose face. After all, he took a lot of pride in having all the right answers.

In reality Ed didn't care too much about the other side of the valley, but he cared more than he should have, given the fact that he rarely ever went over there anymore. Of course, as children he and Ben had spent a lot of time exploring and hunting in the woods on the west end of town. Life was good back in those days. They had been free to go anywhere and do whatever they wanted.

But that all changed when a developer bought the farms and woods on the West Side and turned them into a suburban community. Then all these "come-lately" people showed up out of nowhere. Ed often wondered, *Where were they living before they migrated here? Why did they have to move? Were they chased out of some other community?* He was often heard saying, "Those people who moved in on the West Side didn't just create more traffic and taxes for everyone, they changed *everything*. They always think they can fix every little thing, but most of the time they make it worse."

Of course the suburbanites also blamed the old timers for "being stuck in their ways and not wanting to think or plan ahead on any issue important to the future of the town." As a result, a wall had emerged over the years, an invisible wall of blame between the people who occupied the opposite sides of the valley.

Ed was well known for speaking his mind and defending the East Siders at town meetings. He had known the council members all their lives and often won these debates, regardless of the merits of the case. He was respected as a local hero on the East Side but was a royal pain in the butt to any progressive idea or person. He smiled whenever anyone mentioned either facet of his reputation.

Ed also knew the differences between the East and West side communities. For example, he knew that nearly all the homes on the East Side sported tin roofs, not asphalt shingles, and they only had concrete or gravel roads. No smelly asphalt roads graced his community. He and the other old-timers had told the government to "stay the hell out of our community" when the maintenance crews wanted to come in and pave everything over with asphalt.

These minor differences in construction on the two sides of town become important on the day of The Changes—the name everyone had adopted to describe the impacts of the warming trend. On this boiling hot day, Ed and his neighbors were fortunate; no oil flowed down their streets.

Back at the pavilion, Ed sipped his coffee while formulating his response to what was happening on the West Side. Ben saved him by saying, "Heck with the West Side, Ed. What do you make of the lake? It looks different today. Take a look at the swallows. I've never seen them fly in such bizarre patterns."

With some relief, Ed slowly redirected his attention to the lake. His eyes took a minute to refocus. *By golly, Ben's right, something's happening right here in front of me.* He had been too focused on somebody else's problems to realize there had been a dramatic change right before his eyes. But what was it? After quite some time thinking and sipping his coffee, Ed turned to Ben and said with satisfaction, "I've figured it out."

"Well, what is it?" Ben asked.

"The color's different." After a moment Ed put down his now-empty coffee mug and continued. "We joke about Blue Lake not being blue. As far as I remember, the lake has never looked blue; it's always been green with algae in summer or brown with silt after a hard rain. Today, it's a dirty white color."

All the old geezers mumbled in agreement with Ed's observation of the white lake. They each then started developing their own theories on what could be causing this phenomenon. Thinking their speculation silly, Ed got up and walked down to the lake with his empty coffee mug—a pint-sized Mason jar he always used to save the ten-cent-per-cup fee at the diner.

He filled the clear-glass Mason jar with lake water and peered into it. "It's full of bubbles. The surface is all white foam—like the head on one of Charlie's homebrewed beers."

Ben perked up a bit and said, "You're right. It's bubbling. Something in the lake must be fermenting."

Ed watched as everyone came over to look at the lake water in his Mason jar. They acted like it was a sample of a newly tapped keg of beer.

Examining the bubbling lake waters made some of the guys thirsty for a beer, and they started migrating down the road to Charlie's Bar to get a taste of the real thing. It was late morning and unbearably hot under the pavilion. A discussion about the formation of bubbles would probably come up again as the crew reconvened at the bar.

Ed, Ben, and a few others who remained behind continued to watch the foaming lake. As the day heated up further, an even stranger thing happened.

"Hey, Ben, take a closer look," Ed said. "The bubbling is increasing in intensity."

"Yeah," Ben agreed. "Looks like waves in a turbulent sea.

Must be the heat driving the fermentation."

"Hell, I think the lake's just plain outraged about being so polluted," Ed replied. "It's sick of being used by the people of the town as a sewer and a collector of all the residue that washes off the land. I bet it's going to blow its lid and overflow its banks."

The heat waves coming off the lake on this sweltering morning created a mirage just above the foam. This phenomenon caused the West Side of town, which lay directly across the lake, to completely vanish from sight. Over the next few minutes, the West Side came and went, appearing and disappearing behind the wavering heat waves. It was unsettling to the old men. A chill came over everyone, and they all fell silent. It was a lonely feeling. They weren't sure what was happening.

A stiff wind came up, bringing with it the scent of asphalt. It made Ed remember how much he disliked the West Side of town. He stood and raised his head as if to speak to the gods. After a moment he said in a gruff voice and without a trace of a smile, "You know, I wouldn't be too sad to see the whole West Side of town disappear forever. It would be the end of all of our problems."

* * *

As the old men talked and argued in the pavilion, some of the animal residents who lived in the lake gathered to discuss The Changes as well. One of these groups consisted of 24 greenish-gray snapping turtles. They slowly emerged from the bottom of the lake and methodically climbed up the banks to discuss their predicament.

One of the first snappers to have climbed up the bank said, "What's happened to our lake?"

"I can't breathe," a smaller one complained. "The algae's too thick, and I keep getting my legs stuck in the hydrilla stems."

"This lake's a mess," a third snapper said. "Visibility's down to about three inches. No wonder we keep bumping into each other. We've got to do something."

By this time the largest of these prehistoric-looking creatures had climbed to the top of the bank. He was a male elder boasting a 30-inch shell and was clearly the de facto leader. His 14-inch-long leathery neck, crushing beak, and battering ram head, as well as his 12-inch spiked tail, kept any potential usurper at a distance. He took no grief from anyone—neither beast nor fowl nor human.

A broad scar across his back in the shape of a Z made him even more intimidating. He had earned it in an encounter with a Mack truck while crossing a highway. He walked away from that incident with a scar for life; the truck had ended up in the ditch. From that point on, he was respectfully referred to by the others as "Z." No one in the tribe was old enough to remember his original name.

Z, the granddaddy of all turtles, raised his head up high and slowly surveyed the lake. He cleared his throat and spoke slowly to the others in his deep, waterlogged voice. "I've never seen such hot and foul conditions in all my life, and I've lived in a wide range of lakes, livestock ponds, and swamps. We've got to move—that's obvious. Anyone who doesn't want to go is welcome to stay. I don't want any whiners on this journey.

"And anyone who thinks that going downstream is the answer doesn't know much about how humans treat rivers. This lake is finished. Our lake, our home for the past one hundred years, has become a dead sea. There's no reason to dilly-dally or discuss this any further. Come on, we're moving upstream. Now!"

With that the granddaddy of all snapping turtles took off at a steady rate of 20 feet per minute and never looked back. He didn't care who followed him—but everyone did. He set his mind to get at least a mile or two upriver before nightfall, and at this steady pace, they should make it—even though the younger ones would have to struggle to keep up. He knew the whole tribe was relying on him, and he was taking this drastic action to save them all.

The snappers set off in single file, from the largest to the smallest. Each member of the tribe was instructed that they were responsible for the turtle directly behind them. Z told them they had to stick together—there would be hurdles ahead and they would need the talents of each member of the tribe. Each of them knew there was no telling how long it would take to find another suitable, if not pristine, lake, and none of them had taken such an overland adventure before except for Z. They were anxious but ready to leave the old lake behind. They were looking forward to life in a new and healthier environment.

CHAPTER SEVEN

VIEW FROM THE HILL

A large, glass and concrete, art deco building sat on the hill just south of town, perched like an eagle quietly overlooking and keeping track of all things happening in Sleepy Valley. It was the home of the Hilltop Observatory and Meteorological Station. The building served as the control center for Jim Quartz, chief scientist and director of the station. Wanda Perez served as his communications manager. Due to a series of budget cutbacks at the local, state, and federal levels, all the rest of the staff had been laid off. All they could afford was a summer intern. Last year, Brianne had been selected as the intern and had worked closely with Jim and Wanda.

On the morning of The Changes, Jim knew he had to go in to work. He had been getting texts, emails, and phone calls since early that morning telling him of strange occurrences around town. Even though it was Saturday, his day off, he felt a deep sense of responsibility to help others better understand the nature of the crisis. He needed to access his instruments to assess the situation, so he took off for work at his usual time.

Jim quickly discovered that the main road up the hill to the observatory was covered with oil from melting asphalt. Even his trusty, all-wheel-drive Subaru Outback was unable to get very far up the slick road. Frustrated by his inability to get to work on this sweltering hot but very important day, Jim decided to take a different course. There was a series of secondary, concrete and gravel roads that would get him almost to the top of the hill. He had no trouble driving on them, but there was one short section of melting asphalt he couldn't avoid and couldn't yet master. Every time he attempted it, he lost traction and came to a stop, cursing his failure. It was exasperating. He desperately needed to be in the office, today of all days.

He decided to try one last time. He slowly backed the Subaru up a small hill on the secondary road. He planned to pick up enough momentum coming down this gravel stretch to propel him up the main, paved road far enough to pass the short stretch of asphalt.

Jim, a cautious man, took a deep breath, pushed his hair back, wiped the sweat out of his eyes, and gunned the Subaru with everything he had. The engine raced, the tires spun, and gravel shot out behind the car, launching him forward. The Subaru growled, skidded sideways 20 feet, and then took off, swerving back and forth down the hill.

This was about the most exciting thing Jim had ever done in his life. He was into it big time. He pictured himself like a driver in a NASCAR race. He squinted his eyes and hunkered over the steering wheel. When he hit the melting asphalt, he had to make a sharp right, and as he did, the back end of the Subaru swung around to the left on the oily road. The Subaru was moving so fast that it slid off the far side of the road and onto the left shoulder, where the tires got traction in the gravel.

He pressed the accelerator all the way to the floor again and shot up the hill on the shoulder of the road, spewing rocks, dirt, and weeds behind him and taking out five or six mailboxes and a turtle-crossing sign. He didn't even stop or look for turtles.

To avoid a concrete drainage culvert, he edged back onto the asphalt, but when his tires hit the oily surface, he quickly lost momentum. Frantic that he was going to fail again, he slid off the road and onto the right shoulder, where he took out the welcome sign for the observatory and a dozen old, "Folly for Town

Council" campaign signs. No one had bothered to take them down after the last election.

Jim kept going, gripping the wheel and cursing himself forward. He could see the end of the asphalt just ahead of him. It appeared to be so close that he could almost reach out and touch it. But the Subaru was slowing down fast. "Darn it. I'm almost there. Just a few more feet." In a last-ditch effort, he gunned the accelerator one more time. The back end of the Subaru fishtailed wildly in the wet oil, spinning him around and moving the rear tires forward enough to reach the gravel road just as the oil-splattered car came to a stop.

Letting loose with an audible sigh of relief as his hands released the steering wheel, he sat back to take a deep breath. He smiled. Through pure grit and perseverance, he had made it, and this accomplishment made him feel like he could accomplish anything. After catching his breath, he drove the rest of the way up the hill on a nice clean stretch of concrete at a moderately slow speed, allowing his racing heart to calm down.

Jim was proud of his old Subaru. He had often boasted about how great the car performed in rain and snow, and now he would add this new story about melting streets. The new dents and scrapes provided evidence of the ruggedness and super performance of the car under these dangerous, new driving conditions. He didn't even want to think about what he might have hit on the way up the hill.

As Jim pulled into his parking spot, his phone dinged. It had been dinging all morning, but he hadn't taken the time to read the messages. This time it was Brianne. As his intern last summer, she had been bright and inquisitive, and they had come to respect and like each other. Since he had no children of his own, he had come to enjoy mentoring and hearing the perspective of someone her age, and they had kept in touch. He thought she might continue her interest in science and come back to work at the observatory one day.

While sitting there, recovering and sweating in the parking lot, he read her messages, which were full of questions about all the things she was seeing. He responded: "No answers yet. Just got into work. Will call when i can". At this point all he had were his own questions, so he added her concerns about the melting asphalt, dying trees, and strong winds to his list. It was a lot to keep track of, but he looked forward to finding the answers.

Awkwardly unfolding his lanky body from the front seat of the Subaru, Jim stood there in the extreme heat on the small patch of melting asphalt that served as his parking space in front of the station. He felt his shoes slowly sinking down into the oily mess, so he wisely decided to get off the asphalt before it was too late. It was time to get busy finding answers.

$$* * *$$

The first question bouncing around inside Jim's head was, *How can the asphalt be melting?* He wouldn't have believed it if he hadn't seen it with his own eyes. *Is it just due to the high temperatures, or does it have something to do with the composition of the asphalt or the poor air quality we're experiencing?* He didn't know. Probably some mix of all three.

He decided to measure the asphalt's temperature before he started speculating too much. That was an all-too-common problem—people developing opinions without any data. He grabbed the thermometer that he kept in the back of his car for measuring air and water temperatures around town.

Of course he expected the asphalt to be much hotter than the air temperature since its black color would absorb the radiant heat from the sun—especially on south facing slopes. But he was blown away when the asphalt quickly maxed out his thermometer. The road surface temperature was well over 200 degrees. *That's clearly in the range needed to melt asphalt. And to think I was trying to drive on it.*

He started to realize that, with the climbing temperatures, they were entering a new realm. *Everything is changing, and anything could happen – anything and everything within the laws of science.* At least he hoped that the basic principles of science would still apply in this changing world. But no more guessing. There was a job to do, and the first thing was to find out what else was going on in the valley. He was going to check his instruments and then seek out firsthand accounts of what people were experiencing. He would talk to Max, Doc, Brianne, and Marley to start with, since he knew they would give him objective assessments of what they had been witnessing.

As he entered the office, Jim felt tired after the exhilaration and stress of gunning his car up the hill. He felt that he had made it past the asphalt largely on his willpower, and it had sapped all his energy. His growing concern about the town made him realize it was going to be one of those days when he would have to be attentive to a whole host of issues. He knew there would be calls all day long from people in important positions seeking immediate answers to their questions. He would be expected to have the answers.

Wanda, his lively and very effective communications specialist, greeted him at the door with a look of relief. She must have been worried that he was so late. She would have known he would be coming in to check his instruments.

Jim knew Wanda needed his advice and his insights to do her job well, especially during an emergency. She depended on him to collect and evaluate the data so she would know what to communicate. He was always impressed that Wanda could take his sterile, scientific data and put life into it. It was like magic how she could turn raw data into something useful to others, and he loved that about her—she had real talent. He realized that much of his success here in Sleepy Valley was due to Wanda and her ability to communicate to the public.

He had ended up at Sleepy Valley after suffering a communications fiasco earlier in his career. He had developed a model that very precisely and correctly predicted a storm. However, the news media and politicians in that big city misinterpreted his data, and the governor of the state evacuated the wrong parts of the seashore. It was a political nightmare, and he was the fall guy who took the blame. The mainstream scientific community also shunned him for a while after that experience. In fact he was lucky to have landed this job in Sleepy Valley, even though it was now a backwater outpost to the modern world. Yes, Jim knew firsthand the importance of good communication.

"Am I glad to see you," Jim greeted Wanda. "Thanks for coming in on your day off. We have a lot of work to do. By the way, how did you get in this morning?"

Wanda smiled. "I rode my motorbike as far as I could. Then I walked the rest of the way on the shoulder. It was windy and hotter than Hades, but I got here."

He was impressed by her resourcefulness but didn't say anything. He was a little embarrassed that he had never even thought of walking. He continued, "Boy, do we have a mess on our hands. I'll be checking all the instruments to see what the heck's happening down in the valley. I'm sure we'll be getting lots of calls. Come find me if you need me, but right now there's nothing to report."

Trying to focus his mind, Jim pushed back his thinning hair with his right hand. He did this simple reflex action dozens of times each day. It was partly to keep his hair under control and partly a nervous habit. As usual, he was in need of a haircut; the long hairs in his comb-over flopped down into his eyes. *I wonder when the barber shop will be open again?*

Jim spent the morning checking the instruments located at the station and reading the charts from the remote meters stationed throughout the valley—they were all going crazy. His equipment wasn't new, but he had recently recalibrated all of it, and he knew the readings were accurate. The anemometers spread around town were showing a wide range of wind speeds and wind directions. Jim's hygrometer was measuring very low water vapor content in the air. The barometers weren't making much sense, the atmospheric pressures varied widely, and the thermometers were reading record-high temperatures at all stations.

His equipment also measured the concentrations of a range of air quality parameters including ozone, particulate matter, carbon dioxide, methane, and other volatile organic compounds. He needed to document the concentrations and the trends to better understand The Changes. *It's going to be a long day and night.*

In addition to record high temperatures, Jim noted that wind speeds had jumped dramatically earlier that morning. Wind directions appeared to be highly variable, moving in all directions at once when viewed as a whole. But locally consistent patterns were developing, depending on where you were in the valley.

"I sure wish I had more recording stations around town to make sense of all this," he told Wanda when he reported his findings to her. "We need a bigger budget to give people the information they need to make the right decisions and take care of themselves." It wasn't a new idea. He had been fighting the anti-science cabal in Congress for years—they didn't understand the value of Jim's work and consistently cut the budget for basic and applied science.

In addition to a thermal plume of hot air rising above the town, the data indicated a second thermal plume developing over the lake. The plume over the town made sense—treeless, concrete downtown areas acted as heat-generating "islands." *But what's causing the massive thermal plume rising above the lake?*

Jim also noted powerful downdrafts on the edges of these rising thermals. Their presence shook him to his inner core. He knew full well that mighty microbursts of this magnitude could knock down mature trees, up-end trailers, and sink boats. He had even heard anecdotes of small dogs being sucked out of open windows during these events.

Returning to his work, he pushed the hair out of his eyes again and scratched the back of his head. He was greatly concerned by the data he was recording. The air quality scanner had picked up extremely high concentrations of methane over the lake. This observation puzzled him. Jim knew methane was not only explosive when trapped within buildings but was also a really potent greenhouse gas. *More methane in the atmosphere means more warming. That's not what we need.*

He said to Wanda, "If all the lakes around the world and the oceans are generating this much methane, it will accelerate the warming trend. Game over." He thought about this for a minute and then asked, "The hydrocarbons over the town make sense—the oil is evaporating into hydrocarbon gases. But what's causing so much methane over the lake?" He sat back in his chair, wondering about the causes and the impacts of methane.

"What's going on in this little town of ours?" Wanda asked fearfully.

"It's like we hit a thermal threshold and all hell is breaking loose," Jim replied. "We must have reached a point that triggered these chemical, biological, and physical reactions. These are rogue events with unknown consequences." Then he thought, *I hope we haven't reached a point of no return.*

Still scratching his head, he paced back and forth in the instrument room and then walked outside for a breath of air to clear his head. He took a look down into the valley to see if he could spot anything else that was unusual. He had never felt so perplexed in his life. He knew that all of his fellow citizens were probably even more confused and would be depending on him to get the right answers. After all, he was the senior scientist and director of the once-renowned Hilltop Observatory. The people in Sleepy Valley needed his help to make the best decisions for the health and safety of their families. Their lives depended on him. They needed answers now.

* * *

At the same time that Jim was scratching his bald spot, three big, black buzzards were gliding silently toward Sleepy Valley, hoping to get a free ride on the rising air over the town. These buzzards proudly thought of themselves as the world's greatest efficiency experts, only flapping their wings as a last resort. They were the kings of the air currents, soaring to great heights by riding any thermal they could find. Thermals were their stairways to heaven and to better vantage points for spotting carrion.

Sure enough, the three wandering scavengers found the rising air over Sleepy Valley and hitchhiked on the thermal to several thousand feet above the town. It was way too hot to flap their wings or perform complex aerial acrobatics, so they were very pleased to have the chance to relax, kick back, and ride a super-charged thermal.

The leader of the pack—the oldest of the three buzzards—started to sense something was wrong after 20 minutes of riding the thermal. His nose itched and his tongue had dried out. He no longer felt his normal aches and pains. His eyes bulged as he started seeing a kaleidoscope of colors. At first he was anxious, thinking something might be wrong, but he was enjoying the light show and the other new sensations so much that he just smiled and went along for the ride. But after breathing in the fumes from the thermal for several more minutes, he became dizzy and disoriented. Suddenly, he tucked his wings and went into a steep dive. From his normal, relaxed cruising speed, his plummeting body quickly accelerated to 50, 60, and then past 70 miles per hour. *Wow, if only my mother could see me now.*

His actions befuddled his friends, who followed him to keep a close watch on his peculiar behavior. It was so out of character for him. The head buzzard had always been a pretty laidback sort of guy, seldom encountering a need to rush in his line of work. Seeking out carrion along the sides of roads or nests of eggs in trees does not require speed.

The old buzzard had watched eagles, ospreys, peregrine falcons, and other raptors go into aerial dives many times and had always been impressed with their skill. Now he was impressed that he was doing a dive. It was exciting, especially for an old buzzard like himself. He started imagining himself as an eagle, but all of a sudden he noticed the ground coming toward him at a high rate of speed. Being under the influence of the toxic vapors, he smiled, assuming his body would know what to do. But he had never practiced the art of pulling out of a dive before and was slow to react to the impending danger.

WHOP! He hit the ground, breaking his neck, right at the feet of Jim Quartz.

* * *

Jim jumped five feet into the air. Before he had a chance to scream, two more, big, black buzzards nearly took him out. Running inside, he scanned the skies from behind the large, reinforced, plate-glass windows of the observatory. *Buzzards are world-class gliders. I've never seen them diving out of the skies before. It must be the heat or the air quality. We've got to get an autopsy!* He went back outside, picked up the three buzzards, and put them in a plastic bag in the freezer next to the ice cream. He would have them tested later.

"Wanda, send out an All-Points Code Red Air Quality Alert. No, make that a Code Purple Alert. Let everyone know this is not a day to be outside. It doesn't matter whether or not you suffer from heat, asthma, pollen, or poor air quality. These toxic fumes can affect anyone of any age—they could make people and animals a little daft. Anyone outdoors should wear a mask or use a respirator. No one should be jogging or biking or even driving a car while under the influence of these fumes."

With a few deft keystrokes and a press of a button, Wanda immediately responded by sending out her first alert of the day. It went to thousands of people and all the local media stations. A smile spread across her face—she was helping, she was doing her job. "Done. What's next?"

Jim looked at Wanda, impressed as usual. Almost absent-mindedly, he said, "We have to solve the riddle of why there's such a mammoth thermal rising from the lake."

"Didn't you tell me there are high methane levels in that area as well? Couldn't that do it?"

"Yes, that makes sense. Methane's lighter than air. I've used it as a lifting agent in meteorological balloons. It would rise, creating an updraft and a thermal above the lake. But why would the lake be producing that much methane?" Jim pondered this question as he stood by the large windows and trained his powerful binoculars on the lake. Suddenly, he shouted, "Wanda come look at this. The lake is white. There's a frothy foam on top of it, and it's spreading out in all directions! You're right. The lake must be the source of the methane. But why?"

"Could it be related to the thick algae blooms in the lake over the past few summers?" Wanda asked. "It sure hasn't been much fun to swim in."

"Algae does produce methane when it dies. But I've never seen this much before. This much algae, methane, and the heat will probably cause a major die-off of anything living in the lake."

Jim went back outside, this time wearing Wanda's pink motorcycle helmet to protect him from any more dive-bombing buzzards. He scanned the town and his whole body froze. He locked in his binoculars and focused on where the park had been. "What's happened to the park?"

Throughout his entire tenure at the observatory, there had always been a large green patch on the north side of town. It had served as a retreat, almost a spiritual home, for him and many of the townspeople. But now the park looked brown. *How could anything have changed the park that fast? It was fine yesterday.*

Through his high-powered binoculars, Jim saw in detail the extent of the destruction of his favorite place on Earth. The living, vibrant, green forest had been replaced by a tumble of dying timbers. He couldn't believe it, and for the first time in his life, he felt scared, as if the rug were being pulled out from beneath his feet. *This is a disaster. What in the world could have killed all those trees in a single night?* Sure, it was hot and the winds were extreme, but something else must have gotten into them to produce that much havoc so quickly.

Jim tried calling Max. No answer. "I hope he's alright," he said in a very slow and wobbly voice. He wondered how any person could have lived through the destruction of a forest. "I wonder if Max spent the night in the park." A shadow crossed his face as he thought of his good friend. "Wanda," he called. "Call 911 and have them send out a search party to find Max. Immediately. He must be in trouble. We've got to locate him."

Jim surveyed the West Side suburbs and realized that the brown, dying-tree phenomenon seemed to be spreading rapidly across the whole area. *The loss of the trees is going to make things a lot worse. They have provided shade and cooling throughout the town. Without them, temperatures will rise even more.* He slowly realized that The Changes were probably just the start of a series of compounding impacts. The result of the hot temperatures was a climatic trend that he referred to as The Warming. A trend that had been going on for decades and would continue as long as fossil fuels were burned. *When will it end? How hot can it get?* And then on a real pessimistic note, he thought, *Can we survive?*

Wanda came out of the building to join him. She had a glum expression on her face as she said, "Jim, we're getting a lot of calls and texts reporting strange events around town. Take a look at some of these." She handed him the list she had compiled.

Feeling dazed and confused and a little off-balance, he started to read the notes. He felt as if he had fallen down a rabbit hole into some other strange land; much of what he read didn't make any sense. *Could any of this really be happening?* He hoped he was dreaming or, more accurately, having nightmares. He pinched his arm and frowned. He wasn't asleep. The list of messages included the following, "thousands of crawfish are crawling out of the lake." "Dozens of eagles are dining on dead fish."

A text had come into 911 and had been forwarded to them from a woman who wrote, "My ninety-year-old father was on the porch when a mini-tornado came by and swept him and my favorite rocking chair away. Can't find either of them."

Many messages reported that swimming pools, ponds, birdbaths, and watering troughs had dried up. Reports also came in from all around town about sightings of black squirrels, black pigeons, black cats, and black dogs; apparently, they were all covered with oil.

The normally two-foot tall eternal flame in the memorial garden downtown was now 40 feet tall, fueled by the river of oil passing close by. The flames were threatening to take out the overhead utility lines and the tree canopy.

Jim was forced to accept the fact that a range of complex problems had begun to impact his town. Animals, humans, and plants were all being affected and were responding in their own ways.

He marveled at how it all seemed to be connected and how such a wide range of events were all triggered by something as basic as rising temperatures. He turned to Wanda and asked, "What's next?"

Jim knew all too well that in any collapse of a natural system, a series of cascading events could produce a whole range of unpredictable changes. *It's hard to guess where this series of events might lead. I wonder if it's too late to stop or slow down The Warming. Can we turn back the clock or turn down the temperature?* He was starting to wonder if the town, civilization, and even life on Earth could be saved.

He snapped out of his momentary depression to ask Wanda, "Can you start a master list of these strange occurrences and tie them into locations on our base map of the valley?"

She pointed to the conference table that held a big screen for showing his weather models. "I've already started. Is that map good enough?"

He walked over to the table. "This is great. I'm going to add my best estimates of where the thermals and downdrafts are occurring to see if we can produce a model that explains it all."

They got to work plotting the data. It soon started to look like quite a hodgepodge—much like a drawing by a classroom of three-year-olds. But it proved to be of tremendous value in helping them assess the parts of town at greatest risk. Jim's goal was to warn people if he thought they were at risk of bodily harm.

* * *

His cell phone rang. It was Brianne. He picked up and said, "Brianne, don't go outside today. The air is full of toxins, and the winds are dangerous."

"Yeah, I know. Marley and I have been out all morning. It's scary, Jim. Everything is collapsing around us. It's pretty extreme. We're kinda freaking out. Marley's on the line too."

Marley then took the time to relate what they had seen. He didn't know Jim that well but knew that Brianne considered the scientist to be an expert on weather.

Brianne then unloaded her questions as well. "What's causing all this, Jim? How long will it last?"

Jim took a minute to respond, wanting to be as honest as he could. "I don't know for sure. But I'm working on it. The rising temperatures must have triggered something. It might all be related to some thermal tipping point."

"What do you mean by tipping point?" asked Marley. "That doesn't sound so good. It sounds like something's going to fall over and crash." He was concerned about Jim's choice of words.

"Well, in this case it would be the critical temperature in the warming of our climate that triggers a chain of events," Jim replied. "It also infers that the events may be irreversible. There will certainly be more changes. You can count on that."

"That sounds pretty scary," Brianne said.

"We've known this could happen for years," Jim continued. "But people didn't take it seriously enough—it was just too abstract a concept. Therefore, we didn't take steps soon enough to prevent it."

"Well, the future is now, and it looks pretty awful," Marley said. "I hope there's something we can do to stop it." He always looked for solutions to any problem he encountered, and this was starting to look like a pretty big problem.

"Well, there are still things we can do," Jim assured him. "The very first thing is to understand what's happening. Be sure to let me know if you find anything else unusual going on."

"We can do that," Marley said. "We'll text you whatever we find. Please keep us in the loop as you figure it all out."

"I will. And be careful out there. I don't know what's going to occur next. It's all happening way too fast. I'm afraid we've not seen the end of The Changes yet. Oh, and if you're going to be outside and have the chance, check in with Max out at the park. I haven't been able to reach him." Jim went into some of the detail about what he had seen in the park but didn't say too much because he didn't want to alarm them. "I'd also love someone to check what's happening out at Blue Lake. But don't put yourselves at risk."

"We can do that. If not today, then tomorrow," Marley promised. "I'm also worried about my uncle and aunt's farm. Can you see anything from there?"

"Do you mean Alexander's Last Chance Farm?" Jim asked, focusing his binoculars on the farmlands just outside of town."

"Yep."

"No, I don't see much happening there. Wait a second. It does appear that dust devils are sprouting in Luke's fields. He must be on the edge of a thermal, and the winds will only get worse. You might warn him about how bad the wind was where you were this afternoon. In fact I'll have Wanda send out a High Winds Watch and a High Fire Alert stating that open flames are not allowed in and around town due to the dry nature of the forests and fields and the high winds.

"In addition to that, please encourage anyone you see to stay inside. The fumes are toxic and can mess with your mind. In fact, keep a close tab on each other. If either of you start acting strangely, you should definitely go inside. And with the winds blowing down trees, it's really not safe for anyone to be out in this."

And then, as if nature were trying to emphasize the point, another buzzard fell from the skies and landed right in front of the observatory.

CHAPTER EIGHT

SAVING THE FARM

M arley's Aunt Betsy and Uncle Luke and their preteen boys—collectively known as the Alexanders—ran Last Chance Farm, just on the edge of town. They raised cattle, sheep, pigs, and champion Rhode Island Red chickens. The Alexanders also grew a variety of vegetables and grains. In addition to the old farmhouse, the farm consisted of a large barn to store hay, a grain shed with a tall silo for corn, and 350 acres of pasture and cropland.

All the family holidays were held in the old farmhouse and Marley had great memories of spending summer days on the farm. He got to drive the tractor, round up the sheep, and play in the hay barn. He'd always wanted to jump into the 50-foot-tall silo half-filled with kernels of corn but had never been allowed because of the danger of suffocating or "drowning" in all the loose corn.

Betsy and Luke ran the farm together. They loved living there but also knew their operation was hanging on by a shoestring. The warming climate and the prolonged drought made this a perilous time to be a farmer; most farms in the valley teetered on the brink of bankruptcy.

The recent spate of high temperatures had already dried up all of the Alexanders' crops for this season—vegetables died on withering vines. They had nothing to harvest and nothing to sell. The dry earth on their farm appeared to be dying of thirst. A network of hexagonal mud cracks had opened in the ground as if the Earth's pores were gasping for breath. It had become the heat wave from hell.

Now as Luke listened to the howling winds building up on the morning of The Changes, a shiver went down his spine. He was concerned about his buildings, livestock, and even his precious topsoil blowing away. "Betsy, I'm going out to batten down the hatches before everything gets damaged by the wind. Keep the boys inside."

"Sure. I'll be out shortly, Luke. As soon as I put the food away."

Luke, a stocky, no-fear sort of man, was unnerved as he struggled to open the front door and then again as he encountered the gale force winds which tried to bully him to go back indoors. He leaned into the wind, sand buffeting his shaven head, and wondered if this was what it was like crossing the Sahara Desert in a sandstorm. But he kept going, fighting the wind with every step, feeling responsible for the future of his farm and his family.

A bad feeling coursed through Luke's body as he surveyed the farm. He had learned how to farm over the years from his father and grandfather and normally knew what to expect. But now it seemed as if the rulebook had blown away in the wind. *Everything has changed. These winds, the droughts, what am I supposed to do? Maybe I should have gone into a different business.*

As Luke fought his way around the farm, his faded-blue overalls flapped violently in the wind. He put a calico handkerchief over his weathered face in order to breathe without coughing. It appeared to be the only way to keep the dust from clogging his eyes, mouth, and nose. He thought about it for a moment and realized he had never had to do that before. It had never been this bad. "Stay inside," he shouted to Betsy. But his voice was swallowed up by the wind.

Between opaque clouds of dust, Luke glanced down the driveway to check on the roadside vegetable stand. He couldn't see it with all the dust blowing. He loved selling eggs and vegetables to his neighbors from the old, lopsided stand. The tilted, tin-roofed structure was a relic from a time long ago before either he or Betsy had been born. He figured his great-grandfather had built it. The stand had grown to be an important landmark for the community—all his neighbors loved to stop by, chat, and buy whatever was in season from whichever Alexander was tending the stand.

The air cleared. He took another look. "What? Is that possible?" The stand wasn't there. Nothing was left of a century-old structure that had met a commercial and social need in the valley. The wind howled at Luke as if boasting of its power to destroy.

As Luke approached his eight-foot-high manure pile in the barnyard, it spontaneously combusted. He stumbled backward to keep from getting burned. As he watched the mounting flames, his knees buckled at the magnitude of the blaze. The fire grew in size, quickly igniting all of the straw in the pile, and then the rest of the smoldering manure combusted, fueling the fire.

The flames from the roaring inferno grew so large they threatened to burn down the barns, the house, and what was left of the bone-dry fields. Tongues of flame lapped out at everything as if they were starving and looking for more fuel to consume.

Luke did his best to control the spread of the fire by desperately pumping water from his livestock pond, but he ran the pond dry. The flames reached 30 to 40 feet high, whipping around in all directions as the wind continued to blow without mercy.

In an act of desperation, Luke turned all his livestock loose and let them run out of the barnyard to the safety of the back pastures. He hoped the animals would have a better chance of survival out in the open. But it was too late for some—several cows had already fallen over from heat exhaustion. Several pigs tried to quench their thirst by drinking from the tributary to the Sleepy Valley River, but they quickly died from the toxicity of the waters. Their bloating bodies rolled into the river, and the current carried them downstream.

Two skittish sheep ran in zigzag patterns, not knowing which way to turn. They got too close to the burning volcano of manure and straw, and they instantly caught fire—their fleeces went up like puffballs.

Burning fibers and embers filled the air, starting new fires wherever they touched down on combustible fodder. The farm might have needed rain—needed it badly—but right now a cessation of the unleashed winds that carried the flames would have been a greater blessing.

Betsy must have seen Luke heading to the hen house and with instantaneous foresight leaned out the door and screamed, "Don't turn them loose, Luke. Bring them into the basement. We can live on the eggs."

But her warning came too late. Luke had already opened the gate, and their prized Rhode Island Reds could be seen blowing across the barnyard, tumbling like tumbleweeds. The only reason they could still recognize them as chickens was that they cackled indignantly as they bulleted past.

Betsy stood and watched as some of their champion hens bounced over fences and soared high into the air as the relentless wind and dust storm carried everything away with it. One hen got stuck in the basketball hoop, a second in the chimney. Another got sucked up in a dust devil, spiraling ever upward, and disappeared hundreds of feet above their heads. They heard ghostly cackling for several minutes after the birds had disappeared from sight.

Luke glanced at the house and saw Betsy bracing herself in the doorway, holding onto the screen door with both hands, immobilized by the chaos. He had always viewed her as a strong woman, still pretty with her natural red hair and robust figure, but it was obvious to him that she was in shock. All the color had left her face.

Later in life she would recall, "Along with the hens and the topsoil, I saw the mailbox, the family collie, laundry from the line, backyard furniture, flowers from my flowerbed, and the flamingo windmills from the front yard all fly past. It was as if all my life's favorite memories were passing right before my eyes."

When Luke came in to check on her, she was sitting at the kitchen table. Quite uncharacteristically, she had begun to cry. "I felt useless out in the wind," she told him. He noticed that her tears evaporated even before they left her eyelashes—one of the few benefits of the hot dry air.

He told her he was able to grab the last half-dozen prized chickens after hearing her advice, delivered belatedly on the wind. In fact he was still holding them by their feet. Now he threw them down into the cellar and fastened the latch to the basement door with a double-bolt lock. The chickens were quite content to stay in the dark basement, away from the chaos, away from the noise, in a place where they could regain their composure. Luke then hugged his wife and told her "Stay put I can't afford to have you blow away as well." Then he went back outdoors to see what else he could save.

Once she was alone, Betsy started to cry again. Her husband was a man of few words, and that was the nicest thing he had ever said to her. This time a whole host of tears appeared in her eyes. They flowed faster and didn't evaporate until they got all the way down to her cheeks.

CHAPTER NINE

ASSESSING THE DAMAGE

After an exhausting day exploring The Changes in and around town, Marley was tired and anxious, but he stayed up late working on his skateboard, trying to make it work better on the oily streets—he felt he was going to need it since cars were not much good during the heat of the day. Although it was difficult to ride in these conditions, he had done far better than people on foot or in cars.

While he was tinkering, Marley also struggled to make sense of all he had seen during the day. Earlier in the evening he had talked with his parents about what had happened and what could be done about it. The trees had all blown down in their yard. One was blocking their driveway, another had smashed their big back porch, and their lawn was covered with broken branches. But their house was still standing, and they had enough food for a week or two, as long as the freezer kept running.

They were all shaken up by the dramatic turn of events. Neither his mom nor his dad wanted to go out on the streets under the current conditions. He, of course, couldn't wait to get outside to understand what was happening.

His mother was a nervous wreck and had to find things to keep her hands busy. She still hadn't heard from her brother about how the farm was faring, and she was distraught with worry. She kept asking, "Why haven't they called? How come I can't reach them? They must have lost all power. I wish we could drive out there to check on them."

Marley's father had asked him to cut up the tree in the driveway so they could get out of the garage if they needed to drive somewhere. That actually sounded like fun to Marley. He liked using the chainsaw, and he liked having another excuse to go outside.

His father was angry that the town had done nothing to prevent or prepare for this onslaught of catastrophes and had done nothing yet to fix the problems. "What's the town doing about all of this? I keep calling and can't get through to anyone in the municipal offices," he said. "Their press releases just claim they're studying the problem to see what would be best for the town.

"I realize I never paid much attention to tree-huggers or doomsday predictions," his father continued. "I always just assumed the town would have taken the necessary steps to prepare for weather-related disruptions. That's part of their job, to protect the citizens of the town from natural disasters and to help the town recover if one happens.

"A warming planet just wasn't on my radar as a high risk. I thought things might change, but I didn't think it would be this bad or happen this quickly. I never thought a one or two degree rise in temperature would threaten our jobs and our lives. Somebody should have been more on top of this."

Marley didn't know what to say. He hadn't really thought much about it either. But he did think that maybe his parents' generation should have prevented things from getting this bad.

After a few moments of reflection, his dad continued, "I guess we all should have done more. We all should have paid more attention. If we had all taken it seriously and spoken up, then the government might have done something."

"It's going to be hard on people if they can't get out to shop for food," Marley's mother said. "What are we going to eat? What happens if our water supply gets cut off or dries up or if we can't flush our toilets? What if we get sick or have a bad fall?"

"Mom, calm down. It's certainly not going to come to that. We'll figure something out." Marley thought that if he didn't calm her fears, she wouldn't be able to sleep that night and would be worse tomorrow.

His dad had a similar reaction. "The government's got to step in and get things moving again. They need to convene a meeting and then create a plan for responding to this disaster. In the meantime we all should stay inside and wait. We don't want to do anything that could make things worse."

His mother and father both encouraged Marley to stay home the next day. That was what they had heard on the news. It was about the only thing they took away from all the advice they were getting, even though they both had been glued to the news programs all day. They had heard how bad things were in Sleepy Valley and also the news from all around the world. There were dramatic events occurring everywhere. It was depressing news, but they kept listening, trying to find a silver lining.

As far as Marley was concerned, the talking heads on TV didn't seem to know the extent of the problems as well as he did, at least on a local level. Of course he was going back outside tomorrow.

He also understood that as the infrastructure failed, the news would get harder to access. Many conventional phone and electric lines were already down due to the extreme winds and falling trees. Some cell towers had toppled over as well. Everyone's ability to communicate was slowly disappearing as batteries died. Marley charged his phone every chance he got.

In the discussions that evening, Marley realized that neither of his parents had any idea what could be done now to reverse The Changes. They had no plan as to what the family should do in an emergency of this scale. The problems seemed way too large to fix or even to plan for. They both felt the town or the state would have to jump in to save them. They believed there was just no other option.

* * *

When he finally got to sleep, Marley tossed and turned as vivid, nightmarish dreams flashed across his disordered, oil-fume-marinated brain. On Sunday morning he stumbled around, confused about what he had dreamed versus what he had actually encountered the day before. He was having a hard time separating fact from fiction. It all seemed like some strange science fiction movie.

In addition to being tired and having a headache from the fumes, Marley noticed a rash on his arms and legs. He tried to ignore the redness, but it itched. So he scratched. He didn't think he needed to treat it. He assumed it would just go away with time, so he didn't mention it to his parents. A rash certainly wasn't going to slow him down from getting outside and checking out the status of the town.

Marley was one of the few people who had been out and about on Saturday, so he had become the eyes and ears for his friends and the neighborhood. He was constantly texting what he was seeing and everyone was passing on his texts to others and sending him back the things they were seeing.

Marley was anxious to get going; he wanted to know what else might have happened overnight. He wanted to see what people were doing about the oily mess on the streets, the dying trees, and the bubbling lake. The media was full of speculation on what was happening, but he had firsthand knowledge and a considerable network of friends passing him information. As a result, his information was much more reliable than the media pundits'. But things could have changed overnight, so he needed to get out again and see for himself.

Grabbing his skateboard, Marley escaped the house before his parents woke up. He carried the board under his arm out to the street, excited to try the board after modifying it the night before. He surveyed the neighborhood. Yes, that was the first reality check. The oil *was* real. It was still dripping from the rooftops, especially the roofs facing south that were not tree-covered.

His phone rang and an anxious Brianne said, "Marley, the oil is seeping into our basement. I went down to do the laundry, and there must be a foot of oil down there. I just disconnected the sump pump and flipped the circuit breakers. This old firetrap could go up in smoke at any time. We're pretty scared."

"You guys better get out of there. I'm sure you could stay with us. I'll have my mom call your mom."

"Thanks, but we're moving in with Mom's best friend from work. If that doesn't work out, I might take you up on your offer."

"Let me know how I can help."

Next he got a text from Colin. "We lost our trees. One crashed the garage into a pancake."

He called his friend. "Wow. How are the other guys?"

"When Grant's big oak went over, it ripped up his water line and ripped down his power line. He's getting buckets of water from a neighbor, and his father is over here at our house, using our phone, trying to reach the power company."

These stories emphasized the harsh realities of The Changes. Marley realized that everyone was going to have to help each other out until some sort of relief effort could be organized and deployed.

"I think this is the end," Colin told Marley. "I predict full-on chaos and anarchy by the end of week when everyone's food supplies run out."

No way. Marley didn't want to think about it. Colin was always a little over the top, but this prediction didn't sound too far-fetched. He was hoping everyone would get out of their homes and start helping each other clear the roads, fix the lines, and get food delivered. In other words, take matters into their own hands and fix everything.

But that wasn't the case today. For the second day in a row, he saw very few people outdoors. The fear of walking and driving on the streets had expanded to a fear of the heat, falling trees, and the toxic fumes from melting asphalt and was, unfortunately, now a general fear of the outdoors. His neighbors must have also listened to the news accounts that focused on the dangers of going outside. *What's next, a fear of our neighbors?*

Riding downhill on his board, he felt like a lone warrior after the apocalypse. This was not what he had expected his life to be like after graduation. At least his board, now modified with its larger and thinner wheels, was an improvement, and he was moving a bit faster.

The news reports had apparently left most people too confused and too scared to do anything. Marley wondered how long this inaction would last. *Who will do all the work that needs to be done to clear the streets? Who will deliver food?* He was frustrated that the media didn't even address causes or solutions to the problems. They just showed what was happening today—the sensational stuff. No one was thinking about the bigger picture. They all talked about quick fixes; nobody was talking about the steps needed to actually cool things down. Nobody was asking if something could be done to slow down the warming trend, maybe even reverse it. No, all the talk was about fear, how to fix the streets, how to get back to work and get the kids back into school, and how to return magically back to the way things were. Nobody wanted to admit there was no going back.

* * *

Marley's phone rang. It was his mom. She was hysterical, and it was hard to understand what she was saying. First of all, she was upset that he had left the house. But more importantly, she said, "The farm's gone. It's all wiped out. Burned to the ground." Her voice was trembling as she told him, beside herself with grief over losing her childhood homestead and worried sick about her brother's family. "What will happen to them?" He hung up, not knowing what to do: go home to comfort his mother or go to the farm.

Brianne's call decided for him. "Jim saw smoke coming from the farm. We better get out there fast. Maybe we can help." They agreed to meet in front of her house as soon as he could get there.

After he hung up with Brianne, Marley heard the voice again, asking the same question as the day before, "What are you going to do about it?" This shook him up again as he struggled to think of an answer. He didn't know what to do. He'd never been in such an alarming situation. All he could think of was to be with his family and people he cared about during this time of shock, grieving, and fear of the future. He went to meet Brianne, and they took off for the farm in her mom's Jeep—it was one of the few vehicles in town that could handle the roads.

Marley's hands were shaking as he tried to get his head around the idea of such a tragedy. Although he had not experienced a family crisis in his life, he often feared that something bad would happen. *But not the farm!* He loved going there, loved working with his aunt and uncle and being with his younger cousins. He couldn't picture life without the farm. This tragedy to his cousins was hitting him hard. He couldn't begin to imagine what the farm would look like after a fire. He almost didn't want to see it.

His worst fears came true as they rounded the curve in the road, and the farm, or at least what was left of the farm, came into view. It took him a moment to recognize the family homestead without the huge barn, the grain shed, and the corn silo. They had all been made of wood and had burned to the ground, leaving only smoldering piles of gray and black ashes. He was disoriented. Those farm buildings had held many of his best childhood memories. He recalled climbing all over the barns and the silos with his younger cousins. Those images were now brutally shoved aside into hazy corners of his brain by the sight of the devastation laid out before him.

The earth was scorched as far as he could see. Marley saw no crops, fences, or livestock anywhere. It was hard to get his bearings without the gigantic, 150-year-old sycamore trees that had lined the driveway and the two large farm buildings that had always framed the barnyard. The house, the only remaining structure, looked small and forlorn, its white clapboard siding blackened from the smoke of the burning barns. Everything looked so different. He was unable to recognize this alien wasteland as the paradise where he had spent his holidays and summers. Aside from the memories of happy days still stored in his head, all else was lost.

In shock and in silence, Marley and Brianne went slowly down the lane. They walked around what was left of the farm, kicking up ash, metal hinges, and nails. Much of the litter that had been sucked up yesterday by the thermal had sifted back down as the wind subsided overnight. A layer of leaves, dead birds, and trash covered the land.

They looked at each other. A pile of sweet-smelling corn was still smoldering where the tall, cylindrical corn silo had stood. Brianne cried and looked closely at Marley's face, probably to see how he was taking it. He was silent, but his sadness was mixed with confusion and anger. He felt his face warm from the smoldering pile of ashes. He stared down at his feet as he tried to absorb the seriousness of what had happened to the farm. "How could this happen to such good people? There's got to be a way to save what's left of the homestead, and maybe even rebuild the barns," he muttered.

They hesitated at the door to take in the panorama of the now-barren farmland. Without trees or buildings, the land looked naked, stripped down to the basics, just undulating ridges and valleys as far as they could see. Marley noted that in stark contrast with yesterday's fiery violence, a profound silence had settled on the land. He sensed a deep loneliness as they huddled there together on the doorstep of the orphaned farmhouse.

Without a word they turned and entered the house. There they found an exhausted Betsy and Luke collapsed at opposite ends of the kitchen table. Marley's aunt and uncle didn't even acknowledge them with a hint of greeting. They didn't move. They just stared down at the surface of the red Formica-topped kitchen table. The heavy silence that had descended upon the farm outside had also crept into the kitchen and settled on Luke and Betsy. It had invaded their bodies and had extinguished any remaining spirit within them.

After scooting Rhode Island Reds off the two remaining chairs, Marley and Brianne sat down. He'd never seen his aunt and uncle so dispirited. Normally happy and unruffled people, now their eyes and mouths drooped, their cheeks were stained with tears, and it seemed like all life had drained out of their bodies—they were clearly at the end of their tethers. Aside from the house, everything they had inherited or built, everything they had lived for, everything they knew how to do, was gone.

Marley and Brianne looked at each other and realized it was up to them to wrestle with the silence. They would have to fight the doom and gloom that had descended on the farmhouse in order to bring some hope, some purpose back into the lives of his aunt and uncle.

Marley reached over and put his hand on his aunt's arm, squeezing it ever so gently, "Aunt Betsy, how did you save the house?"

There was a pause that went on for well over a minute, and then without looking up, Betsy explained, "Luke sprayed water from the well onto the roof. He was out there for hours, keeping it from catching fire. We were lucky that the well lasted and that he didn't get burned too badly. It was like a roaring furnace out there."

Marley, sensing there was little joy in her heart, said, "It worked. That's miraculous, given how bad the winds blew. At least you have the house to live in." There was no response from either end of the table. He didn't know what else to say.

Brianne leaned in close to Luke. "Where are the boys?"

Marley noticed that the hair on both of Luke's arms and his forehead had been singed and he had no eyebrows left. His face and clothes were covered in ashes.

Luke mumbled, "I sent them out to count the livestock we set loose in the back pasture." After a few moments he continued, "I wanted to keep them busy. Of course we have no place to put the animals, even if they can round a few of them up."

"Well, let's start rebuilding this place. We came over to help. I think we can salvage some wire fencing and build a simple barnyard at least," Marley offered.

Betsy explained that it wasn't worth the effort. "Once the bank hears we lost our barns, all of our crops, and most of our livestock, they'll move to foreclose. There's no way for us to pay our mortgage."

It was clear that Betsy and Luke had given up. They were in shock and in a state of grieving for all the things they had lost. They were too tired to sleep. They were too worried about the future to relax. They saw no way out of their troubles. They needed some new way of generating income, at least through the next season, or they would lose the farm.

Not knowing how else to help, Marley and Brianne kept talking, hoping to infuse some hope into the older couple. They wanted to help bring them back from the catatonic state of despair they had fallen into.

"Goodness, Uncle Luke, what're you going to do?" asked Marley.

"I don't know, Marley. I just don't know. It seems impossible to try to start over, with no money in the bank and carrying a huge debt already. We're not a good risk for the bank."

"But I'm sure you'll be able to find a way out—you always have. You have to. So many people depend on you and this farm. I bet all the neighbors will come and help."

"I hope you're right," Luke responded. "I keep thinking that my father and grandfather experienced even worse times than these. Somehow, they made it through the Great Depression and both world wars. But we don't even have a plan."

"With the changes in the weather over the past few years, we're not sure what we can do with this land," Betsy added. "We keep challenging each other for new options. We're trying to consider every idea, but nothing seems possible right now. We're out of ideas."

"What have you considered?" asked Marley.

"We have two difficult challenges," his uncle told him. "We have the immediate challenge of how to cope with the crazy changes that are occurring—we don't even know when the winds, drought, and fires will end. Then we have the long-term challenge of how to get back to earning a living. We don't even know how to get food for our family."

Betsy explained to Marley and Brianne that they couldn't

even sell the farm. "No one wants to buy it now. The land developers who were circling like vultures, trying to buy it before The Changes, will be gun shy now. They'll be concerned about the future of the town, whether this area can recover."

"None of the local farmers want to buy any more worthless land if this area is going into a prolonged drought as predicted," Luke told them. "But we keep telling ourselves there must be something we can do. We don't want to give up."

Marley sensed a spark of life growing in the conversation. Brianne must have sensed it too, because she leaned forward and spoke up, trying to fan the spark. They worked in tandem, trying to help Marley's relatives find the dream that would re-energize their spirit, give them a thread of hope—something to fight for. Sitting around the kitchen table was the perfect setting for brainstorming. They needed to discuss any and all options they could think of for generating income.

Brianne asked, "In the short term, would it make sense to get jobs in town, just till you get your feet back on the ground financially?"

"I think we would be open to doing that," said Betsy, looking at Luke.

"Yes, we would," Luke agreed. "Anything to save the farm. But my guess is that jobs will be moving to places far away if the town doesn't find a way to keep its economic base humming."

With a look of hope on his face, Marley offered another idea. "On the way over here, we passed the RV campground. It was built on the floodplain of the river, and now it's been destroyed. The oil has coated all the campsites, and their picnic tables have spread for miles downriver. I doubt they'll rebuild it. Your land lies above the floodplain. This is a great location for a new RV park, right next to the river. I'd be happy to help out."

"Thanks, Marley," Luke said. "I love the idea. But the river's no longer such an attractive outdoor recreation site since it's filled with oil. I don't know how long it will take to clean the river and for campers to return. It could be years, maybe decades. Who knows?"

Brianne spoke up next, trying to lift their spirits with another idea for the farm. "How about a Christmas tree farm? You could do a Cut-Your-Own-Tree operation. Everyone would love it. I can picture families running all over the farm, selecting the perfect tree."

"That's another good idea," Betsy said. "We've talked about that in the past. But again, even if we got enough rain for the trees to grow, the cash flow would be nil for a while because trees take five to eight years to grow to a size that people want. We don't have that much staying-power. There's not enough money to feed the family *and* the bank for five years."

"We must sound like a couple of pessimists, citing all the reasons why we can't do any of these things," Luke apologized.

But neither Marley nor Brianne were ready to give up. They had gotten the discussion going with their enthusiasm and had brought Betsy and Luke out of their silent depression. They had started them thinking and dreaming again.

"Well, you could take advantage of the hot, dry conditions and build a solar farm," Brianne offered, hoping to stumble onto something that would both cheer them up and meet their needs. "That would be a great use of your barren land, and you could still keep some land for a scaled-back farm, with smaller gardens and fewer animals. You could probably generate enough electricity to meet much of the town's needs."

Marley noticed that Betsy became more animated at the mention of the solar option. She had obviously been investigating it already. "We could install a solar farm fairly quickly and make revenue from it this year," she said. "The bank would like that, especially if we can find an investor and a purchaser for the electricity we'd generate."

"It's worth taking a closer look," said Luke, looking as though he were trying to get his head around the idea of farming the sun. He was hesitant, probably for good reason. What did he know about that business? "I wonder who we should talk to about that possibility. Our local utility, SVE—Sleepy Valley Energy—should be interested in another source of power. Their old power plant won't last forever. I would hope we could work with them."

"I don't know, but I think you should find out. Let us know how we can help," said Brianne.

Marley noted that solar was the only option still afloat at the end of their discussion. He smiled at Brianne. They had found something his uncle and aunt could focus on—a business for the farm that could make economic sense in a warming climate. It was also clear his aunt and uncle had a lot of work to do and not a lot of time to make it happen before the bank stepped in and took the farm away from them.

But he sensed that Brianne's enthusiasm had worked a miracle; his aunt and uncle were engaged. With renewed energy and hope, they were no longer despondent. The brainstorming had provided them with a lifeline. They had risen from their chairs and were milling around the kitchen, making coffee and making plans. Marley knew Betsy and Luke would now do whatever they could to pursue the solar option. Maybe there was a way to save the family farm after all.

CHAPTER TEN

MAX EMERGES

A lonely male woodcock flitted around the dried-up, splintered remains of the forest. He poked his ultra-long beak here and there into piles of woody debris, looking for food. The bird had completely lost his orientation in this wind-tossed landscape of dead wood. Only his internal GPS told him this was, or at least had been, his home. However, he didn't recognize a thing that looked like home. *Where are the tall trees, the meadows, all the other animals, and most importantly, that dreamy female woodcock I was courting the other night?* He felt lost, puzzled, and disappointed at the state of things. But being a woodcock, he focused on living in the present, which meant food and mating.

A rumbling groan emanated from deep within the pile of broken timbers. The woodcock went to see what might be the source of these sounds. Not much appeared to be alive on the upper levels, so he fearlessly explored deeper and deeper into the woody debris.

As he hopped from dismembered trunk to limb to branch, he recognized the camouflaged Peeping Tom who had been watching him during his last intimate mating ritual. *Maybe this human who distracted my intended mate knows where she is now.*

He jumped down to get a better look and noticed a bronze Ranger nametag on the man's khaki-colored shirt, identifying him as "Bunyan." The woodcock decided to wake the man up. He landed on Max's boots, then jumped from leg to arm to chest to chin, and then stared Max directly in the eye and called out, "PEENT! PEENT!" as if to say, "Now what do you have to say for yourself?"

* * *

Max woke on Sunday morning to the sound of the woodcock's call—it sounded like he was being heckled. Blinking his eyes, he realized he was under a huge pile of trees. *I can't believe it. How could I have lived through the nightmare of losing an entire forest? Those darn beetles buried me well. And their venom kept me in a motionless, delirious state the whole time.*

He slowly remembered that every crash of a tree throughout the night had felt like another rusty nail being hammered through his broken heart. Now, as his mind started to clear, he realized his body still felt comatose after those long hours of torture, lying trapped on the forest floor, listening to his forest fall all around him.

He checked his phone—he had been in a coma for 36 hours. No wonder he was sore. He stretched each limb of his stiff, aching body. Amazingly, everything still worked. He hadn't suffered any serious physical wounds to his body, but mentally, he was a total wreck. He remembered that at some point during his ordeal, he had given up, not willing to expend any energy whatsoever to save himself. After all, what was there left to live for? The forest had been his home and the fauna and flora his family. He guessed that over 99% of the living creatures and plants in the park had died or been blown away. He had suffered a terrible loss from which he might never recover. Now, in this desperate state of mind, he had nothing to motivate him and was dejectedly waiting for the end.

Max's burned-out mind slowly began to focus on the bird, the only other living thing within eyesight. *Now what's this bird up to? Oh, right, I recognize him. He's a male woodcock. I wonder if he's the same one I was watching when all hell broke loose. I bet he is, and now he's coming back in search of his mate. Unfortunately for him, I'm the only other remaining party of that affair. Must be sad for him, too. He gave a brilliant display and got nothing for his efforts.*

Max's tortured mind went off on a tangent. He revisited memories of the good times and the struggles he'd had preserving and maintaining the park over the years. But then, with another "PEENT, PEENT," his recovering brain came swirling back to the present and to the woodcock. *Well, he's certainly all business, checking things out, not letting this catastrophe get the better of him. What a great example of life carrying on — pretty impressive. He might be the only bird left living here, and he might just make it if he's lucky. I hope he does.* Just thinking about the perky woodcock and the resilience of life energized Max a little. It must have been his Thoreauvian side—he loved watching and learning from nature.

With this newfound energy, Max's mind began to picture all the other wonderful parks he had visited. He realized none of them were native stands of trees. Almost all forests today were the result of someone's efforts in the past.

And that was the moment Max had an epiphany. *Aha! This desolate place — this pile of debris — could once again become a beautiful park. It would take decades of hard work, and the rebuilder might never see the fruits of his labor. But so what? It would be like building a cathedral. It would be solely an investment of love. A gift to future generations.*

A few moments later Max fully emerged from his stupor and took an inventory of his current state of being. He checked to see if he could move his limbs and discovered that he could; he wasn't permanently trapped under the timbers. With great effort he rolled over onto his belly, dust and leaf debris falling every which way. He now faced downwards and decided to rest again to catch his breath and at the same time marshal all his strength for his next move. While he caught his breath, he looked carefully at what lay right in front of him.

Max focused his eyes on the dead limbs, branches, and debris lying just inches in front of his face. After a while he started to notice green and white spots in the midst of the splinters. As he examined them, he began to wonder. *Are they moving? Am I hallucinating? Am I crazy?* No, he wasn't losing his mind. The dots *were* moving, or growing at least, reaching upward ever so slowly.

He watched as a small army of green mosses and white fungi climbed up and engulfed the dead wood, sending mycelia tentacles deep into the dead branches. They were all reaching up to consume the debris and break it down into the basic elements needed to feed new life. He remembered that's what mosses and fungi do. *It's their job. And here, right in front of my nose, they're starting the process of rebuilding the forest. Hurray!* They were indeed the first responders to this catastrophe, and they were already onsite and busy. He was impressed.

The more he looked, the more he saw. As usual, nature was instructive. He noticed hundreds of thread-like mycelia climbing up towards him, starting to wrap their tentacles around branches, bark, and even his motionless fingers. The eons-old rebuilding process that occurs almost everywhere on Earth had begun. And just like that, his choice became crystal clear. He could get up right now and join in the rebuilding process, or he could just lie there and be consumed by it.

Damn it! It's time to get the heck out of this prison and build something great. I'm going to lead the charge. I will find a way to get rid of every last one of those blue beetles, and I'm going to build myself a new forest. Something the Greater Sapphire Beetle cannot destroy. Something that will be attractive and beneficial to all people and animals. Something natural and exciting for our kids and grandkids to enjoy years from now.

And with that vow to the universe, Max rose from the dead forest. He stood up, and all the branches and timbers fell off him. He climbed out of the graveyard of trees and headed back to park headquarters with a fierce determination. He had turned his anger into something constructive. He was going to rebuild his forest.

The woodcock must have sensed his passion, because he followed close behind. "PEENT! PEENT!" He didn't know exactly what Max was up to, but he wanted to be part of it. At least someone was taking action to rebuild the forest.

*** * ***

Later that afternoon, on their way back from the farm, Brianne and Marley passed along the frontage to Sleepy Valley Park. Both their families had spent many weekends in the park over the years and had many memories of camping and hiking there. They often recalled crackling campfires, wind moaning in the treetops, and animals, foraging at night, sounding much bigger than they were.

In more recent years, Max had engaged Brianne and Marley as camp counselors. As a result they both felt like it was their park, their backyard. But where was Max now? Marley was concerned because they hadn't heard from him since Friday night. Jim had described what had happened to the park, and it was hard to imagine anyone living through the total demolition of a forest.

Marley struggled to get his bearings as he came up the road into the park. The large sentinel pine trees at the entrance were gone. The brown cedar buildings had been smashed beneath the falling timbers. No trees stood in this place that had once been defined by trees. Nothing was left that could help him get oriented. The park was devastated; it looked like a rolling hillside wasteland. Everything was covered with debris.

"I'm feeling sick just looking at what's happened," Brianne said. "Max must be here someplace. He would never abandon his park. Where should we start to look? The cabins are destroyed."

Beyond being shocked, Marley was furious, just as he had been when he first saw the devastation at the family farm. "What happened here? How could this place change so fast? We were here just a few days ago. It was so beautiful."

"The trees are gone. All the trees. The birds and animals are gone, too. It's so quiet. Marley, our park is gone."

Marley just looked around dumbfounded, unable to answer her, even to look at her or to express his deep sense of loss in words. He kicked at branches strewn all around on the ground.

He didn't want her to see how depressed he was and how useless he felt. His two favorite places on Earth were destroyed.

As they came up the lane toward the park, they saw a dust cloud brewing in the middle of the debris. The more they watched, the more they recognized it as human. A manmade duster, with a lot of yelling, grunting, and cussing emanating from the cloud. As they drew closer, they both broke into smiles. It could only be Max, and yes, there he was, scurrying around as fast as they had ever seen the big man move. He was hustling about, cleaning things up. He threw a branch one direction and dragged a limb another, literally going non-stop, moving the dead wood off the road and out of the way.

They both yelled at the same time, ecstatic to see he was alive. Marley was even more amazed to realize that Max was beyond the denial and anger stages and had marshaled all his energies to take action, to rebuild the forest. How could he have processed his anger so fast? They were impressed, and his enthusiasm was contagious. They, too, wanted to help.

"We're so glad you're alive," Marley shouted to Max. "But what a mess."

"Yeah. How can we help?" Brianne asked.

Marley then realized Max wasn't alone. The first thing he saw was a woodcock flying around Max's head, eating any insects that might be bothering the big man. Then Marley noticed that Luke's biggest steer, a crossbreed between an American Bison and a Black Angus, was assisting Max. He was big and had a beautiful, bluish-black hide. He must have gotten out when the fire destroyed Luke's farm.

"I think the steer belongs to Luke," Max said. "He just showed up this morning and seemed like he wanted to help, and I need as much support as I can get. He's a great volunteer."

Marley did get the feeling that the steer enjoyed working in the park.

"I call him Buff because he looks like a buffalo—albeit a very large one." Max had outfitted his newfound friend in a wooden yoke with long ropes. Buff was dragging the large trees over to a place where Max could stockpile the wood.

Apparently, Buff could pull anything, sometimes two trees at a time. Just by watching them for a few minutes, it was obvious to Marley that the two of them had bonded and had enthusiastically begun the daunting task of restoring the park. Marley was impressed with their drive and ambition.

Without stopping, Max shouted to them with a look of crazed determination. "I need to get the roads cleared so people can come and inspect the damage. They need to have a gut-level reaction to what happened here, so they'll fund the replanting of the forest."

"You know," Marley commented, "there are a lot of other disasters in town as well that people want the town council to fix."

"Yep. We have a big sales job to do. That's why we've got to get the council members out here soon. Time is of the essence because gut reactions don't last long! When faced with so many problems, people tend to just move on to the next catastrophe, and with the warming weather, we're sure to have more."

"Max, we can't stay and help now," Marley said. "Mom's waiting to hear our report about the destruction of the family farm. You might have heard that most of it burned down. But be sure to let us know how we can help. We'll be back."

"Sure thing, Marley. And let your uncle know his prize steer is over here helping out."

CHAPTER ELEVEN

LIFE ADAPTS

When Marley and Brianne got back to Marley's house, they sat down with his mom and dad and described what they had seen at the farm. Marley's mom was most concerned about how Betsy, Luke, and the boys were doing and how they were going to survive with the farm mostly gone. Marley assured her there was a plan for rebuilding. Turning to his dad, he asked, "Dad, is there any way you could help get the financing for a solar farm? It sounds like it should be a great investment."

"I don't know, Marley. I agree it sounds tempting, but there's so much uncertainty right now with all the changes taking place. People with money are going to be real hesitant unless they feel it's a sure thing. They'll definitely need a contract in place for selling the electricity to the utility company."

Marley didn't mention to his parents how distraught the Alexanders had been when he and Brianne had first arrived at the farm. He didn't want to get them any more alarmed than they already were, but he did discuss what the farm looked like.

Marley's mom, near tears, got up from the discussion and said, "I'm going to make a few casseroles that you can take over to help feed them during these tough times."

"Mom, that's great. I'm sure they don't have much to eat at this point, aside from the canned vegetables and the fruit in their root cellar. I'm guessing all of their sources of food are gone except for the few chickens they kept for eggs. They're hoping the well will continue to provide them with enough water for household needs."

"I wonder what else we can do for them and for others in their situation," Brianne said. "There are a lot of people in need right now."

"That reminds me," Marley's dad said. "Did we tell you that several of our neighbors have been trying to reach you, Marley? Evidently, they saw you were the only person outside yesterday, so they started calling, looking for assistance with a range of errands. They realize cars are way too dangerous on the melting roads."

Marley liked the idea of being able to help—it gave him something to do, something to take his mind off the destruction of the farm and the park. It also gave him a good excuse to justify staying outside. He would go crazy cooped up in the house all day. "I'd love to help them out."

"I'm not so sure about that. You don't need to be exposed to all those fumes," his mom cautioned.

"I don't know if the fumes are any better inside than out," Marley replied "I've noticed both of you itching your arms, and neither of you were outside yesterday."

"We'll leave it up to you, Marley," his dad said. "But keep an eye on how you're feeling and come inside if your symptoms get worse."

"I can help by taking calls, arranging for pickups, and scheduling stops," Brianne offered. She too seemed pleased to have something to do, some way to help.

"That would be great. Let's get started," Marley told her. "We can take over the den as our call center." The two stood up and moved into the adjacent room, closing the door behind them.

"Let's call these people back and start booking the day," Marley began. Then he noticed her shallow breathing and how hard it seemed to be for her to catch her breath. "Brianne, your breathing doesn't sound so good. Are you okay?"

"It's just my asthma coming back. I'm short of breath, but I'll be okay as long as I have my inhaler."

"You inhaled too much of the polluted air yesterday."

"Probably. All I know is that when I woke up this morning, everything seemed out of kilter. When I glanced at the clock, it appeared to have slumped downward, almost as if it were flowing off the bureau and onto the floor. My whole bedroom felt surreal, like the clocks in a Salvador Dali painting. It took a while for my vision to clear up, but I'm okay now. I'll just take it easy today."

"I know what you're talking about. I felt pretty woozy this morning too. I'll try to pick up some backup inhalers at the drugstore for you. They'll certainly be running out of supplies soon. Who knows how long this will last."

"You better get yourself some cream for those rashes on your arms, too," Brianne told him. "I've noticed you've been scratching a lot."

"It's not so bad." Marley smiled for the first time that day. He liked working with her. She listened, she cared, and she was fun to be with, even when things were bad. He was so glad she was helping to take the calls and find stores that were open. She was much better talking with people on the phone, and he just wanted to keep active, out on the streets.

Brianne found she had to resort to stores on the edges of town and near the interstate exits for most of the things people requested. The oil was not as thick in those places, and the employees were able to get into work.

People were also borrowing items from each other. It took a lot of calling and coordination. But by the end of the day, she had a network of folks who could help her figure out who needed what and where the best place was to get something. Everyone was helping out.

They were both surprised by the number of calls, mainly requests for food and medicine. Everyone wanted to stock up on anything they thought would be in short supply.

Mr. Truby called to ask, "Can you pick up a prescription for me at the pharmacy? It's way too hot for me to go out. I can hardly breathe."

Gertrude and Bertha Hall, down at the Tea Room, requested 20 pounds of pastry flour.

Audrey Webb asked, "Is the postal service working? Do you think you could mail a package to my niece?"

Marsha Bell called, asking, "Can you actually get around in all this mess? I need new batteries for my fire alarm system and a pound of sugar for a birthday cake I'm baking for my son."

Even though Marley encountered a great deal of fear, it felt good to be able to help. He knew most of the people who called. Equally important, the errands got him out and involved during this challenging time. It gave him a deeper appreciation for the daily struggles of the people in his neighborhood during The Changes.

The neighbors also loved talking with Brianne. She had a cheerful way of instantly lifting their spirits while meeting their needs. Mr. and Mrs. Truby both commented to Marley, "You could hear Brianne's smile shining through the phone."

A large number of requests were for creams to treat skin rashes and for medicines for bronchial problems. Marley realized his rash and Brianne's asthma were not unique occurrences; they were just symptoms, part of a widespread health epidemic resulting from The Warming. The high concentration of toxic fumes was affecting the health of almost everyone in the community, one way or another. The patients and doctors all focused on relieving these symptoms. None of them discussed that the best solution would be to take steps to improve the local air quality or move to healthier areas. The doctors, like everyone else, must have felt that the big-picture solution, the global nature of the problem, was beyond their responsibility.

During a break in the action, back at Marley's house, Brianne asked, while attempting to clean the oil off her shoes, "Why do you think this is happening?"

"I don't know," Marley said. He reached over and took a few of her potato chips. "Doc says there's a point with most natural systems where they get out of balance. He believes we've gone too far and the atmosphere's just responding to a long list of human impacts, including the release of huge amounts of fossil fuel emissions."

"I guess we're all in this together," Brianne said. "We caused it, and now we have to work together to fix it. That's even more reason to help each other out."

Later that day, when Marley stopped by the Truby home and gave them their medicine, Mr. Truby gave him a nice tip and asked, "Can you buy all my groceries later this week? I'm scared to go outside until the streets are cleaned up. Who knows when that will happen? At my age I'd rather stay home and starve than risk breaking a leg."

Marley started to realize that food delivery was going to be a long-term need for his neighbors. He wondered how long he would be able to meet that need and whether he even wanted to do it for long. It gave him a sense of purpose in the short term, but he would have to see. There was a lot more he wanted to do with his life than run errands for neighbors. "Brianne, we need to find some way to get groceries and other supplies delivered better, more efficiently. I'm thinking of some sort of cooperative network where people could all pitch in to get food to everyone in town. We can't run our limited delivery service forever."

"You're right. How can we build on everyone's interest to help their neighbors? I think we already have a good network growing. Let's keep expanding it and get even more people to help. We can call it the Neighborhood Network."

Marley was intrigued trying to figure out how the network would work. If the stores closed up, food could be delivered to neighborhoods, and then neighbors could help distribute it. This could be done at nighttime when the roads were safer to drive on. Eventually maybe all deliveries could be done by drones. But for now, the key was to strengthen the human aspects of the network he and Brianne were establishing and then expand it. It had to be based on trust and a desire to help each other. Using money was great as long as everyone had it. But at some point it might not be available.

Marley also struggled with trying to envision what might happen in the long term. *What is life going to be like in a month, in a year, in ten years?* He kept coming back to three questions: *Will Sleepy Valley ever get back to normal? If not, then what will the new normal be like? Can anything be done to stop, slow down, or even reverse these disasters?*

He was increasingly concerned, not just about what could be done to fix things in their town, but who was going to do it. *Someone else, someone older, should be in charge of figuring this all out. But is anyone in charge? Aside from Max, Jim, and Wanda, no one seems to be taking any action. The town doesn't appear to be doing anything at all.* That concerned him. His vision of a neighborhood network wasn't going to be enough to save the town. There was a lot more that needed to be done.

When Marley had thoughts like these, he went to Doc. He and Brianne had come to respect Doc ever since Doc started hosting the Friday Afternoon Seminar Series at school. Doc was cool. He had this understated way of engaging the students, challenging them, and giving them respect when they deserved it. He also went off on tangents that helped to tie each topic into real-life choices. Marley and Brianne loved it. The seminars had inspired them both to organize their thoughts and think about bigger issues, as well as making them more comfortable when speaking in front of others.

In search of answers, Marley and Brianne went to find Doc, who just happened to be standing next to his mailbox when they arrived. The mailbox was now completely covered in vines, but Doc had managed to find the latch and open the door. He was a bit anxious since, due to the street conditions, no mail had been delivered the day before. Like everything else, no one knew what they could count on anymore.

Doc acted surprised to see them, but Marley knew he was interested in what else was happening around town.

"Just reporting back, Doc." Marley then proceeded to tell him about all the things they had seen, including the destruction of the farm and the park.

"Doc, what's going on? Is our city dying?" asked Brianne.

"And what can we do about all The Changes?" Marley added. "We can't just let Sleepy Valley melt or blow away."

Doc looked tired. Marley assumed he had been up late, trying to put his thoughts about a very hot, dystopian future into words. But Doc stopped what he was doing and took the time to hear them out and honor their concerns. Doc, of course, would want to inspire them to get engaged during this crisis, not to shut down like so many others were doing.

After a few minutes mulling over an appropriate response to this barrage of new information, concerns, and fears, Doc said, "Helping your neighbors is great. You need to continue and expand those efforts. In fact, you need to organize the entire community to help one another. But as important as that is, it's only a temporary fix.

"The town has to look at all the facts and decide what they can do, both in the short term and the long term—how to best use their resources to help us recover. There won't be any easy solutions to these events. The first thing our elected officials should do is call a town meeting to listen to and address our concerns."

"When will they do that?" asked Brianne. The whites of her eyes completely encircled the dark pupils. She was clearly bewildered that nothing had happened yet.

"I don't know, but it should be soon. Let's hope they're already assessing the problems and evaluating their options. How soon they hold the meeting really depends on how many people contact them. I bet their phones have been ringing constantly. People may not be outside, trying to fix things, but you can bet they're on the phones, trying to get the town and the state to take action.

"The next thing you might want to do is to call the people on the council, encourage them to act. The more people they hear from, the sooner they'll respond."

"I'm all in," Brianne said. "I think it's a great idea, and it's easy to do. I'll find the phone numbers for our local and state representatives and start calling. How about you, Marley?"

"I'm not getting involved with the council," Marley replied. "I'm going to stick with helping my neighbors. That's the best use of my time, and Brianne, I need your help. I hope you're not abandoning our community-support efforts."

"No, I still want to help the neighbors," Brianne said. "But give me an hour or two to make these calls. I think both steps are important."

After a moment or two, Doc continued, "When they do hold a meeting, you two should go. Your voices need to be part of this discussion. You're the future of this town, and what we do now will determine what kind of future you'll have."

Marley fidgeted with the wheels on his board for a moment before he replied. "As I said, I don't do politics, Doc. It's all corrupt. I don't want anything to do with the council."

"You already do politics, Marley," Doc told him. "You care. You talk to others. You help your neighbors. You speak out on issues important to you."

"Yeah, but I've never spoken at a meeting," Marley said.

"Trying to convince the politicians to do the right thing is just another level up from what you're already doing. It's an opportunity to be more effective and help even more of your neighbors," said Doc. "Don't tell me you don't do politics. Just ask yourself if you want to have a greater say in your future and what gets done around here."

Marley looked down at his feet, unsure whether he followed Doc's logic.

"Doc's right," Brianne told him as she walked over to him. "We should go and make sure they hear our concerns. It's a big deal. I know you care a lot about our town. If not us, then who's going to do it? We've seen more of what's happening in town than anyone else."

Doc checked the empty mailbox for the third time and then laughed. "I finally realized today's Sunday," he said. "No mail delivery—even if they were still delivering the mail. But back to our discussion. Politics is a noble thing in concept, a way for more people and more ideas to get heard—it just requires people like you two to share your ideas and make sure it works well."

"If you want to go, Brianne, I'll go with you, but I have no idea what I'd say, or for that matter, what they should do," Marley said reluctantly. "I also kind of doubt they'll listen to us. Nobody's going to pay attention to a couple of teenagers."

Doc chimed in one last time. "It's actually more important that you ask questions and engage in the discussion than go with your minds already made up."

"Why's that?" asked Brianne.

"Democracy works best when people come together to listen to others and discuss a full range of options as they seek to find the best solution." With that final message, he banged the mailbox door shut and turned toward the house, leaving Marley and Brianne to contemplate his comments and determine their next steps.

"I'm going to focus on the neighborhood," Marley decided. "That's where the biggest need is."

"Go for it. I'll help when I can," Brianne said. "But right now I'm going to focus on making calls and sending messages to get the town and state to take action."

They waved to each other as they headed back to their respective homes.

* * *

When old Ed Perkins took his "daily constitutional" stroll the morning after The Changes began, he encountered a much smaller group of old men at the pavilion. He realized the missing ones must have taken Jim's air-quality warnings seriously. *Or maybe they've already felt the effects of breathing the polluted air. After all, breathing isn't always easy for old people, even on good days.*

Ed suspected that many of his associates would be selective about which of Jim's health warnings they listened to. The air-quality and high-temperature alerts encouraging folks to stay home also warned them all to stay hydrated. Jim had suggested that everyone should avoid coffee, Coke, alcohol, and energy drinks, which all increase dehydration. Ed doubted any of his friends would listen to that advice.

As Ed walked along, his breathing was more labored than normal, but he ignored it. "Nothing out of the ordinary," he would say when someone mentioned it to him. When he arrived at the diner where everyone was, he announced, "Some of the men are scared to go outside. They've probably been listening to the radio again."

Ed's respiratory system was further challenged by the bad air quality around the lake. As he walked down to the pavilion, he encountered the stench of four-foot-high windrows of dead fish decaying on the beach. The fish had died during the night, unable to breathe in the methane-charged and algae-clogged waters. The oxygen-starved fish had floated to the surface of the lake and had been blown onto shore by the strong winds. Thousands of shiny, dead fish were now drying out in the hot sun. The horrific aroma had attracted feral cats, rats, buzzards, and even a few eagles that had come from miles away to gobble up this tasty feast of decomposing fish. Ed didn't find the stench attractive at all.

Ben was there, of course, with his cup of coffee, but he sat farther away from the lake than usual. Before retiring, he had been the agricultural extension agent, so he knew the new agent would want to know what was happening in the lake. He snapped pictures of the windrows to send off to the agent, along with his personal commentary of events. "Ed, the word I get from the state is that our lake isn't carbonated. The bubbles are probably methane from the decay of all the algae and dense grasses that have been snagging our fishing lines over the past few years."

"That makes sense, Ben, but what's causing the massive algae blooms in the first place?"

"The ag agent tells me its nitrogen exhaust from cars, the power plant emissions, and excess fertilizer from our yards and fields. It all washes into the lake and feeds the algae."

"I knew the West Siders were to blame for this mess," Ed said, his voice rising. "They have more cars over there and use most of the electricity from the power plant. Without them we wouldn't be having this problem. This valley's not big enough for all these new people. It just can't handle all the growth."

"They do account for some of the pollution," Ben agreed. "But all the water pollution comes from our side of town. We just use too much fertilizer."

"It's hard to believe people would waste fertilizer," Ed argued.

"Fertilizer's cheap, so everyone uses way too much. The ag agent's been trying to get people to use less and to slow down storm-water runoff. It carries the fertilizer into the lake."

"It's hard to get folks to cut back on fertilizing," Ed mumbled. "Farmers think they need it. Gardeners think they need it. Hell, even people with just grass think they need it. They never think of the consequences."

"I hope the fear of losing the lake serves as a wake-up call. What would our town be like if we didn't have a healthy lake?" Ben replied.

"House values would fall, and we couldn't go fishing. It's a darn shame to lose all those fish. I never knew so many lived in the lake."

Ben nodded his head. "It's a mess, a *preventable* mess. Why's it so hard for people to change their behavior? Does it always take a catastrophe?"

Old Ed groused as he turned to go. "Hell, even a catastrophe doesn't help much. Nobody wants to believe they're responsible for any of these problems."

"Where're you going, Ed?"

"Think I'll keep walking. Find someplace upwind, away from this stench." Ed then winked at Ben and said, "Be careful, Ben. Don't light a match around all that methane. I'd hate to see you go up in smoke."

As the two old men went their separate ways, a boy glided by on a beat-up skateboard. He was there to see for himself what had happened to the lake and the life it once supported.

✳ ✳ ✳

Over the weekend, Sleepy Valley's downtown morphed from a busy and prosperous commercial center into a ghost town. It was the second day of The Changes, and few people felt safe enough to venture outside.

The downtown pigeons found this refreshing on the one hand and disappointing on the other. They weren't being chased by kids, dogs, or cars. But they missed the sugar and trans-fat-saturated, fast-food rejects they had come to depend on. They were getting thinner by the minute.

Being bright animals, it didn't take long for the pigeons to learn not to land on the streets or on asphalt-shingled roofs. It was too hard to lift off once they stepped in the sticky goo. The decomposing, oil-soaked bodies of several of their careless friends remained memorialized on the streets and rooftops. These foreboding black statues served as a warning of every pigeon's fate if they made a misstep and got covered with oil.

The smarter pigeons learned quickly to limit their roosting to telephone wires and historical monuments, slowly covering the famous humans of the past with a fresh, white, guano veneer. The monuments turned into ghost-like apparitions that haunted the deserted square day and night.

As the velocity of the winds increased with the warming of the day, it became a challenge for any bird to keep a perch on the now-overcrowded telephone lines. Pigeons found they needed to hold on so tightly that they often got leg cramps and couldn't release their grip. Cramped legs and clenched claws became a big problem when they lost their balance. Pigeons could be seen twirling around the wires like pinwheels. It was exhilarating at first, but most birds got dizzy and found it hard to stop and regain control once they started spinning.

Many pigeons got so tired of balancing on top of the wires that they gave up and hung upside-down, like sleeping bats or backyard laundry. Others who were able to release their grip flew to more protected areas outside of town.

With the double whammy of oily streets and roofs and high winds, life wasn't easy for those pigeons who remained in Sleepy

Valley. One could just imagine that, in their morning discussions while perched on the telephone lines, they increasingly spoke of migrating to someplace else—but it wasn't clear where they could go.

The squirrels were having an even harder time adjusting to The Changes. Like most other animals, squirrels had lost their traditional transportation routes: the ground, treetops, and roofs. They had the additional disadvantage of not being able to fly like pigeons.

There were numerous examples of clumsy squirrels stuck in the oil all over town—their fur now coated in black. Most squirrels, however, quickly learned to stay in the branches of downed trees that served as solitary islands in the sea of oil. They learned to adapt to life, a life of higher risk closer to the ground. Any slip, of course, and they were goners.

CHAPTER TWELVE

THE GLOBAL VIEW

On Sunday night Marley's mom invited Brianne to stay for dinner. Mrs. Jones had been on edge all day—ever since she'd heard about the damage to the family farm that morning. She said she wanted the four of them to have a frank talk about what was happening in their town and what they should be doing to stay safe. She knew Brianne's presence would be key to getting her son and her husband to sit down and fully engage in a serious discussion. She wanted to know what risks they faced and their plans for the future.

Marley was cool with that. He wanted answers too. He just didn't know if his parents had any answers. But he sensed this was important to his mom, and he agreed they should have an emergency plan if conditions got worse.

Marley also knew Brianne would be delighted to join them. She had told him it was always fun to hang out with the Jones family. This didn't happen all that often because Marley, like most teenagers, was often embarrassed by his folks. He always worried they would say things or ask questions that would be awkward for him. But they were all feeling the stress, and it was a good idea to be together.

The dinner went well. Most of the discussion centered on Sleepy Valley and what could be done. It was a good time to air their fears to one another. Up to this point Marley had just been thinking about himself and Brianne. He hadn't really appreciated or taken the time to listen to his parents' concerns. It was helpful, and they did come up with an agreement to check in with each other during the day. They also picked locations where they would meet in case of an emergency.

Right after dinner Marley's dad said, "Let's watch the national news and see what else is happening around the world. Let's see if it's as bad in other places around the country."

Each of them had been getting information, of course, all day long on their newsfeeds, but none of them had found the time to read any of it in detail. It was a good opportunity for all of them to sit back and think about what was going on in a more global context.

Marley sat down on the couch next to Brianne. "Do you mind if I sit next to you?"

She smiled. "That would be fine as long as you bring the popcorn."

He laughed as he sank into the couch. The discussion that evening had been cathartic. It felt good that he had a family and a good friend to go through these challenging times with; it felt like a load had been lifted off his mind. It was also the first time he'd had all day to sit and relax. He even thought he might fall asleep.

However, that state of calm didn't last long. When the news came on, with full screen images of what was occurring around the world, he leaned forward, not wanting to miss anything. It was pretty shocking. No part of the planet appeared to be immune to the impacts of The Warming. They all sat silently and watched to see how the pieces of the global-climate puzzle fit together.

"It's pretty confusing," Marley said, turning to Brianne. "It's not just that everything's heating up. In some places it's colder than normal, and in other places it's hotter. Some places are drier and other places are wetter."

"It looks like our climate is changing to one with more

extreme weather events, not just a warming trend," Mr. Jones added.

"Well, that's what the models have been predicting," Brianne told them. "More evaporation as the oceans warms leads to a more saturated atmosphere resulting in more extreme storms."

Marley stood up and walked over to the screen, pointing to the interior of the U.S. "I really don't understand all the different maps they're showing, but it looks like large areas of the country are suffering from drought, much like Sleepy Valley."

"Yes, and look at the northeast and Gulf Coast areas. They're getting drenched with torrential rains, floodwaters, and storm surges," Marley's mom observed.

"I remember looking at an earlier version of this picture last summer during my internship," Brianne told them. "It's complex and hard to comprehend, but the models have been consistently right on."

Mrs. Jones stopped her knitting and said, "Look at the pictures of the flooded towns. How are all those communities along the coast dealing with these events? The flooding there looks much more threatening than what we're facing."

"No one has plans for battling that amount of water," said Brianne.

Marley's dad took up the conversation. "The problem now is that these events are so widespread. It's impossible to marshal the manpower you need from other parts of the country because everyone needs help. FEMA and the Red Cross aren't prepared to handle all of these disasters at one time. Rescue and rebuilding efforts will all have to be managed and supported locally."

Marley had started pacing around the room while his dad spoke. Now he said, "That's kind of the way I feel here. The only help I've seen is what we're providing our neighbors. Our town's government hasn't done anything yet."

"Did you hear that all the insurance firms in the country declared bankruptcy earlier today?" Mrs. Jones commented. "There'll be no funding from any of them to help people recover."

"I'm numb just listening to this. It's worse than I thought." Marley sank into the couch. "It really is all up to us to save ourselves, isn't it?"

"Yeah," Brianne agreed. "To save ourselves, our neighbors, and the masses of people migrating northward and toward the interior of the country."

"That's a good point," Marley's dad said. "How're we going to be able to help them when they get here? Most of us are already running out of food and suffering from our own extreme weather challenges."

They were all quiet, thinking about how things could get even worse. The newscaster could be heard speaking in the background. He was talking about how many businesses and essential services like hospitals, power plants, and sewage treatment plants had shut down. "No one knows when things will, if ever, return to normal."

"I doubt they ever will," Marley said quietly.

The last report they heard before turning off the news described mountain-scale ice sheets that had slid into the seas off Greenland and Antarctica, creating tsunami-type waves that rolled across the Atlantic, Pacific, and Indian oceans, devastating coastal villages, cities, and fishing fleets. Hundreds of oil supertankers were already missing, and huge oil slicks, some the size of Delaware, had been seen in many of the Earth's oceans.

In a very shaky voice, Marley's mom said, "We need to make an even more detailed back-up plan than we discussed earlier. I think we're going to need it. We should stock up and start eating more frugally. And we can fill the bathtubs with water."

"You're right," Mr. Jones agreed. "We should consider our options in case the town doesn't figure out how to fix all The Changes. First thing in the morning I'm going to take some cash out of the bank and keep it here in my office in case money gets tight. I might also look around to see what my options are in case I need to find a new job. You two may want to do the same thing. It wouldn't hurt, especially if your colleges don't open in the fall.

"This is really depressing, Dad," said Marley. "First the farm and now our own home. I've had enough shocks for one day. I'm going down to the basement." He turned to Brianne and asked, "You want to come?"

* * *

Marley and Brianne went down to his shop. He needed to get away from the bad news—maybe distract himself by working on his board. He was struggling with the doomsday nature of what he had just seen on the screen. "We've got to talk to Jim. Maybe he can help us see through all these events to the future, if there is one. Watching the news is just numbing us all into inaction. I came away from watching it with a sinking feeling in my stomach, a hopeless feeling—like there's nothing I can do."

"You're right. I'll get him on speaker."

Jim picked up right away, almost as if he were waiting for Brianne's call. "Hey. What's up?"

"Hey, we're both here at Marley's house. We're getting a little scared."

Marley found himself staring into Brianne's eyes. She was looking at him as well. He sensed her fear, and it made him want to find a way through this nightmare and save both of them, as well as the town.

"Jim, we need to get your perspective on all these things that are happening," Marley said. "These aren't just local problems. Is there any hope? Or are we in survival mode already?"

"Sounds like you've been watching the news," Jim said.

"Yes, Brianne and I have been watching for the past hour. No place on Earth is normal anymore. A lot of people are already suffering. It's all changing."

"The whole world has tipped. I think that's pretty clear," replied Jim.

"Marley and I are wondering if we're going to make it through these events," Brianne admitted.

"A lot of people are asking that same question. I believe humans have the ability to weather this storm," Jim said. "Of course, a global event of this magnitude will change us and our quality of life. But we can survive if we take the right steps and act soon enough."

"What do we do?" Marley asked.

"We've got to learn how to slow down The Warming as much as we can and then adapt to The Changes."

"How do we do that now that all these changes are upon us?" asked Brianne.

"You're right. We've known about The Warming for years and never had the will or the consensus to act before. But now maybe we will. That's why we all have to get more involved in the political process."

"Oh no, not politics again," Marley groaned.

"Yes, politics. That's how you get things done in a community," Jim said. "That's what you and Brianne have been doing, organizing your neighbors."

"That's politics?" Marley asked.

"Yes, it is. In contrast, our main job here at the observatory is just to understand what's happening, and I think we have a good handle on that.

"Our second job is to use that understanding to advise people what to do to protect their families. We've been trying to do that with the alerts we've been sending out and our press releases to the media."

"Yeah, you guys do that all the time," Marley said.

"Now what we need to do is to develop a plan on what actions the council should take to resolve the problems as we understand them. Then, based on our input and input from other sources, they'll decide what to do."

"Well that would be great as long as they listen to you guys," Marley replied.

"Unfortunately, they don't always do that."

"If I understand you correctly, there is hope and there's a process for recovering from this series of events."

"I think so. We have to try our best. Why don't you two get some sleep. We can talk tomorrow to see if we can create a plan."

"Okay. Okay. Thanks, Jim. Sorry we called so late. We'll check in with you in the morning."

* * *

Wanda had been up talking with Jim when Brianne called. They were feeling pressure to do more to help the town. There was no way they were ready to retire for the evening.

"I'm really concerned that all this information is just scaring everyone into inaction, which is bad," Jim told her. "Or even worse, it could spark riots, looting, anarchy, or maybe even mass exodus out of town."

"I agree, Jim. We have to figure out how to share what we know about these events in the context of a plan for getting through these tough times. They may not appreciate it yet, but The Warming is going to change everything. We have to come up with a plan to help our town survive." She saw Jim looking at her and realized he was at a loss and that he was expecting her to come up with the answer. After all, she was the communications expert.

"How do we do that?" he asked.

"I've been thinking about it all day," Wanda told him. "Let me draft something for you to look at. I'm going to keep it brief and to the point."

So while data continued to pour in, Wanda stopped reading reports and sending out alerts and focused all her energies on creating a simple plan. She wanted a plan that the council, the citizens, and all the other interested parties could understand and support. She knew that to be successful, she would have to mobilize the whole community around a single game plan with specific actions.

When she finished the first draft, she passed it to Jim. He stopped what he was doing for the first time that day and read it, knowing how important it could be.

Wanda's plan included three parallel tasks. The first task was to get everyone in the town organized so they could help one another survive in the short run. She had been delighted that

Marley and Brianne had initiated the Neighborhood Network. It could be expanded to reach all members of the community. That was a great start.

The second task was to find ways to reduce or stop the Warming—steps that everyone could take. There was no reason to try to fix anything unless they were also taking steps to slow The Warming. Jim had already come up with that list, but it had not been implemented.

The last task was to create work teams to start rebuilding roads, water supplies, power lines, wastewater treatment plants, and other infrastructure as needed for the future. She realized these tasks would require leadership, cooperation, and adequate supplies. The key to the plan was to get everyone to adopt it. The challenge would be to get everyone to understand that all three tasks in the plan were essential.

"This is great," Jim said after he finished reading. He gave her the first real smile of the day. "If we could get everyone to work together on this, it would be great." Then she noticed his smile turn flat. "I just wish we had time to get everyone on board with it before the meeting. The town council just notified us that they called for a meeting tomorrow night. That doesn't give us much time to talk to others. Worse yet, they may have their own plan that doesn't take into account all the needs of the town. They may not want to listen to yours."

They both collapsed back on the couch and sighed in frustration. What could they do in the next 24 hours? Was it enough time to get everyone on board with their plan?

Wanda's excitement about creating the plan turned to a look of concern. She knew from past experience that, without a lot of cajoling, this council would probably not make the right decisions, even if they looked at all the data. What was needed now was real leadership and the marshaling of all the town's resources. It was unlikely that the current council would do that. They were known for always taking the easiest and slowest way out of a problem, and this wasn't a good time for that kind of drag-your-feet politics.

She looked at Jim and spoke slowly. "For us to make any headway, it will be critical that the council hears from other knowledgeable citizens as well. You've got to get your allies there. We'll need solidarity on this issue to carry the day."

Wanda was referring to several other occasions when Jim had teamed up with Max and Doc to argue against or in support of an issue. This had often been the case when the science was clear but was ignored by certain anti-action factions in Sleepy Valley. This was going to be another case where multiple proponents would be needed to create a rational solution to the problems.

"I'll do my best to get Max and Doc and hopefully others to show up and testify as well," Jim promised.

"Good. That's a start," Wanda said. "But it's going to take more effort than that. It's going to take a real spokesperson from the community. At this point, I don't have anybody in mind." She sat there anxiously and cringed. She hated the fact that she wasn't fully prepared.

PART TWO

THE DECISIONS

CHAPTER THIRTEEN

MARLEY FINDS HIS VOICE

M arley was greatly relieved when he heard first thing Monday morning that the town council had called a meeting for 7 pm that evening. *Finally, someone's acting as if they're in charge. It's about time. Surely, they'll find a way to fix the problems. Maybe they'll even figure out how to prevent these events from happening again.*

He returned to skating around town and helping his neighbors. He didn't think any more about the meeting. Now that it was finally happening, he actually had less interest in attending. After all, in his mind town meetings were pretty much an adult world, and as a teen he didn't feel like he was part of that world yet. They didn't need his input, and he had better things to do. He and Brianne were busy building a network to help people through the tough times.

While running an errand, he heard the voice in his head again. But this time it said, "You have to go to the meeting. What if no one shows up, or worse, the people who do go convince the council not to take any action? That would be terrible. What would happen to the town?"

He contemplated this for a while. *Maybe I should go. After all, I do have questions about what steps should be taken and about what caused The Changes in the first place. Someone must have the answers.*

Marley was starting to think that someone—or maybe

even everyone—in town should have acted more responsibly. *Somehow, we screwed up. Could all this chaos have been prevented?* He started to feel the tightness return in his chest. It made him angry that his town hadn't done anything to prevent The Warming.

Marley kept struggling with these questions and whether or not to go to the meeting. Wasn't he doing enough, just helping his neighbors? That's what he was best at, after all, and it was keeping him plenty busy. He couldn't do everything.

At one point in this internal debate, when inclined toward attending the meeting, he caught himself, puzzled about why he was getting involved all of a sudden in politics. It wasn't that he didn't care about community decisions; he did. But he couldn't be everywhere at once. He had always just left politics up to his parents' generation. And yet his parents never went to town meetings either.

Marley heard the voice again. "You cannot trust the council to make the right decisions. After all, they caused these problems with their inaction. You have to go, and you have to speak out, speak out for your generation."

It was true, he had the impression the council was part of the problem. Just thinking about the meeting, he became more and more intrigued—he could see the severity of the problems and their direct impact on his family and friends. Marley's anger was building; he was ticked off about what kind of world he was inheriting. *It's just not fair. This debate isn't about politics; it's about people's lives, it's about our future. It's about my future.*

Marley scratched his rashes and tried clearing his mind of the anger. What was happening to him? He had never cared about politics before. Was someone influencing him? Was it Doc and the course in school that he'd taken that was encouraging this independent thinking? No, Marley didn't think so. It was more like an inner voice, but that made no sense to him. *What could it be?*

The more he thought about it the more he became convinced someone was talking to him. Marley decided to test this theory by tricking whoever it was to reveal their true identity. He found a quiet place with nobody else around, stopped walking, and said quite clearly to no one in particular, "That settles it. I'm not going."

Marley listened carefully. There was nothing at first, just a few blue jays calling in the distance, a breeze blowing dry leaves, no other sound. Then he heard a voice, the same voice; it was as clear as if he were listening to Brianne.

"You have to go. There is no one else we can trust. You must have a voice in this or nothing will be done."

Marley's jaw dropped. His eyes widened. He was baffled. He'd heard the voice clearly enough. Whoever had spoken had not been him—they even had a slightly different accent. It was more formal. They had also used pronouns like "you" and "we." His trick had worked! *But who's trying to convince me to take action? There's no one else around. I must be going crazy.*

Marley decided to lay it out straight to whoever was speaking. "I'm not going to the meeting unless you tell me who you are and why I should listen to you."

Again, silence. A plane flew over. He just waited.

More silence.

Then, with sounds of frustration and acceptance, and maybe a tinge of desperation, the voice came through loud and clear. "My name is Joe."

* * *

Marley started walking in circles, trying to clear his head and focus at the same time. It had been bad enough when he thought he'd been talking to himself—he suspected everyone did that. But now he found himself talking to someone he couldn't see. Someone who wasn't him but maybe, just maybe, was *part* of him in some way. Marley started to think he must have a split personality. *Maybe I should talk to someone about this.* He found himself in a quandary, so he stopped walking and decided to proceed with caution.

Speaking very slowly, he said, "Okay . . . Hi, Joe . . . Can you tell me anything about yourself? Like who the heck you are . . . And where you are. Something that might actually be helpful to me in this situation." Marley listened carefully.

After a pause, Joe responded, also slowly and deliberately. "Well, let me apologize, Marley, and explain everything now that I have blown my cover. I was not elected to reveal who we are but just to try to motivate you to do the right thing."

"What? You used the term 'we.' Do you mean there are more people involved in this discussion? Now I'm really lost."

"Please, please, let me explain. You are not crazy. In fact, I believe, I mean *we* believe, that you are one of the more rational people around. But when you say 'more people,' you are a little off base. You are the only person here. I am, I mean we are, actually . . . not people. We are part of you, but *not* you."

Marley spun around in a tight circle, scratching his head as well as his arms and legs. He collapsed onto the grass, his head tilted downward, weighed down by the impossibility of the conversation. He felt he must be deranged.

Joe continued. "I belong to the colony of microbes that live on your skin and also inside of you."

"Microbes?"

"Yes. We are very small—you cannot see us. But there are trillions of us."

"Trillions?"

"Yes. We have co-evolved with humans over millions of years—our job is to keep you healthy. We help you digest food. We help you fight off bad things, like disease and illnesses. We help you live fully as a 'person' in this complex, interconnected place that you call Earth. You need us and, of course, we need you. We are in this together, and that is precisely why we are talking with you."

"WHAT? You've lost me. I'm having a hard time picturing this. If you and your friends are inside me, and you represent this legion of microscopic bugs, how can you be talking to me?"

"I happen to spend most of my time living just inside your left ear, so it is easy for me to talk with you. But we are everywhere. Just think of us as covering all of your exterior and your interior systems like your respiratory and digestive tracts."

Feeling a little squeamish about this whole idea, Marley asked, "You guys are really inside me?"

"Sure. We know you pretty well. From the inside out, you could say, and much like you humans, we continue to evolve. Natural selection has resulted in a few microbes that can speak to our hosts. Like me."

"Am I a host?"

"Yes, you are. I consider you a great host, compared to many others, and that is the problem. We have had to evolve because humans, in general, are making some bad decisions that threaten the existence of all of us. Humans are doing things that, in fact, threaten all species.

"But the greatest threat to all of us is the human role in the rapid warming of the planet. We may no longer be able to protect you from viral and bacterial invasions that are starting to move north from the tropics. The number of bacterial mutations is happening so fast that we may not be able to adjust. Furthermore, we think millions of you are going to die as the Earth warms and whole regions of the world are forced to migrate toward the poles."

"I get it. I get it. So what're you planning to do about it?"

"Your microbiome council has selected me, as one of the few who can speak and, may I add, has taken the time to learn English, to work with you. We do not want to be presumptuous, but we would like to help humankind make better decisions. For your sake—and for ours."

This conversation was way too crazy for Marley. He didn't buy this microbiome stuff—microbes can't talk. It didn't all fit together. He thought he might *be dreaming or h*allucinating but couldn't put his finger on why. *It must have been that old yogurt I ate this morning.*

Then he remembered Jim's advice to stay indoors due to the toxic petroleum fumes rising from the streets. *Of course. That's it. I should've taken Jim's advice. I'm delusional. If it's not food poisoning, it must be the air I'm breathing. Maybe I should've stayed inside like Jim recommended.*

Marley had heard on the news that animals and people all over town were behaving oddly. Even Brianne had said she was disoriented. That was the only logical argument he could think of that made sense to him. So Marley assumed he was halluci-nating. *You can't talk with a microbe.* He stopped engaging in the conversation and decided to head home and take a nap until his head cleared up. *Crazy.*

* * *

Marley retreated to his home and spent late Monday after-noon in his basement workshop, tinkering with stuff. It was cooler there and he felt he was safe from the fumes. He was examining and taking apart a drone Brianne had dropped off. She had found it stuck in a hedgerow and thought he might be able to fix it. He didn't know the first thing about remote controls but was quickly learning a lot about how the drone propelled itself. Colin had been over to the house earlier, and they had discussed all sorts of things one could do with a drone. He had become pretty jazzed about it.

Marley had successfully avoided thinking about the crazy conversation that may or may not have occurred that morning with Joe. He stayed preoccupied by focusing on other things—and the drone was fascinating. He already had it apart, and pieces were scattered all over the shop. Unfortunately, this state of calm curiosity was not to last.

"Hey, Marley. This is Joe. We think it is time for you to get ready for the meeting tonight."

Marley bolted upright and then sat back on his stool, per-plexed. He had hoped the voice would never return. But here it was, and he wasn't sure what to do. He felt okay. He didn't think he was hallucinating. But he needed proof that Joe was real. He wasn't about to accept this whole microbe thing, based just on a leap of faith.

"Joe, is there something you can do to prove who you say you are? I'm sorry, but I'm not ready to believe you. It's way too bizarre."

"Sure, Marley, I understand. This must be weird for you, too.

Let me see what can we do? Hey, boys, send up a belch."

Marley belched.

"Now make him pass wind."

Marley popped.

"Now make him sneeze."

Marley sneezed three times.

Joe waited a moment for a response and then said, "Now make him vomit."

Marley's stomach started to churn. "No, no, no! I believe you! I believe you!" Immediately his stomach started to calm down. "That's amazing. You certainly appear to be who you say you are. But it's going to take me some time to get used to this idea." After a few moments, he asked, "Why me?"

"Because you are curious, logical, you care about things, and this process might take a while—maybe even your whole lifetime.

"Wow. So what is it you want me to do tonight?"

"We, and I mean you and the rest of us, have to make sure our voices are heard tonight at the town hall. We are going to listen, but if people are not making sense or, even worse, thinking of not doing anything useful at all, then it has to be our job to speak up and convince them to take action."

"I won't know what to say."

"Well, that is where I come in. I will coach you on what to say. We have a lot of experts at our command. Just remember, there are many more microbes in your biome than there are humans on Earth. We are all very specialized in our knowledge, so collectively, we know a lot more than all the people in the room. And we have allies. I am counting on all the microbes in other people's bodies to help inspire their hosts to make good decisions too."

Marley started to scratch his arms again, but then he thought twice about it, not wanting to hurt any of the microbes on his skin. "Joe, excuse me, but are you sure about this game plan? It sounds a little far-fetched to me."

"We have put a lot of thought into what we are proposing.

Yes, we realize that this is an experiment. It has never been tried before, as far as we know. But you can see why we are pretty excited about the potential of working together with you."

"I'm not so sure this is going to work."

"Marley, please understand. We have been preparing a long time for tonight. You have been helping us. Every time you sneeze or shake hands with other humans, our scouts fan out to meet their cousins that co-inhabit the body that shook your hand. In turn, when those humans sneeze, some of our scouts come flying back.

"Our goal, of course, is to create a large cadre of microbes that will help us convince more humans to live in balance and co-evolve with the rest of life on Earth. That is the only way all the different species on Earth can continue to exist. It is the only way for all of us to thrive."

"You're starting to sound like Doc."

"Who?"

"Just one of my teachers. But it doesn't matter. I'm game to try this. I just hope it works."

"Great. Then we should get going to this meeting. There is no time to lose, especially if we want a good seat."

CHAPTER FOURTEEN

TO GO OR NOT TO GO

M arley and Joe were now committed to going to the town council meeting, but Marley was worried he might need others to help him have an impact on the proceedings. He assumed Jim Quartz would be there. That would be key, but he didn't know who else would show up. He left a text for Brianne and Collin and wondered about Doc, Betsy, and Luke. He hoped they all would be there and speak up. He also hoped they would be there to back him up in case he spoke and got any tough questions. He sent them all a text.

Marley also didn't know if Max would come. After all, Max was rebuilding a forest; what was more important than that? Max had also told him that he disliked meetings. "Meetings are often a waste of time and I never like being confined indoors. I'm also not a fan of the democratic process—too many decisions made with incomplete information. Decisions made without regard to the impacts on our critical life-support systems. Trees, plants, animals, streams, wetlands, soil, air, and water are not well represented at meetings." But that was why Marley wanted him there. He could be the voice of nature, the voice for a healthy future. Max got a text, too.

Max knew he had to go. He had to get the council to buy more trees. Who else could make that argument as well as he?

Max knew the town needed trees—a lot of trees—to survive. They needed trees to clean the air, the water, and the soil, to stop erosion, and most importantly, to cool things down. He had stayed up all night, calculating how many trees would be required. Sleepy Valley would have to plant about 360,000 trees in total just to get back to the status quo before The Changes: 180,000 trees to replenish the park and another 180,000 to replace all the trees that had died in and around town. He also had to deal with the beetles. Someone on the council would be sure to ask about them. He needed an answer and he needed it soon.

His phone rang. "Hi, Max, this is Jim up at the observatory. I hope you're alright. I can't believe what happened to your park. From here it looks like a total disaster."

"It is, Jim. We were overrun by Greater Sapphire Beetles, millions of them. There's not a tree left standing. Can you believe it? All from a nasty little blue beetle, the heat, and the strong winds."

"I can't," Jim said while peering out the observatory window at the remains of the park. "Max, I hope you're going to the meeting tonight. We need your voice to get the council to save our valley. You know, if left on their own, they won't do a thing."

When Max didn't reply, Jim pushed a little more. "I bet the park isn't even on their radar. Most people, including all the council members, haven't seen the devastation—they haven't even left their homes. We have to make sure they know what's happened over there. Maybe you can load some of the debris into the back of your pickup truck and bring it to the meeting to show them. It's critical we get their attention and get that forest growing again. Max, you need to come. You need to come and speak for the trees."

"I hear you, Jim. You know I hate meetings—too much talk and too little action. But I'll be there. We need funds to buy saplings."

"Great. Of course, you also need a way to combat the beetles, or replanting won't do any good. Do you have any ideas?"

"Nothing yet, but I'm working on it. Everything has a predator."

"I've heard that other towns are facing this same issue. Someone will come up with an answer."

"We've got to. Let me know what you find out."

"I will. By the way, Max, do you think you can get Doc to show up?"

"I'll try. But he's been keeping a low profile ever since that run-in with the school board."

"Yeah, I remember. Several parents tried to shut down his climate-studies class. So far, he's prevailed. Most people value the course. He's a great teacher."

"I agree he needs to be there. I'll call him. We need his perspective on what might happen. He cares a lot about these things too."

Jim hung up and Max called Doc. Max was delighted that, with only a little convincing, Doc agreed to go to the meeting. Doc told Max he knew this would be an important milestone in the town's history, and he wanted to support Marley as well as Max.

As the time for the meeting drew near, Max decided to walk. It would be good for him to calm his mind and prepare what he was going to say. He needed to think through what it would take to plant 360,000 trees by himself. He liked the idea and the challenge of building a forest. A broad smile spread across his face for the first time since his rebirth from his premature burial in the valley of dead trees. He took off on foot to walk into town.

As he walked down the gravel road leaving the park, he noticed the oddest damn thing right in the middle of the road in front of him. He saw—or thought he saw—what appeared to be an armored rat, or maybe even a groundhog. Or maybe it was an armored beaver walking towards him.

"Oh my goodness," he said with a twinkle in his eye. "It's an armadillo. I've never seen them in these parts before. They must be migrating north with the warming climate."

As soon as he said that, Max stopped still in his tracks. It was as if he had hit a wall. He stood there motionless, studying every movement of the armadillo. Max had learned this stop-and-look behavior from a long career of watching and listening to nature. Just freeze and take the time to observe the animals, and nature will treat you to the wonders of the universe.

As he watched he realized the armadillo wasn't walking but was scurrying about on its short legs. It was chasing after something, running this way and that, having a feeding frenzy. The size of Max's eyes started to grow. They opened wide and wider still until there was no place for them to go unless they popped out of his head. *Is it possible? Could it be true? Is this the solution I've been searching for?*

A big smile, the second one of the day, spread across his face from weathered dimple to weathered dimple. The armadillo was feasting, with a great deal of relish, on beetles. And not just any beetle. It was feasting specifically, and without any doubt, on the Greater Sapphire Beetle—and this one little fellow couldn't get enough.

Nature was finding a balance.

* * *

Over at the farm Betsy and Luke had been working non-stop at the kitchen table, studying all aspects of solar farming. The boys were lost in their video games in the basement, so the house was quiet except when Betsy broke into a verse of "Let the Sunshine In." Her singing not only helped lift her spirits but got the hens clucking as well.

Betsy had been reading online about solar equipment installation, maintenance costs, and payback. She had studied the impacts of cloudy days, volcanic eruptions, earthquakes, dust storms, locust swarms, nuclear winter, and bird droppings. Luke had read every page of *An Introduction to Electricity*, an online reference book he had downloaded from the library. Betsy and Luke wanted to understand it all—what caused the successes *and* the failures of solar ventures.

"Luke, I'm getting buried under all the reports we've col-

lected, but I'm sure there are many more we should be reviewing. What other questions should we be asking?" Betsy's head
was spinning, trying to make sense of it all. It was pretty dry
stuff, written by engineers and economists. Whenever she finished a chapter, she would get up and stretch, walk around the
kitchen table, pat the chickens on their heads, and then sit down
again to read. To create some sense of order, she made piles of
their notes on the countertops, spread topographic maps across
the kitchen table, and organized reference papers in the kitchen
cabinets. Not wanting to take the time to shop, they lived off
eggs from their hens, who had taken up nesting on the couch in
the living room.

It was an exciting and scary time for them. As Betsy went
about her tasks, she retained a glimmer of hope, but a constant
pit of fear, lodged in her stomach, reminded her they were under
the gun with the bank.

Their neighbors grew concerned about Betsy's and Luke's
health and stopped by to drop off food; some wondered if the
Alexanders were losing their minds as well as their farm.

Betsy's strong will and determination had convinced Luke
that solar was their only option, their only hope for staying on
the farm. So both were putting their hearts and souls into the
project and did nothing else. At times she was so immersed that
she could feel the presence of her ancestors there in the room,
struggling along beside her, trying their best to help save the
farm. They were a great comfort to her.

At one point Luke caught her talking to her great-aunt
Dorothy and her uncle David. He thought she had lost her mind
and said so. "Who are you talking to? There's nobody else in the
room. Are you going crazy?"

After that Betsy stopped having these conversations when
Luke was around, not wanting to scare him. He had too much
pressure to deal with already and didn't need to be thinking she
was going looney on him. But the ancestors were a big help to
her, they served as a sounding board and offered her a lot of
encouragement.

Betsy stayed focused on the mission. She told Marley when he called, "Our next big hurdle will be to get approval from the town council. That means we'll need the support of our neighbors."

"After all these years of helping one another, I'm sure they'll support you," Marley assured her.

She knew that might be wishful thinking; it wasn't clear if they would. She woke up at night, sweating, wondering who her real friends were. She said to Luke, "To get financing, we'll need a firm agreement that the town or SVE will buy the clean, solar electricity we generate. The bank has asked us to provide a twenty-year commitment from one of them."

Betsy was beginning to understand the complexity of working with the neighbors, the council, the bank, and the utility all at the same time. Luke drew up meticulous plans, and Betsy created beautiful sketches of how the solar panels would look. It was true their farm was no longer going to be the pastoral place they had treasured for years, but it could still be a home, their home.

Their kitchen was overflowing with ideas. Betsy papered the walls, windows, and appliances with sketches, plans, and long lists of the benefits of having a local source of clean energy. With the yellow-paper-covered windows, their house glowed like a spaceship to people who passed by at night. Betsy was starting to feel as if she were in some sort of purgatory, floating above the farm, not knowing where or when this all would end.

She did take a few short breaks to walk over and talk to their neighbors and explain what she and Luke were trying to do. These discussions helped her realize the array of questions and challenges they faced. After one such meeting she told Luke, "Everyone has different concerns. Safety, loss of pastoral views, traffic, reflection from the panels, and vandalism. There's a lot of skepticism and pushback, and a strong fear of change. It seems like everyone wants to support local farms, but that support weakens when farms become industrial looking."

Betsy and Luke realized that calming their neighbor's fears wouldn't be easy—they had some of the same concerns themselves. But The Changes were forcing them to find a new way to eke out a living on their farm. Furthermore, the pastoral views were already gone, destroyed by the weather and the fire. Those views weren't coming back anytime soon.

Betsy knew they had to attend the town hall meeting. She looked at Luke quite seriously and said, "We need a seat at the table to build support for our plans. We need to be part of the solution."

CHAPTER FIFTEEN

THE TOWN HALL MEETING

The Sleepy Valley town council met at the historic grange hall, located right in the center of town. The white clapboard siding on the outside and white plaster-covered walls on the inside preserved the feeling of an old community meeting place. It had served as the gathering place and marketplace for area farmers before there were any other buildings, aside from the general store and saloon, which were no longer standing. The grange was the only remaining testament to the early pioneer days of the town.

Marley had passed by the grange hall many times but had never been inside. He had never really known what it was used for, but he was starting to realize it was where important decisions were made.

The council had been meeting monthly in this hall for almost 150 years, dating back to the time when kerosene replaced whale oil in lamps. Dances, weddings, and hangings had all taken place here. It was easy to picture the town's founding fathers and mothers milling around and debating in this very same hall back in those early days. Unfortunately, the interior hadn't been painted for decades. The dirty white walls and old fluorescent lights reflected a gray pallor on the faces of all the people who came out to discuss The Changes.

As the clock struck seven, Marley and his newly discovered microbial friends slid through the side door of the meeting room. He parked his skateboard in the front corner so he could keep an eye on it. When his neighbors in the front row saw him coming, they made room for him. Most recognized him as "that kid with the skateboard" who had been running errands over the past couple of days. He had become a local hero. They were surprised but happy to see him at the meeting.

Brianne, who had been standing near the back, slid in next to him and rested her hand on his arm in a form of silent greeting, support, and camaraderie.

He glanced at her hand and smiled, imagining Joe's army of scouts running out to meet members of Brianne's microbiome. He wondered what they were saying to each other. Of course many of them would already know one another—this wasn't the first time Brianne had touched him innocently and unsuspectingly.

He imagined that their respective microbes were probably closely related by now. He wondered how her visiting microbes might have already influenced who he was. What role had they played in his relationship with Brianne? He assumed the microbes were probably breaking down barriers and building invisible bonds between the two of them. He smiled, wondering what she would say if she became aware of the routine merger of their respective microbial colonies. He wondered if he would ever tell her about Joe. But right now, all he said to her was, "You made it."

"You too. I thought you said you'd never come," Brianne replied.

"I'm just here to see what happens," he said as he looked around the room. "I can't believe so many people showed up. The place is at least half full. It's amazing this many people came in spite of the travel advisory to stay home. We're lucky the temperatures cool down a little at night and the oil hardens back to tar. There's no way all these people would have made it for a daytime meeting when the roads are so slick."

"They're here because they're angry or scared," Brianne told him.

"It's a big deal. Everyone *should* be here." Marley looked around the room; it was loud and bustling.

The attendees were happy to see one another and anxiously waiting to see what would happen. Many of them, especially the ones from downtown and the West Side, wanted the council to do something about cleaning up the streets. It did not appear as if the council had done anything yet. A chant started up in the front of the room. "Fix it. Fix it. Fix it."

Several folks from the East Side countered from the back corner, "No more taxes. No more taxes." The people from the East Side didn't have a melting road problem and didn't want to have to pay for problems that only existed on the West Side.

A few people from each group stood up and shouted at each other, waving their hats and gesticulating wildly. Tensions grew, but eventually calmer heads prevailed, and everyone sat back down and stopped chanting.

At the front of the hall, Marley saw a raised platform with a long table and four chairs behind it for the council members. The members of the council who were already present looked uneasy, constantly adjusting their ties, scarves, and the paperwork in front of them. They looked concerned that the meeting might get out of hand.

"Serving on the council can't be an easy job," Marley said. "It takes the members away from their families in the evenings, and on nights like tonight they're going to have to listen to a good deal of complaining."

Brianne agreed. "Some of them are probably wondering why they ever ran for office."

Marley was sweating. The hall was hot, the air was still, and everyone in the room was uncomfortable. A few fans were brought in but didn't do much good. Some of the council members stared out at the audience with blank looks on their faces as if they were wearing death masks. They had clearly heard too many late-night testimonies over the years. Some looked as though they had perfected the art of sleeping with their eyes open.

Maybe it was due to the heat, but Marley imagined, in his slightly dazed state, that their faces almost appeared to be melting, losing their shapes and flowing slowly downward toward the floor.

Marley and Brianne sat with the suburbanites from the West Side who occupied the three front rows of the room. His neighbors wanted immediate action on cleaning up the oily streets and had a petition signed by their friends who couldn't be there. They were well organized, much more so than the other groups in the room. The suburbanites were dressed respectfully in business casual but had a few outliers like Marley, who had come tonight sporting a Grateful Dead T-shirt and looking like the skateboarder he was. A faint but distinctive odor of asphalt permeated their hair and clothes.

Marley was usually not relaxed in crowded, public settings, and tonight was no different. He still wasn't sure why he had come or what he could do. He fiddled with his shoes and hair and kept tugging on his left earlobe, checking in to make sure Joe was still there.

"Take it easy, kid. I have your back, and you have friends here to support you. We will not abandon you."

It felt great to have Brianne right there with him, as well as many of his neighbors. Marley was starting to feel glad he had come. He laughed to himself when he saw that even Doc had shown up at the meeting, and he wondered what could have made the teacher leave his house at night. Doc always encouraged others to engage, but he seemed wary of the process. Marley noticed Doc had his notebook in his hands and was scribbling in it. *What's he doing?* Almost as if he felt Marley's gaze, Doc looked up and nodded to him.

Marley also noticed that Jim Quartz, the meteorologist, was sitting right next to Doc. They seemed quite comfortable together, as if they were friends or collaborators. Marley wondered how well they knew each other. He didn't know Quartz as well as Brianne did but had always respected him as a weather expert. Seeing them both there was comforting—they would probably have his back if he did speak tonight and got tough questions.

He let go of his remaining fears and, with a sigh of relief, settled back into his chair. He realized that, with all the people who had come out tonight, he probably wouldn't have to speak up at all. He slouched in his seat, arms folded in front of him, waiting for the action to begin.

The meeting didn't start on time; the chairman had not yet arrived, and latecomers were still filing in through the back and side doors. As the room filled, Marley noticed the hall also filled with noise. So much noise that it was hard to hear the person next to you. There was so much hot air and talk spewing forth from the people in the room that Marley envisioned the walls and the ceiling bulging outwards like a balloon. He wondered, in fact, if the old grange hall might burst at any moment. It certainly wasn't built to last forever or to hold all the energy and anger of this many citizens.

Marley recognized a few of the members of the downtown business community occupying the seats right behind the suburbanites. They were sitting on the edges of their chairs and talking anxiously with one another. This group included food vendors, lawyers, several nail spa entrepreneurs, insurance brokers, retail store owners, bankers, and representatives of the town's once-booming manufacturing and furniture firms.

The business owners' discussion was quite animated, apparently revolving around what should be the top priority for the council. They wanted to put their collective muscle—and pocketbooks, if necessary—behind the fastest way to get their businesses back up and running. They looked scared, as if concerned they would lose all their cash flow if people wouldn't leave their homes to shop. Their discussion focused on quick, short-term solutions for making the roads passable again—leaving all the other issues to be taken care of in the future.

Joe pointed out to Marley that some of the businessmen were so lathered up with deodorant, perfume, and cologne that he feared for the health of his friends who were part of their biomes. "Some of them have no natural scent at all. They must have killed off all their microbes with antibacterial soaps and antibiotics. It is tough to maintain a healthy biome if you are poisoning it all the time." Joe continued, "Why do humans do that? How can you know someone well if you cannot detect their pheromones? It is like trying to assess someone's body language over the phone."

Marley sat listening, intrigued by the discussion. Then he whispered under his breath, "Well, I only know a few of them— the two with the ties. They seem like okay guys."

"Keep talking, Marley. Tell me more. I need names. I am trying to make note of all the people you know. We need to network with them all."

"Okay, Joe. You might want to start by checking in with my orthodontist, Dr. Ashai. I bet your guys have already met members of his biome. We've had lots of up-close-and-personal time together recently—he's been straightening my teeth.

"Which one is he?"

"He's the guy with the big, shiny-white smile and perfect teeth."

"I am on it."

Marley smiled at Joe's efficiency. He then turned even further around in his seat and waved to his Aunt Betsy and Uncle Luke. They sat with the farming community, in a group about halfway back in the crowd. They waved back but didn't make a move to join him. They were busy warmly greeting their neighbors, whose support would be critical to their hopes of staying on the farm.

Of course they weren't the only farmers trying to make a living on their farms. All the farmers present looked equally nervous, worried about their futures as well. Many came tonight hoping to learn more about solar farming from the Alexanders.

Marley noticed that a cloud of dust and insects seemed to float over the farmers.

The town's old-timers, mainly from the East Side, sat near the back of the hall, emitting a whiff of dead fish. Marley didn't know many of them but recognized Ben, the retired ag agent, who sat next to old Ed Perkins's son, Sam. They seemed quite relaxed, leaning back in their chairs, casually chatting with each other. Sam sported a crewcut and an array of tattoos on his sagging muscles. He was no friend to skateboarders; he thought they were just nuisances on the roads, so Marley stayed clear of him. *Why would Sam have any interest in this meeting? He's the last one I'd expect to be here, especially since nothing's melting on the East Side.*

Marley thought about this for a while and then realized the East Siders had their own problems. They would want the lake back to normal—especially if it didn't cost them anything. In fact everybody in the room would want something fixed. He also guessed Sam was there to figure out how he could make money off any of the fixes the council voted for.

Marley watched as the two representatives from SVE, the local utility company, worked the room with warm smiles and hearty handshakes. The woman and the man were good looking. Maybe a little overdressed for these hot conditions, but they were pleasant to everybody, partly because everyone in the valley was a SVE customer. For over 100 years, everyone in this town had bought electricity solely from SVE. The SVE reps' job tonight was to maintain the monopoly and to protect and expand their business.

While scanning the room, Marley realized the one group not well represented were young people. He felt a little deflated. "Brianne, we're the only teenagers in the room. Where's everyone else?" Even though he had initially not wanted to come, he was starting to realize that matters important to his future, to everyone's future, were going to be decided here in this room. It was sad to think that so many of his friends were off in their fantasy worlds of video games while the real world was changing rapidly all around them. He started texting his friends to come, even if they were late. The reality and chaos in Sleepy Valley was much more important than escaping to some alternative digital universe.

"Well, at least we made it," Brianne replied. "We'll have to represent our whole generation. You think we can do that?"

At that moment the room fell quiet. Marley and the rest of the attendees turned toward the back door to see what had happened. Mr. Folly, longtime chair of the town council, and usually the last one to arrive, had just waddled in, and the sergeant-at-arms was closing the door behind him. Folly's gait was slow. Like everyone else, he was having trouble walking with his oily shoes sticking to the floor on every step. He trudged onward, probably not wanting to admit the oil was a big deal. He had delayed the meeting as long as he could, hoping the oil would just go away or the temperatures would cool back down to normal. But no. Here he was, at the center of a major challenge with no apparent game plan or easy way out.

Marley found it painful to watch as Folly slowly made it to the front table, shimmied sideways into his seat, and then slowly and gruffly called the meeting to order. He was short of breath when he spoke. It was obvious that his lungs weren't operating at full capacity. Silence settled on the room so all those present could hear him better. Marley grimaced when he realized this was the man in charge.

As he began to speak, Folly's voice was quickly lost in the street noise outside the window as old Ed Perkins rode up on his Harley, late as usual. The motorcycle's deep rumbling penetrated the thin walls and open windows and vibrated the floorboards, seats, and all the attendees at the meeting. Exhaust floated in the windows and dust sifted down from the rafters. The disruption caused everyone to readjust in their seats and shift their focus. Their eyes were now drawn to the side door while they all waited for Ed to come in. He was infamous for creating a grand entrance when he arrived at events or meetings.

Ed turned off the Harley but didn't come in. There was an awkward silence, so Folly started again by clearing his throat. "Ahem. Thank you all for coming. We are here today to discuss what many of you have been referring to as The Changes. Thank you for your messages. There have indeed been a few unusual occurrences in town."

"That's a heck of an understatement," shouted a rough-looking character leaning against the wall. "Open your eyes, man. The town's melting away."

"Order in the hall," Folly said as he hit the gavel on the table, re-establishing his control. "The council has been in constant contact with each other, as well as with officials from the state and federal governments. We want to start off by assuring all of you that we have compiled a list of unusual occurrences, and our town engineer is trying to make sense of what's happening."

"What're you going to do about the melting roads?" shouted the man leaning against the wall.

Folly struck his gavel again. "Let's keep this meeting orderly. Everyone will get a chance to talk. If you disrupt the proceedings again, I'll have the sergeant-at-arms escort you from the premises."

Marley was surprised at how the man had challenged Folly. To Marley, Folly was an intimidating presence, especially with his gavel.

Folly continued. "I understand that everyone's concerned, but we need to realize that these events are not limited to Sleepy Valley. They are happening everywhere. We are therefore waiting for the federal and state governments to develop a plan. We are expecting them to declare Sleepy Valley a federal disaster area, and that will release funding for us to use to reclaim our town. We will keep you posted as we determine what, if anything, can be done here on a local level."

Marley turned to watch as a local economist stood up and said, "I wouldn't wait for or count on any assistance. It simply won't work in this case, since every town in the country will be applying for those non-existent dollars."

"The beauty of the federal government is that they can always print more money," Folly replied. "Let's give them time to recommend something. In the meantime we should discuss what we can do here by ourselves."

Marley sensed that Folly was warming up to his job. Joe had told him that all Folly cared about was keeping control of meetings and getting re-elected.

"I also promise you that we won't go off half-cocked and start spending your hard-earned money on something that might not be necessary. We don't yet know what the long-term impacts of The Changes will be. We will closely monitor these events and wait to see what else might happen in our town." Chairman Folly looked down the table at the other members of the council and then continued. "The council is holding this open meeting to listen to your concerns. Please keep your remarks to under two minutes. Who would like to speak first?"

Marley didn't move and there was no prompting from Joe. When Marley saw a dozen other hands go up from all quadrants of the room, he relaxed, delighted so many others had things to say. Maybe he would get off without having to say anything. He would just sit back and wait for Joe's advice.

One energetic young man jumped up and started talking, even before being acknowledged by the Chair. Nobody objected, so Folly let him speak.

"We've got to act, and we've got to do it now," pleaded the well-dressed, anxious businessman. He owned a shoe store downtown and Marley recognized him as the guy who had tried to clear the oil from the sidewalk in front of his store. Sweat had beaded into a series of droplets lined up like an army across his furrowed brow. He was all arms, gesturing wildly in an effort to make a point. "No one is venturing out of their homes to shop. My walk-in business is dead. I'm afraid my customers will turn to online shoe companies—who don't pay any taxes here, by the way. If we don't clear the sidewalks and fix the streets, all local retailers will fail. That puts the town at risk. We can't let that happen."

"What do you suggest?" asked Folly as he wiped his brow.

"We've got to clear the sidewalks and the streets. We've got to get people out, moving about the town and spending their money here."

Marley appreciated the need to clear the streets but wondered if that was really the first thing that should be done.

"Cleaning up the streets will cost a lot of money, and then keeping them clean if the heat wave continues will cost much more," Folly told the businessman. "We don't know how long the melting will last. Or what happens when the weather cools down this fall. Maybe all we have to do is wait for temperatures to drop."

"We can't wait that long. We'll all be ruined," said the shoe salesman.

"I understand. We don't want that to happen. Let's ask the budget director how much money we have in reserve to spend on clean-up projects."

Marley watched as the serious-looking, bow-tied, town budget director got up to speak. "I know these issues are important to all of you, but we can't afford to do anything at this time unless we raise funds to do it."

A short man in the middle of the hall shouted, "Where did our tax money go? Don't we have an emergency fund?"

The budget director replied with a blank expression on his face, "We spent our reserve fund on our Fourth of July parade, fireworks, and the cleanup of the ensuing forest fire."

An older woman said, "We should have listened to Jim Quartz when he warned us against shooting off fireworks in the middle of extreme drought conditions." A supportive murmur snaked through the crowd following that comment.

A fast food vendor Marley recognized stood up. He was still wearing his greasy work apron, and he swayed back and forth as if he were flipping hamburgers and cooking fries at the same time. "Borrow the money, create a bond, you guys know how to do that. That's what we small businesses have to do all the time, get a loan and pay it back over time. Regardless of where the money comes from, I think all the downtown businesses agree we have to make the streets passable again. We need to clear away the oil, and . . ."

A woman along the other wall interrupted, "It won't do any

good to clean the streets as long as it stays this hot. The streets will keep melting. It'd be like pouring money down a sinkhole. You need a better plan than that."

Old Ed, dressed in his weathered, black leather Harley Davidson vest, chose this moment to make his entrance through the side door. Marley was impressed with Ed's entrance. He had seen the old man before but didn't know much about him.

Sauntering to the front of the hall, Ed nonchalantly interrupted the speaker and went off on a monologue, addressing the council. No one tried to stop him. "I've been on every street on the East Side of the valley today, and we don't have any problems with rivers of oil. We don't want any of our tax money wasted on West Side repairs. It's as simple as that. The West Siders should have known better, importing asphalt from some foreign country when they could've used local concrete. I never did like the smell of those asphalt roads. Stupid decision. If you're all so anxious to spend money, fix the lake. That benefits all of us."

With that Ed walked to the back of the room and sat down with his friends. Hoots and hollers rose from the East Siders sitting in the audience. Nothing but silence came from the West Siders in the front rows. They were just hoping Ed would go away. Marley was disappointed by the divisiveness. He felt they all should be coming together to find solutions. Evidently not. Ed seemed to be speaking the mind of his conservative East Side buddies. His rant did not bode well for building a consensus on what to do.

Folly banged his gavel again and said, "Let's give everyone a chance to speak."

Ben stood up. "To restore the lake won't cost much—we just need a campaign to get everyone to stop using fertilizer." He sat down, thinking he had made a rational proposal. Sadly, no one followed up on his suggestion. The lake didn't seem to be a high priority for most people in town today. It didn't directly impact anyone's livelihood.

"We should at least find out what can be done to fix the biggest challenges," said a concerned citizen who worked down-town. "We need a plan. Times like these demand government action to help us help each other. Once we have a solid plan, the town can borrow the money to fix the problems or raise taxes. But if you don't do anything, the whole town dies. We lose everything."

This made sense to Marley, but he heard an undercurrent of mumbling at the reference to raising taxes. No one wanted to pay more taxes. In contrast to something as real as taxes, the vision of what it meant for a town to die was way too abstract. No one could picture that, and it sounded like fear mongering. Clearly, something could be done to save the town. After all, it had been here for what seemed like forever.

A number of angry people stood up and began shouting.

"Clean up the roads."

"Save our town."

"Create a plan. That's your job."

A cloud of defensiveness rose from Folly and spread over the other councilmen. Marley was glad he wasn't in Folly's shoes. This whole process felt a bit dysfunctional. How could anything positive come out of this debate?

Folly gruffly interrupted the series of outbursts and turned to the very quiet, mustached, and bespectacled town engineer. "I would like to ask the town engineer what we could do if we had the money?"

The engineer, who had been taking notes, looked up and replied, "We could clean up the oil from the streets if and when it stops melting—probably this fall sometime. But we would need a much larger budget."

A local school teacher called out, "We can't afford that. If we raise new revenue, it should go to the schools."

The engineer continued, "The lake is a different challenge. I don't know how to get everyone to reduce their fertilizer use and curtail storm water runoff from their land–probably some mixture of education, incentives, and regulation."

Folly interjected loudly, "Let's make it clear, we sure don't want any more regulations, and it's not our job to tell people what to do. The lake is not affecting commerce, so let's put that on the back burner." A wave of murmuring suggested that not everyone agreed with him. He held both hands up with the palms facing the audience as if he were calming a classroom of unruly kids. "Let's figure out if there's anything we can do without spending money."

Jim Quartz, exasperated with Folly's words, stood up and stated, "Responsible government action is the most sound approach for a town to take in times like this. We have no other choice. We need to spend the time and money to fix these problems now. That will create more jobs and allow the town to grow and prosper."

Wanda leaned over and said in Jim's ear, "You can't browbeat him, Jim. You can't force the council to do anything by telling them how to do their job. They'll just stop listening to you."

Before Jim's remarks had a chance to settle in, the representatives from Sleepy Valley Energy stood up, almost as if choreographed and timed to avoid this battle of where to spend money the town didn't have. They got up armed with a series of charts, proposals, and smiles.

Marley and everyone else turned to watch the presentation. "We would like to offer a solution that won't cost any of you—or the town—a thing, and it will fix your two biggest problems. Take a look at these charts. We propose to collect all the oil and burn it in our power plant. The town doesn't have to do a thing.

"We also propose to collect the gas from the lake and use the methane to run our turbines. If you let us do this, your problems go away, and everyone will be assured of cheap electricity for years to come." The SVE folks smiled, passed out handouts that summarized the savings, and then sat down in unison.

Folly quickly jumped on this bandwagon—as if he had known it was coming. "Now we're talking. That plan is clear and is an excellent way to clean up the streets and the lake."

"They're missing the point," Marley whispered to Brianne. "We need to focus on the disease, not the symptoms."

Folly then tried to wrap up the meeting by directing the town engineer to review the SVE proposal and report back to the council.

But before he could pound the gavel, Joe shouted into Marley's ear, "Jump up!"

CHAPTER SIXTEEN

MARLEY SPEAKS OUT

M arley jumped up as if he had been kicked in the pants. All heads in the room turned toward him. He took a deep breath to calm his nerves. What had he gotten himself into? He had no idea what to say, so he scanned the room for help. "S . . . Sir, may I speak?" he stammered.

"Why sure, young man. We're always glad to hear from the younger generation," Folly told him. "But keep it short, we don't want to be here all night. What do you have to say?"

Joe, as promised, began to feed lines to Marley, who then repeated them to the crowd gathered there. Marley was hesitant and spoke softly at first, so everyone strained to hear what he had to say. He was nervous, and his hands were clammy and shook a little bit. After all, this was his first town council meeting. "Hi. I'm Marley Jones. I just graduated from Sleepy Valley High three days ago, and I've lived here all my life." He stopped speaking but was encouraged by the smiles of support he was getting from those around him.

"I've been all around town over the past three days and have a sense of the problems. The discussion tonight and this proposal seems focused on just two of The Changes . . ." Marley stalled for a moment as if he were thinking—or listening to an inner voice. "Of course these issues are important, and we need to find a way to deal with them. But just discussing two of the symptoms, the impacts to the lake and the roads, appears to me to be short-sighted. There are a range of problems that have hit our town. Furthermore, if I understand this correctly, there will be more changes if we don't fix the root cause of it all."

There was a hush in the room as everyone contemplated this idea. One old man commented loud enough for most people to hear, "The boy makes sense. But what does he mean by the cause of our problems?"

Folly said in his most paternalistic voice so everyone in the room could hear. "What do you think is the cause of our prob-lems, young man?"

Marley scowled. He didn't like Folly's tone. It felt like Folly was trying to intimidate him. But he took another deep breath to keep his cool and, with Joe's careful prompts, continued. "Things are getting warmer—we all know that. If we don't reduce the warming, then these problems will get worse and additional problems will arise."

There was a general murmuring around the room, which gave Marley a feeling that people were actually listening to him. What he said must have made sense.

Brianne jumped up and stood right next to him. The crowd hushed. Some wondered who this young woman was, but many of them had seen her before—just never in a setting like this. She seemed more mature, not like the little girl they remembered. Brianne showed a lot of poise and addressed the audience as well as the council. "I agree with Marley. If all these things are the result of this warming trend, then the first thing we need to do is to focus on slowing it down, cooling things down."

Brianne took her time as she slowly scanned the audience. It was as if she were trying to connect with each and every per-son in the room. "If we could cool the temperatures, we would reduce the current problems, prevent future damage, and spend less money in the long run."

There was a warm and supportive applause following her comments.

Marley smiled. *She's good.* He was impressed and wondered, just for a moment, if she had a microbe coach as well.

When she had finished, Marley continued, "Does the town have a plan to stop the warming trend? What are other towns doing? What can each of us do? It makes no sense to just clean up the roads and the lake without a plan for lowering the temperature."

Joe took a deep breath. Marley did as well. He was gaining confidence, standing a little taller and speaking more clearly. Joe was doing his best to stay one step ahead of his protégé. Marley, however, was learning to talk while he listened. He was starting to feel confident enough to add his own thoughts. In fact, he was on a roll and only partly listening to Joe. It was as if Joe had stoked the fire in Marley's belly and now the fire was starting to roar.

Marley and Brianne's comments inspired Max, who stood up to support their suggestions. Sawdust fell off his beard and his clothes. "They're right," Max said in his deep, baritone voice. "We should listen to these young folks. So far we've only talked about two impacts. We haven't discussed what's happening to our farms, fields, woods, backyards, and rivers. We can't forget them—they're all important. Addressing the rising temperatures should be our top priority."

Marley just wanted to jump up and cheer but realized no one else was cheering, so he stayed in his seat.

Wanda, delighted by the change in direction and the growing grass-roots support, stood up too. She wanted to keep the momentum moving forward. "We have also not addressed the impacts to our health. Just sitting here, I've been listening to some of you struggling to breathe. Others are scratching your skin rashes. I'm suffering too. This is serious. These are symptoms of real health impacts that we need to address, all resulting from the heat and the bad air quality. These symptoms are probably just the beginning—the tip of the iceberg."

Marley was looking around and could see that Wanda was touching a chord with many of the people in the room. Everyone could relate to her very personal health-related comments. It felt so good to see the crowd shifting their attention to these often-overlooked concerns. "It's crazy to even consider burning the dirty oil in the power plant," she continued. That would contribute to the warming and create even worse health issues. It's time to think about your health and what kind of future you're leaving for your kids." Her comments appealed to the parents in the room, who enthusiastically applauded as she sat down.

Max's voice rumbled through the hall again. "There are undoubtedly more impacts coming if the warming continues, and therefore, we need to focus on prevention. It's always better to prevent a forest fire than to fight one. If we just react when the problems show themselves, we'll all end up playing a never-ending game of whack-a-mole. We need to act now to cool things down. We need to slow down The Warming."

There was a wave of support for Max from around the room. After all, he had a commanding presence in his ranger uniform, and they could all relate to a never-ending game of whack-a-mole.

Not liking the direction the debate was heading, old Ed Perkins shouted from the back of the room, "You guys are crazy. Sounds like you're talking about climate change. Get real. There's nothing we can do about global warming. Stop wasting your breath. The weather's always changing, and we just have to get used to it."

The East Siders cheered. Marley thought, *Oh-oh. Here we go.*

After waiting a moment for the hall to quiet down, Jim stood up to counter Ed's comments. "I think it's clear that the cause of all of these problems is rising temperature. It's been going on for some time."

Marley was glad Jim was there to rebut Ed's opinions. Jim had the facts, the reputation, and the gravitas to win a debate with Ed. Marley felt relieved that he had not had to engage in the debate with Ed, someone with a larger-than-life personality.

Jim continued, "It's also clear that the warming is due to human activities. None of us like to admit that we're responsible for something bad, but the good news is that if we caused it, then we can fix it."

"Even if climate change is manmade, there's nothing we can do to offset the pollution coming out of China and India," Ed shouted.

Jim continued talking to the council and the audience. "It is both a local and a global problem, and therefore will require both local and global responses. Many towns and countries have already taken steps. We need to catch up. Ignoring the need to reduce The Warming will cost more money and require more government involvement in the long run, so we need to act now."

Jim then addressed Ed directly. "Even parents in China care about the health of their kids. China is taking The Warming seriously. All of us have to act. Sure, there are big steps that governments and businesses will need to take—and many steps have already been taken. But we can't wait for them. We have a very important local role to play as well.

"Isn't it too late to reverse global climate change?" one council member asked Jim.

"You better hope it's not too late. But I agree we should have taken action sooner. It would have been easier and far cheaper to have slowed The Warming before it hit a tipping point."

When Jim raised his hands in frustration, Wanda leaned over and whispered, "Jim, don't blame anyone. That won't help our cause. They'll just get defensive and dig in their heels. Just address their questions. Just state the facts."

Jim took a deep breath and continued, "We're in uncharted territory. We may not be able to reverse The Warming, but we can slow it down, so the worst impacts don't wipe us out."

"It sure can't get worse than what happened here this week," Ed observed.

Jim went on. "The Changes could get much worse. They could be more expensive in terms of loss of life, severe health impacts, and business disruption. The cheapest thing to do is to prevent these disasters from happening in the first place." Marley had the feeling Ed wasn't even listening, but Jim continued. "So it's even more important now to take steps to reduce The Warming, manage The Changes, and build resiliency into our town. If we don't do all three, we'll be forced to move out of Sleepy Valley. We would have to go to areas that do care about the future and are willing to take action to reduce these impacts."

"I'm not going anywhere," Ed shouted.

Jim turned to face Ed again. "Well, if you want to stay here, as I do, we need to take a look at how we can save our valley. The do-nothing approach got us into this mess. It's time to take action to get us out of it. Ed, we need to find some path forward where we can work together."

Wanda stood up beside Jim. "Ed, there are good examples from towns all over the world that have already made progress. I agree with Jim that it's time we did something here in Sleepy Valley. If people everywhere had been proactive years ago, The Changes would never have happened. Betsy and Luke wouldn't be losing their farm. The streets and rooftops wouldn't be melting. Blue Lake wouldn't be dying. Life as you knew it in the good old days would have continued. But we didn't do enough."

"So what can we do?" asked Marley.

"Wanda and I would be happy to summarize what other towns are doing, and what we can do to slow down The Warming," Jim told everyone. "Wanda has put together a plan for the town to follow. I have a list of things that each of us can do on our own. We'll get the plan and the list out tomorrow for each of you to consider. Let's just hope it's not too late."

Marley was amazed at how the meeting was going. He realized that his comments had changed the direction of the discussion. And yes, all his allies had jumped in to support him. Joe's plan was working. It was pretty exciting.

Marley then noticed Mr. Folly loosen his tie with his thumb and middle finger and then squirm in his seat. It was noticeable to everyone in the room that he was growing very uncomfortable. After all, Jim was blaming him for not taking action in the past and was demanding that he take action now.

Marley stood up again and said, "I would like to thank the council for holding these hearings, and I look forward to working with you all on a solution." He watched the chairman carefully, looking for clues as to how he would respond. He knew Folly didn't want to intervene, spend money, or do anything at all, even with these extreme conditions battering their town. But had their testimonies convinced him that some action was in order? He sure hoped so.

Folly appeared to be looking for an escape—a strategy to delay any decision. He picked up the gavel and moved to close the meeting by saying, "Thank you all for coming tonight. I think we need time to see what else happens and to study our options. How about we meet again a month from tonight?"

A great moan, tinged with anger, bubbled up from around the room. No one except Folly thought they should wait that long. They all wanted an answer now.

Marley stood. "It can't wait a whole month. How about this Thursday?"

The room erupted with clapping and support, so much so that Folly was forced to adjust. "Okay, okay, this Thursday. Bring proposals for what can be done to reduce the heat and fix The Changes. Ideas that don't cost the town anything will be favorably received. Same time and same place. Meeting adjourned." Folly struck the gavel once, turned, and slowly extricated himself from his chair.

As people left, Marley noted the SVE reps were approaching Folly. Joe whispered, "They've been fighting for years to keep their coal-fired power plant open. It should be shut down, but they've been dragging their feet. Their proposal would help them keep it operating. We need to find out who in SVE is looking at the bigger picture. They must have individuals focused on clean energy and the future. It's only a matter of time before they'll welcome a solar farm."

"We have to speed up that process," Marley replied. "We have to save Betsy and Luke's farm *now*. They can't hang on much longer."

"Then let's do our homework on SVE," Joe continued. "I have to get my troops into their microbiome. It would help us, Marley, if you went over right now and shook hands with both of the folks from SVE. Stand as close as possible to them. Sneeze if you can. We will do the rest."

Marley felt this was a weird request, but he had come to respect Joe. After all, they had gotten through their first public meeting together and had made a difference. Marley told Brianne he'd catch up with her in a few minutes, and then he casually approached the SVE reps.

CHAPTER SEVENTEEN

FOLLOW-UP

Marley went home and collapsed on his bed, but his subconscious mind kept running, thinking about solutions to The Warming. During the night he had three dreams. In the first dream he pictured himself as a mile-high giant, huffing and puffing and blowing the carbon dioxide that had accumulated in the atmosphere far out into outer space. He then charged around the countryside, stomping on all the old, coal-fired power plants, finally shutting them down for good. When he woke up at the end of the dream, he smiled. *If only it were that easy.*

Later that night, when he started to dream again, he was the king shouting out edicts. He banned all use of fossil fuels, ordered the army to install solar panels on all buildings, and charged the navy with building offshore windfarms. Practically overnight, the country ran on 100% renewable energy and health, power, and national security costs dropped dramatically. He was hailed for his actions for the next millennium.

When Marley woke up from that dream, he was so disappointed to find it wasn't real that he growled angrily. *But I'm not a king. I live in a democracy.* It was so frustrating to him because many of the solutions were straightforward. It just required creating a plan and getting everyone to follow it.

Then Marley fell into another dreamy stupor. This time, his

subconscious conjured up a picture of himself as a prophet in a long white robe, a graying beard, and leather sandals. He was walking through the Dust Bowl deserts of North America, carrying a banner on a pole. The banner's display, in bright red letters, simply stated, "Summer's Coming." He was also handing out clay tablets on which "Ten Steps for a Cooler Planet" had been inscribed.

That was the last image he remembered of a wild night of sleep.

* * *

A few hours later Marley yawned. It was now Tuesday morning, and after a fitful night of sleep, he was up and on the road. Brianne had picked him up early in her mom's Jeep. They were going to go help Jim and Wanda at the observatory.

Now, in the Jeep, Brianne nudged him when he started to nod off again. "Hey, wake up."

"I'm awake. Just groggy. You know, I've never been inside the observatory before. I'm looking forward to seeing where you spent all your time last summer." He also wanted to spend more time with Jim and Wanda. Their comments at the meeting had inspired him. He realized that if anyone had the answer to how to slow down The Warming, it would be Jim.

"Aside from being with friends during these scary times, I also want to help out," Brianne said. "Besides, I think Jim and Wanda could use a little encouragement right now."

"Why's that?"

"I don't think they have any family in town, and I don't know if they have any social friends. They just work all the time. This is clearly a time to be with family, friends, and allies."

"Well, I'm glad we're going. I think they're both pretty cool. Thanks for inviting me."

She smiled over at him.

"I'm also glad there's more I can do to help than just deliver groceries."

After struggling to make it up the hill, they went inside the unlocked front door of the observatory.

"Good morning. Anyone here?" Brianne called as she came inside. Marley noticed she had a big smile on her face and a bounce in her step—it was like she was coming home.

They stopped just inside the lobby and looked around. Marley was shocked. The place was a wreck, papers everywhere. Jim was asleep on the couch, his shoes and tie scattered around the room. It looked as if a cyclone had hit the place.

Jim sat up groggily. He looked like he was trying to remember where he was. Although barely awake, with hair astray and bags under his eyes, he perked right up and gave a crooked grin when he saw Brianne and Marley. He looked delighted to see them and acted as if they were long-lost friends—a couple of kindred spirits. This must have been a very refreshing change for him from the unruly crowd he had faced last night at the meeting.

"We came to see if we could help out," said Brianne. "You look tired, Jim. Did you spend the whole night here?"

"I am tired, and yes, I spent the night here. There's so much to do. It's great to see you both." He seemed excited that they cared enough to offer their help. "Welcome to our little observatory in the sky." He turned to look out the window. "What's it like out there? Is it as bad as yesterday?"

"I think it's going to be worse," Brianne replied. "It's hard getting up the hill. We had to walk the last stretch. By the way, did you know someone took out your sign? Looks like someone slid off the road."

Jim just nodded, looking a little guilty. Of course he was the culprit; no other cars were in the parking lot.

"It's more of the same," Marley added. "The streets are still empty of people. I'm afraid that, with all the oil and dry wood, the town could go up in flames at any time."

"I think we'll have to get used to the heat and a high level of risk in our lives," said Jim.

Marley started walking around the observatory, looking at everything. "Wow, this place is really cool. Look at the large windows. You can see the whole valley and beyond."

"I'll show you around when we get the chance," Jim told him.

* * *

"How can we help?" asked Brianne, clearly looking forward to getting involved.

"It's great to have you back here. There's an awful lot you can do to help us get organized," Jim said. "Let me get some cold drinks first."

Brianne smiled. "I thought I got you organized last summer."

"You did." Jim laughed. "You were a great help. But we're really buried now." Then he looked at Marley. "You both can be a big help by encouraging your friends and neighbors to read my 'Ten Steps for a Cooler Climate' and to come to the next meeting. It's only two days away and we have to inform more people about what's going on and get them to come out, speak up, and take action."

"I know," said Marley. "None of our friends came last night. It was so disappointing that they didn't feel it was important enough. Of course, I almost didn't come either."

"We did invite some friends at the last minute," Brianne added. "Many of them didn't even know the meeting was going on. They didn't show."

"Yeah, it's too bad. Most of us don't follow local government unless it directly affects us," said Jim. "Of course, The Warming is affecting us all."

"Several friends told me they didn't think anyone would listen to them," said Marley.

Jim pushed his hair out of his eyes and replied, "And yet you both came. Your testimonies were significant, and people listened—you got everyone thinking. Most importantly, you stood up at the crucial point in the debate and changed the course of the discussion. That was a big step forward. You made a huge difference.

"I think you both should be talking about these issues with your neighbors and friends as much as you can. See how many will come on Thursday. If five more people had stood up and supported what you said, we might have won the debate."

"We can certainly do that," Brianne said and immediately began texting her friends and neighbors about the next meeting. She even asked Marley's parents and her mother to show up.

Marley pulled out his phone too, but first he asked, "Jim, can you send me your 'Ten Steps to a Cooler Climate' list so I can include it in my texts?"

"Sure thing. The more people who see the list, the more likely they'll read it and take some of the actions."

Just then Wanda came in from the back room. "Wow, this is a big surprise. It's great to see you guys. I hope you got more sleep than we did."

Brianne skipped over to give her a big hug. "You stayed here too? Well, of course you did, there must be so much to do. We should have brought you both breakfast."

"We're getting by—mostly on adrenaline," said Wanda. "We're living on Cliff bars, gorp, and iced coffee." She grinned then turned serious. "By the way, your testimonies were spot on. We needed spokespeople from the community, and you both stepped right up and filled the gap. I loved it. We couldn't have planned that any better."

Marley thought Wanda looked and sounded a lot more put together and awake after a short night than Jim did. "We were so glad you two were there, setting the stage and backing us up. I don't know what I would have done if I'd had to debate Ed Perkins alone."

"I'm not much of a public speaker," Jim admitted. "I just get too upset. It's hard to debate someone as self-assured, opinionated, and charismatic as Ed Perkins. We need to prepare better for the next round."

"Well, we're here to help out. What can we do?" asked Brianne.

Wanda quickly replied, "It would be great if you could read through these reports to find out what steps are paying off for other towns? We need any ideas that might be helpful to reduce The Warming, manage The Changes, and strengthen our infrastructure."

"Sure, we can do that," said Brianne. "Where should we sit?"

"Sit at the central table." Wanda pointed to a big table in the middle of the room.

"Look at that screen," said Marley as he walked up and reached out to touch it. "You've got all the big events shown on one display. That's the most detail I've ever seen of our local weather patterns."

"It's pretty amazing how much can be shown at once, isn't it?" Wanda said proudly.

"Now I can see why the farm got wiped out. It's right on the edge of this big thermal," said Marley. Both he and Brianne were mesmerized by the detail of the weather model and stared at it for a few minutes. Then Marley noticed that Brianne was smiling at him.

It was the first opportunity she'd had to share this place with him, and Brianne was clearly pleased that Marley seemed as excited as she was to be here. She pointed out the shorthand symbols Jim used to represent different data sets.

Wanda cleared a space at the big table and encouraged them to start sorting through reports from Jim's network. Marley and Brianne both felt as if they were trying to solve a mystery—what might happen next and what could be done to prevent it.

They read reports of people, towns, states, and even whole countries that had taken The Warming seriously for years. They also read reports about places that hadn't done anything. They focused on the reports that described what had been done to slow down The Warming and limit the damage.

Marley took the reports that discussed successful shifts away from fossil fuels. Brianne focused on efforts that towns pursued to become more resilient. The room grew quiet for several hours as they hovered over monitors and stacks of paper.

As Marley read about what people had done, he got more and more animated, sitting up straighter and tapping his fingers on the table. He was the first to break the silence. "Do you realize that Germany, Costa Rica, and Denmark have led the move toward renewable energy? Their grids approach one hundred present renewable at times. China is rapidly ramping up, too. They're all way ahead of us."

"So how are we doing in this country?" Brianne asked.

"Wind power's taken off, with Texas, Iowa, California, Illinois, and Oklahoma leading the pack. I didn't realize it, but the Great Plains has the greatest onshore wind resource in the country.

"How about solar?"

"The leading solar states are California, North Carolina, Arizona, Nevada, New Jersey, and Massachusetts," Marley said.

"New Jersey and Massachusetts?" Brianne repeated. "Why isn't Texas big in solar?"

"I don't know, but it's clear there's a lot of effort going into renewables. The economies and work forces have grown in those states, debunking the myth that reducing our use of fossil fuels wouldn't be good for the economy."

"Why haven't we done it here in Sleepy Valley?" Brianne asked.

Jim broke in. "This is just the type of information our town and the state need to see. I hope it will encourage them to move away from fossil fuel."

"Don't they already know that?" asked Marley.

"The members of the council can't seem to make the connection between their everyday behaviors and the warming of the climate. Do they even realize that driving gasoline-powered cars and using electricity generated from coal-fired plants is a big part of the problem?"

Wanda reminded him that he drove a gas-powered car.

"Yes, yes, yes, I know. But I love my old Subaru. I want to keep it going forever. My *next* car will be electric."

"But, Jim, that's part of the problem," Wanda replied. "The warming climate never seems bad enough or urgent enough to make us change our behavior in a timely manner. You're a good example of that."

"You're right," Jim agreed. "I am a good example. It's hard to change our behaviors. At least we insulated this building and cut our heating and cooling bill in half."

Brianne offered, "I've been reading about the Great Plains as well. Droughts over the past few years are wreaking havoc on the oil- and water-dependent, big corn business. Evidently, the aquifers are running dry. Some ranchers are converting their dried-up farmland back to native-grass rangeland to raise bison. The deep roots of these grasses help the plants withstand extended droughts, prevent soils from blowing away and, along with the bison, replenish nutrients in the soils."

"We've got to send those stories to Betsy and Luke," Marley said. "If they can't make the solar happen, maybe they could run buffalo on their land." He was excited to find some options for the local farmers.

Brianne added, "Of course, as you get closer to the coasts, they have the opposite problem. They're seeing too much rain."

"I doubt anything can be done to prepare for those mega-storms," said Marley.

"Actually, some towns restricted building along shorelines, on floodplains, and on steep slopes. By expanding their green infra-structure network of buffered streams, wetlands, and forests, they've been able to reduce flooding and polluted runoff."

As Marley listened he became angry and his body grew tense. "It does seem that planning ahead is paying off for other towns. I don't think we've done any of that here in Sleepy Valley. Why not?"

Jim was now up and walking around the table where they were working. "That's right, we haven't. Our town council needs to hear these stories. They haven't done enough. Their head-in-the-sand approach is causing our people to suffer."

"And now it's too late." Marley said, feeling despondent that his town wasn't prepared.

"Maybe not," Jim said, handing them his 'Ten Steps for a Cooler Climate' list. "Take a look at this list. This is the cover page of the report that I am sending out to everyone in the valley. How can we get these points across to the council and get all our neighbors to start doing these things?"

"Jim, I'm really glad you created this," Marley said. "I'll take it home and see what we can do.

"And don't be fooled. The list seems simplistic, but I wanted simple, easy-to-take steps so more people will implement them and develop an awareness that they can help. There are no silver bullets. It all comes down to each of us doing what we can do—taking a series of small but consequential actions. That's how you nudge cultures to change. I do have a more thorough report of global actions. Things like creating clean and sustainable technologies, more walkable cities, and shifting to more plant-based diets. It even discusses population, immigration, and the empowerment of women worldwide. They're all important. But I doubt many people will read it all. My 'short list' focuses on steps that Sleepy Valley residents, businesses, and the town could take immediately."

Dear Neighbors:

All the data we have indicates that rising temperatures triggered each of The Changes we have seen over the past few days. If you want to reduce a continuing cascade of damaging local and global events, we all need to take actions to decrease this man-made warming trend. Every person, business, and town that does nothing makes it worse for all of us.

A large component of The Warming is the misuse and overuse of fossil fuels like coal, oil, and natural gas. There are no quick solutions, but we can have a big impact if all of us reduce fossil fuel usage at home and the office by taking these ten steps:

Your neighbor, Jim Quartz
Chief Scientist, Hilltop Observatory

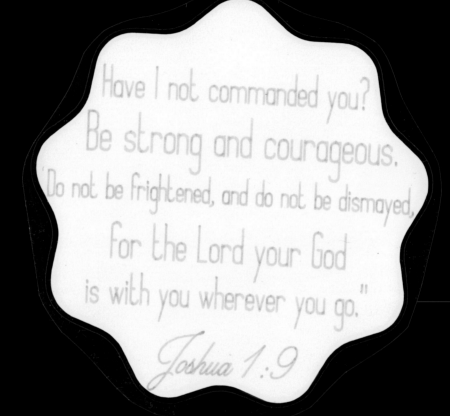

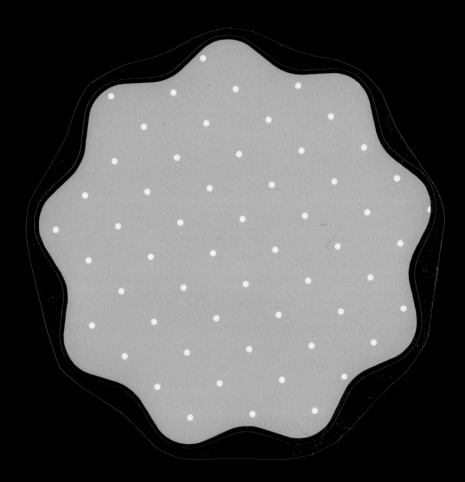

TEN STEPS FOR A COOLER CLIMATE

1. Reduce energy usage: insulate, drive less, use hybrids & electric vehicles, unplug

2. Switch electricity supplier to 100% solar or wind

3. Buy only the most sustainable products to incentivize businesses to make more of them

4. Plant native trees and shrubs to clean our air & water and cool things down

5. Support local and national environmental non-profits

6. Reduce meat consumption and food waste

7. Encourage businesses and governments to support solar and wind energy development

8. Encourage energy-efficiency upgrades in all buildings and vehicles

9. Support the expansion of interconnected green infra-structure networks

10. Implement a national "carbon cap and dividend" pol-icy or a "carbon tax" to pay for the real and hidden costs to society of using dirty fuels

Brianne and Marley stopped what they were doing to read the list. They were interested to know what they could do. As far as Marley could see, his family hadn't done anything that would have helped to reduce The Warming. When he finished reading, he said, "Jim, some of these actions seem doable, but others are beyond our control."

"You're right. So focus on what you *can* do. You can then encourage your representatives at the local, state, and national levels to get the rest of them done. We have to do both."

"But is this enough?" Brianne looked at Marley with a disappointed look on her face.

He knew exactly what she meant; the list was a little underwhelming. He too was hoping for something a little more dramatic. "Even if we did all of these items, it feels like it would be just a small drop in a very big bucket. I was hoping we could do some big things with big impact."

"I understand," Jim responded. "But that's the point—all these actions are small. Small enough so that each of us can do them. There will be a big impact if everyone in Sleepy Valley— if all seven billion people on Earth—take these steps. Remember, the Warming is the result of seven billion people living in a way that, day-by-day, collectively pumps massive amounts of greenhouse gases into our atmosphere. We can stop that by changing our behaviors. Each of us, as individuals and as businesses, can help fix things by voluntarily taking these small steps."

"It sure would be easier if the government just took care of this by stopping businesses from polluting our air and sending industry a clear and consistent message to invest in clean energy," Brianne commented.

"Yeah, but don't hold your breath. Congress hasn't been able to agree on a plan for decades," Jim replied. "We need to do exactly what you two are so good at doing—organizing and inspiring others to act. We can also have a big impact on business. Just buy from firms that operate sustainably or that sell energy-efficient items."

"These are certainly things we can do right now. We don't

have to wait on others," Marley said, looking at Brianne and starting to understand Jim's strategy. "I think we can get our friends on board with these steps, too."

Jim concluded, "It's all possible. We just have to get everyone working together."

Marley got the picture, but he had a sinking feeling in his belly. Was it too little, too late? He had a bad feeling that they should have acted years ago.

CHAPTER EIGHTEEN

THE SECOND TOWN HALL MEETING

On Thursday night Marley was in a state of dismay as he set off for the meeting. In the past 48 hours, he had watched with growing sadness as life in Sleepy Valley continued to deteriorate. Fear had invaded every home in town. Everyone was now facing problems with food and water supplies, intermittent power, poor air quality, and the oppressive heat. The hall wasn't big enough to hold all the anger flowing from the town and into the room.

As he approached the grange hall, Marley marveled at all the people and especially all his friends who had shown up. He noticed a number of his classmates standing outside the hall with posters saying "Save our Town" and "It's Time to Act." One had a cartoon of Chairman Folly melting away into the asphalt.

Marley smiled at the signs and waved to his friends. His organizing efforts had paid off. It gave him a sense that people in the valley did care about their future. His texts had motivated not just his friends but several neighbors to come tonight. He spoke with many of them as he entered the grange hall and moved slowly toward the front row.

Colin and Grant, his skateboarding friends, texted him as he came in. They were there, standing in the back. They had heard through the grapevine about the role Marley and Brianne had played in the debate on Monday night. They were excited and proud their friends had helped to focus the discussion.

Bertha Hall from the Tea Room approached Marley and said, "Thank you so much for encouraging me to come. Gertrude and I are very concerned about the town. We're so glad you're involved. That gives us hope that something good will come out of this chaos."

"Thanks for coming," he replied, not sure what else to say.

The feedback he got made him feel like his efforts had something to do with the great turnout. Of course he also realized that the growing impacts of the current disasters had a lot to do with the attendance—the problems were now big enough and widespread enough to get everyone's attention. The hall was standing-room only; people were clustered three rows deep all along the back and on both side walls.

The heat and the tension in the room were noticeably greater than during the first meeting. Concerns about the temperature and the reliability of the electricity had prompted the town engineer to set up generators outside to run the lights and the fans that had been brought in. He clearly didn't want a power outage in the middle of the meeting.

Marley noticed that several attendees wore dust protectors over their faces, evidently to reduce the amount of toxic air they inhaled. Two others had respirators and one even had a gas mask on her face.

Marley listened intently to as many of the conversations going on around him as he could. Most people were discussing how The Warming was affecting them and their families. A few of his neighbors had heard that fires had started popping up all around town from downed electrical lines. They also talked about how the hordes of invasive vines, growing rapidly in the heat and high CO2 levels, had clogged up storm drains, chimneys, roof vents, and even exhaust pipes on cars.

Everyone was having trouble accessing fresh food; shipments

from other areas had become irregular due to the melting streets. The city had started rationing water, and people were scared about where they would get their next meal. They had all come out tonight, wanting answers.

Marley felt the pressure in the room oozing into his pores as the sweat passed it on the way out. He sat there, anxious for the evening to begin.

* * *

Moments after the SVE contingent came in and took their seats, Chairman Folly made his entrance. Folly worked his way through the hot and noisy crowd and sat down at the front table. Marley doubted if there had ever been so many people in this room in all of Folly's years of conducting meetings here.

Folly opened the meeting with an extra heavy bang of the gavel. "The meeting will now come to order. If anyone is next to an empty seat, please raise your hand. There are still more people trying to get in. Let's take another minute or two to settle down."

Folly did not look happy. Marley knew Folly was hoping things would have gotten better over the past few days; they had actually gotten worse. Marley also knew Folly felt blindsided by Jim's letter and Wanda's plan. Jim had shown Marley an irate email he had received from Folly.

It merely said: "I managed to read all the way through the cover letter and then decided not to read any of the detail in the report. Who do you think you are? It's one thing to propose ideas in a discussion but quite another thing to write them down as facts and send them out to everybody in town. Your letter was nothing more than a partisan attack on me."

Now Jim leaned over and told Marley, "Folly has his own opinions and isn't ready to accept any facts, especially if they don't agree with his preconceived beliefs. I doubt whether he appreciates that the scientific method is an objective tool people use to establish facts and to understand how things work."

"It sure has led to a lot of great discoveries," Marley added.

"That's right. He also believes that he and he alone knows the proper role of small-town government. He doesn't think anything can be done here in Sleepy Valley about a widespread climate-warming event. In fact he refuses to accept any personal responsibility for creating the current problems or for fixing them. So be careful. I think he feels like he's backed into a corner, and like a badger, he's going to fight his way out."

* * *

As the noise in the hall dissipated, a hand shot up from the second row. "I'll go first."

Everyone looked surprised when Doc stood up. A small number of people knew he was a teacher, and a few knew he was an author, but no one in town had read his books.

Not knowing what to expect, Folly was hesitant but cordial. "Why certainly, Doc, go right ahead."

Marley was as surprised as everyone else and turned around in his chair to be sure he wouldn't miss anything Doc said.

As Doc stood, he brushed several green vines off his shoulders, paused for a moment then spoke in a quiet and clear voice. "I'm glad to see so many young people here tonight. Pay attention. This is all about your future. What we decide here will have a big impact on your lives." He stopped for a moment, probably thinking he should take attendance. "Jim Quartz's report is an excellent piece of work. I read the whole thing. I suggest everyone read at least the first page which is a list of things we each can do and then leave here today committed to taking action in your homes and businesses. There are steps that each of us will have to take in order to save the valley. You are the primary line of defense to the scourge we're facing."

Marley took a quick look at Folly to note his reaction. Folly didn't change his expression, but he slowly scanned the room, his head rotating like an owl on the prowl. The crowd was quiet, everyone listening. Marley could tell they were all impressed that Doc had read the report and were hoping Doc would summarize it for them so they wouldn't have to.

Doc continued, "It should be clear to all of us that our town is facing disastrous challenges. Our climate is like a runaway train. It's fueled by subsidized 'cheap' coal and it's headed for a cliff. Sadly, there's no engineer on board to slow it down."

He paused, letting the picture of a train sink in. Marley noted that Folly shifted uncomfortably in his seat. "Our town needs that engineer. Someone with the technical expertise to understand and solve our challenges. I suggest we create a position for a top-level technical advisor or consultant to the council. Their job would be to make sure all projects and decisions are done in a way to decrease, not increase, The Warming. He or she should be able to create a plan to reduce both The Warming and The Changes. These critical matters should be decided by technical professionals and not be debated or decided in a political arena." With that, Doc sat down and crossed his legs, clearly waiting to see what Folly would do with this rational suggestion.

No one said anything. It was a logical, if not very dramatic, proposal. But Doc had failed to line up any support ahead of time, so he got none. He had relied on the power of the metaphor to make a difference. But it might not have been enough.

Marley thought Doc's proposal made sense. He liked the image of the runaway train. He and the whole crowd looked to Folly, whose face resembled a stone wall, to see what he thought of the proposal. No clue there. Doc had told Marley that Folly had no appetite to expand the size and expertise of the town's government now, even if it would help prevent more disasters in the future. This was the classic debate that happened all the time in Sleepy Valley, and Folly had never been accused of being forward thinking. His specialty was to let things die.

While everyone waited for Folly to decide what to do, or rather what not to do, Joe spoke softly into Marley's ear. "Of course that makes sense, we should all want a government that knows what they are doing, will plan ahead, and do what needs to be done to protect us from future disasters. We clearly do not have that kind of council now."

Just as the silence started to be awkward, Max opened the side door and rumbled into the room. It was probably one of the few times Folly actually welcomed the arrival of Ranger Bunyan. Everyone's chair squeaked as they all turned—immediately forgetting the proposal Doc had presented. Max's entrance was much more exciting than solving the town's underlying political standoff.

Marley's face softened, edging toward a smile. He noticed that Max looked like a pile of sawdust; when he stopped moving, a shower of woodchips and splinters that had been stuck to his beard, clothes, and boots rained down to the floor. There was a strange-looking bird with a long beak hovering over Max's head and an even stranger looking rodent-like animal scampering around him on the floor. All three of them seemed anxious about being indoors. Max's contingent smelled like the woods and left a trail of debris wherever they went.

Now Max was a large man, about 6'5", which made him intimidating without any accoutrements. But with the woodcock and armadillo circling, he drew the mirthful attention of everyone in the room. And even though most of the audience knew Max, none of them had ever seen an armadillo or a woodcock before.

Upon seeing them arrive in the hall, most of the crowd expected a naturalist talk. A lecture describing life in the park, how the bird and the armadillo fit into the web of life, and the importance of biodiversity. But no, judging by the intensity on Max's face, Marley realized that wasn't why he was there.

Silence pervaded the room. Max cleared his throat and jumped into the pitch he had likely been practicing on his walk to the meeting. "All the trees in the park and the town are gone. As Jim pointed out in his report, we need trees—saplings, that is. We need hardy, drought-resistant trees as an important step to restoring our town. I have done the calculations. We need 180,000 of them. That would be enough to restore the park. You should probably double that number to replace all the trees that have died around town. Trees are the cheapest way to clean the air, the water, and to help cool down this hothouse. Planting trees is the best way to save our town."

Marley wanted to cheer. *How could the council not support that plan?*

Folly thanked Max for his proposal but said, "Max, why should we spend all that money to plant new trees when those blue beetles will just kill them anyway?"

"I've found a solution to the beetles, and it won't cost you a dime. Leave the beetles to me," Max replied, glancing proudly down at the armadillo at his feet.

"Buying 360,000 trees will be expensive. Where's all that money gonna come from?" asked the town's budget director.

"You need to include the costs in an emergency budget and borrow the money," Max told him. "It's an investment that will be paid back multiple times in clean air, clean water, and cooler streets. The sooner we get started replanting the park, the sooner we can start getting this town back to being livable again. If we wait too long, the park—and the town—will catch on fire or be taken over by invasive plants. We'll lose all our investments to date in building this town."

Folly thanked Max for his comments and then recognized the local representative from the Audubon Society, who was wildly waving her hand. Marley recognized her and was surprised she was an activist. But she sure looked the part of a professional birder. She was a woman in her seventies, complete with a *Peterson Field Guide to Birds of North America* in her left hand and Zeiss binoculars hanging from her neck. She got up and seconded Max's idea. "We need trees to attract birds back to Sleepy Valley. They've all disappeared over the past week. Their habitat's gone. What's life without the sounds of birds in the trees?"

"What's life without the sound of money in your pocket?" Old Ed griped loudly from the back of the hall. A burst of chuckles erupted around the room. The woman glared at him. Then Ed turned toward Max. "Who's going to plant all those trees, Max?"

Max replied in his deep baritone, "I'll make you this pledge, Ed. You get me the trees, and I'll plant them." A cheer went up from the audience. Marley smiled. He really liked Max's proposal and thought everyone should. *How could you not support someone who was so dedicated to the cause of a healthy park?*

In reaction to the loud noise, the woodcock buried his head deep in Max's beard, leaving only his tail feathers showing. The armadillo curled up in an armor-protected ball under the pile of sawdust between Max's feet. Folly looked like he wished he could do the same. He clearly wasn't interested in another request for funds, especially one he had not expected. It was going to be a long evening.

"I'll even plant some of them on the East Side, Ed. You guys could use a little shade. Trees will cool things down and will help clean the air coming off the lake."

"Most of us won't be around here by the time those trees do us any good," Ed argued.

The local leaders of the Boy and Girl Scouts, dressed in their respective uniforms, offered Max the full support of all their troops. "This would be the greatest project ever for our youth. A way for us to give back to the community. Our children could all become naturalists and earn their tree-planting merit badges. What a wonderful way to extract our kids from our basements and get them enjoying the outdoors again." All the scouts' parents, ex-scouts, and sisters and brothers of scouts stood up and clapped.

Folly looked around, hoping to end this discussion by calling on someone else.

Marley just sat there with a big grin on his face. He thought Max had done a splendid job in making the case for more trees. He realized his allies were stepping up to the plate and giving it their best shots.

* * *

Marley watched as the businessman who used to sell shoes stood up next. He was now dressed in forest-green overalls. But before he could speak, the clapboard walls started vibrating from another disturbance on the highway. Marley quickly realized that this time it was Sam Perkins mimicking the noisy entrance that his dad, Ed, had executed with his motorcycle so effectively a few days before.

Sam drove his recently converted, *Rolling Coal* Humvee right up to an open window and revved the engine. Black exhaust invaded the hall. Clearly, he was pissed. Upon reading Jim's letter, he had become incensed and complained to anyone within earshot, "That damn weatherman's trying to tell me what I can and can't do! No way am I going to buy any silly hybrid!"

In angry protest to Jim's perceived insult, Sam had spent thousands of dollars over the past few days to create the most polluting vehicle in all of Sleepy Valley, maybe even the state. The first thing he had done was to illegally remove the particulate filter. "Screw the EPA," he said when his friends told him he was breaking the law.

He then installed extremely large and very loud, dual smokestacks on his Humvee so he could spew as much sooty diesel exhaust into the air as possible. He was having a blast, driving around town and drowning anyone in a dark cloud of soot who might be walking, or biking, or driving a hybrid.

Marley had already been a target of Sam's diesel-smoke machine and was still trying to get the diesel fumes out of his clothes. He had advised all of his friends to stay out of the way of this crazy man.

"There's no way I'm going to change my behavior one bit for any pie-in-the-sky theory about why the Earth is warming," Sam belligerently informed his friends. "In fact, what's wrong with a little warming–especially if it extends the fishing and hunting seasons?"

When Jim had heard this, he just shook his head and told Marley, "Sam doesn't realize that most of the fish and game species might be displaced or destroyed by The Warming. Sportsmen should be among the most concerned as their game lands are destroyed."

Meanwhile, inside the grange, people began coughing. They were trapped in the hall by the sheer number of people standing in the doorways, and the hall was quickly filling up with diesel fumes. Marley looked over at Brianne. She was having a hard time breathing.

Marley watched in disbelief as even the termites started swarming out of the floorboards, trying to find an escape route. They made a beeline for any open window or door. Like canaries in coal mines, the termites were serving as the early warning signal alerting everyone to the unhealthy conditions within the grange hall.

Finally, several older women jumped up to close the windows. But by then everyone had gagged on the particulate matter that had already filled the room . . . and their lungs.

Not having the guts to come into the meeting, Sam just sat there, idling. He kept running his air conditioning and periodically revved up his engine to re-emphasize his point, as misdirected as it was.

Marley and Brianne just rolled their eyes every time Sam revved his engine.

* * *

After a few minutes of general grumbling about Sam's boorish behavior, Folly called the meeting back to order and asked the businessman in the green jumpsuit to continue.

Marley smiled as the shoe salesman started off by waving his arms just like he had done at the earlier meeting. It appeared that he was warming himself up by cranking his engine. He then began his pitch.

"I have changed from selling shoes that nobody wants to selling solar collectors that everybody needs. Jim's report helped me to see the light. To be a healthier community and to be resilient as more changes occur, Sleepy Valley needs a local and clean source of energy. The energy resource we have here in abundance is solar. I believe there's a future in solar for all of us. It's the solution to many of our town's problems."

Marley glanced back at Betsy and Luke to measure their response to another solar option.

"We could all switch from dirty, fossil fuel-generated electricity to clean renewable sources like solar practically overnight. In fact I'll prove it by making an offer to every one of you. Sign up tonight at my booth, and I'll lease you a roof-based solar system for less than you're currently paying Sleepy Valley Energy. I guarantee you'll save money.

Marley looked out over the audience and noticed the solar energy marketing booth in the back of the room with the header *Let the Sun Do It!*

"Furthermore, while up on your roof, my teams can replace your ruined asphalt shingles with no-melt shingles and insulate your attics so you use less energy and save even more money. This is a great opportunity for everyone. It's a no-brainer."

Marley could see Folly was getting angry at what seemed like a brazen sales pitch. But the guy was good, and this private-sector initiative was appealing to many people in the audience. Even Folly liked an agile entrepreneur, so he let him continue.

"I'm also here tonight to ask the town council to demonstrate how easy it is to 'go solar' by agreeing to cover the roofs of all municipal buildings with solar panels. That will reduce our town's costs and our taxes."

The business community was impressed. They cheered and many of them jumped to their feet and gave him a standing ovation for being so resilient to the changing market conditions. Finally, a money-making solution to their problems. Nobody liked the air pollution from the local, coal-powered power plant. They all liked the idea of being self-sufficient.

Joe whispered to Marley, "The only people who did not stand were the employees who work in the fossil fuel industry. That includes the power plant, local gas stations, and home-heating-oil businesses, who view all renewable energy ideas as potential threats to their livelihoods. They are against these ideas . . . unless they can figure a way to profit from them. Folly has to be sure to keep those people happy. They represent part of his political base."

Folly complimented the businessman on his resilience but wanted to move on. He asked if there were any more speakers.

Betsy raised her hand, and she and Luke stood up together. She cleared her throat and then spoke directly to the audience.

"You know we've been good neighbors for five generations. We like farming, and over the years we've sold healthy, locally-grown food to probably everyone in this room."

Marley heard a warm murmur of supporting voices all around the grange hall. It made him feel just a little proud that the Alexanders were so well-liked in this town.

Betsy continued in somber tones. "Have any of you been by the farm recently?" She paused as tears welled in her eyes. "There's nothing left. No barn, no garden, no farm stand. The change in the weather here in Sleepy Valley has turned our farm into a wasteland."

You could hear a pin drop; everyone hung on her every word. Many of the other farmers identified with her depth of despair and her fear.

"We've tried to think of everything possible to make a living during these challenging times. It's come down to one last shot at keeping the family farm." Marley realized that everyone in the room was hoping to hear she had found a solution.

Unable to go on, she turned to Luke, who stood up as tall as he could and spoke with as much confidence as he could muster. "Like the last speaker, we also want to harvest the sun. We propose building a solar farm on three hundred acres of our land. It should produce enough electricity for many of your homes. That's a big step. Along with the systems you can put on your rooftops, and the conversion of other farms, we should be able to retire the old, coal-fired power plant outside of town. It doesn't have much life left in it and will fail soon. We need a more secure, longer-term, and cleaner source for our electricity here in Sleepy Valley."

"Shutting down that plant will result in cleaner air and far less asthma and bronchial problems for all of us," Betsy said. "Just like Wanda said earlier in the week, we'll all be healthier, live longer, and have lower medical costs. What we're asking for tonight is permission to become the solar farm pioneers here in the valley. Like the challenges our ancestors faced, we're ready to take the risks of this new venture. We want to pave the way for other farmers to stay on their land as well."

As Betsy and Luke sat down, there was a general vibration of support all around the hall. Betsy could even feel the support of her ancestor's spirits, who were hovering over her. She silently thanked them for their encouragement even though she realized they had no idea what a solar farm was.

Marley could sense the widespread support in the room for his aunt and uncle's proposal. People liked them, and this was such a rational plan.

Brianne whispered to Marley, "They did a great job. How could anyone say no to them? I wonder how SVE will react to both of these solar ideas." They both glanced over at the SVE representatives, who were quietly taking notes.

Folly thanked both Betsy and Luke for their proposal and offered his condolences for the tough year they were having.

Marley decided it was time for him to stand up. "I would like to focus on Wanda's 'Plan for Saving Sleepy Valley.' You all should have received it, along with Jim's action list. She recommended the town pursue three tracks at roughly the same time. It seems to make a lot of sense to me. It puts all of these ideas into an orderly process.

"The first track of her plan is to get everyone in the town organized so food, water, and essential medicines could be distributed to everyone as needed. Brianne and I have already been doing this over the past four days in my neighborhood. It appears to be an effective system. Everyone is pitching in to help their neighbors. But it's getting too large for us to manage. We'd like to turn it over to the town. It could be used as a model that could be expanded to cover the whole town. Who should we be coordinating with in the local government to take this over?"

Several people who had been using the system shouted out their support.

"You should coordinate with the social services department downtown," Folly told him. "It's staffed by only one person, but she may be able to offer some assistance to you."

Marley thanked Folly and sat down, a little disappointed

that Folly wasn't more welcoming of his offer. Then much to Marley's surprise, a very familiar voice spoke up. Marley spun around in his seat to watch his dad join the discussion.

"I would like to say that I had always assumed this town was doing a pretty good job balancing business and environmental health issues. It's been a good place to live. I never thought much about rising temperatures. It wasn't even on my radar. I assumed we could just adjust to a little warming, no big deal. But look around. Life here in Sleepy Valley is now dangerously out of balance. It's hot. It's hard to breathe. We've destroyed our town." He glanced at Marley and then turned to the crowd, "So what do we do now?"

"You can move back to where you came from," Ed shouted.

Mr. Jones ignored the interruption. "What we need is a plan, and I like the one Wanda created. I think the neighborhood network Marley and Brianne have initiated is working. I've watched the impact and the camaraderie that's been created in the process. It's a good model for the whole town. I for one am also willing to reduce my use of fossil fuels. I get it. I found Jim's list very compelling and very doable. There's nothing crazy on that list. We all can do it. I think if we all did, it would go a long way toward slowing down The Warming, the second track of Wanda's plan.

"The third track of her plan may be the hardest. We need to create work teams now to repair the critical infrastructure. I think that track should focus on roads, utilities, and installing solar power systems. We can do it all. But the town needs a plan that includes all three of these tracks. I'm here tonight to say that I'm willing to pay my share of the taxes necessary to implement this plan and save the town. We need to ensure this town is livable for all of us—and the generations to come."

There was quite a bit of head shaking and encouraging comments from the audience. They liked the idea of a detailed plan to help them climb out of the hole the town had sunk into.

Joe was ecstatic. "Your father is right on. I see where you get it."

But Marley was looking at Folly, who appeared to be gravely disappointed in Mr. Jones. Marley's dad was considered by many to be a rational man, a fiscal conservative, and now he was giving testimony calling for action on multiple fronts!

"Thank you for your thoughts, Mr. Jones. But that sounds like way too much for a small town to handle. What we need is a simple, concrete step that doesn't cost this little town a lot of money." Folly called the town engineer up to report on his assessment of the SVE proposal.

The town engineer, a man of few words, wiped the sweat off his face. "I've found the SVE proposal to be technically feasible, revenue neutral, and risk-free to the town. It's the most immediate fix to the two most obvious changes we've been experiencing."

"That's great news," said Folly without even looking at the other members of the council. "At least we have one solid, rational, and low-cost plan to work with."

With these remarks, one could hear all the enthusiasm in the room escape through the doors, windows, and cracks, like air from a balloon that is released without being knotted.

Marley and Brianne gasped. It appeared as though the discussion had just taken a sharp turn. What happened to the other suggestions made that evening? Most people in the audience looked at each other with a sense of impending doom.

Jim got up, his voice shaking, and sternly addressed the town engineer. "Burning the asphalt, tar, and oil will produce an enormous amount of pollution. That added pollution will impact the health of all the citizens in town. We're already at Code Purple! How can you recommend a fix that hurts the citizens, ignores these other good ideas, and fuels the warming trend? That makes no sense."

A local businessman got up. "But that would be the fastest way to get the roads cleared."

Wanda stood up, on the edge of losing her self-control, and said, "Is the town, SVE, or the business community prepared to cover the greater medical costs we'll all incur as a result of the increased pollution? This short-term fix is a death warrant for this town and its citizens."

Go, Wanda. Go, Jim. Marley was excited that they were there fighting, trying to get the town to make the best decisions possible.

"We don't know what the impacts will be on the air quality, but it will be short-lived," the engineer replied. "We'll only be burning the oil during the cleanup phase."

"That could be years," Jim responded angrily. "Have you seen how much oil there is out there on the streets?" He looked around at the faces in the crowded hall and then turned back to the council. "For the sake of all of us living here, I recommend we reject this proposal." He sat down, in a state of shock that the SVE proposal was even being considered.

Brianne got up and pointed out, "The SVE proposal does nothing to reduce The Warming and, in fact, makes it worse. It certainly can't be the only step you take. What else does the council propose?"

Folly looked at his fellow council members. No one from the council had any other ideas.

Marley stood up. He was slow to speak, gathering his thoughts and very reluctant to be in the midst of a firestorm. But he stood on his own volition—Joe had not prompted him. Marley had found his voice. He spoke haltingly, as if trying to get every sentence just right. "We have to adopt a broader approach. We need a community-wide effort to reduce our emissions. Look at Jim's action list. It has several steps that will save each of us money and slow The Warming at the same time. Let's all agree to take those steps. Our main objective should be to reduce further warming."

"It isn't the government's job to tell people what to do. This is a free country," Folly said.

Ed shouted from the rear of the room. "I didn't even read the list, but I'm going to tell you right now that I'm not going to take any of those steps. You cannot control the weather. I can't believe you're even listening to Jim. His weather predictions are wrong most of the time, and we're supposed to follow his list? You're all crazy!"

Marley took a deep breath and continued, "We also need to evaluate the solar options—we can't afford not to. What if the electric grid fails or the power plant dies tomorrow? Let's agree on the need to develop more energy independence and reliability. Letting the business community run with the solar option will help us clean the air and slow The Warming. It's being done successfully all over the country." With that Marley sat down, a little surprised at himself. There were cheers of support from Marley's friends. Joe just smiled; he hadn't needed to prompt Marley at all.

Next it was Doc's turn to speak. "I agree. It makes no sense to pursue the SVE offer. I also agree that the first thing we need to do is follow Jim's list. We've got to stop the train. Only if we can take these steps to slow The Warming does it make sense to start tackling The Changes. We need to think of it as a one-two punch."

Marley watched Folly, who was not smiling. Clearly, the meeting was getting out of hand.

It was time for Folly to retreat. "Well, that's it for the public part of the meeting. These are difficult decisions, but I think the council has plenty of information to proceed. Thank you all for your input. We'll now adjourn to a closed session. You're all invited back tomorrow night to hear our decisions." And with that, Folly struck the gavel and asked all the citizens to clear the room.

CHAPTER NINETEEN

TO ACT OR NOT TO ACT?

After another horrifically hot day, everyone returned the next night, demanding action and anxiously awaiting the final decisions of the council. Marley was pleased his friends had shown up for a second night in a row. It was going to be a big moment, one that everyone had been waiting for all week. Each group in the room gathered in their own clusters, which were buzzing with a mix of excitement and concern.

The nightmare outside the grange walls was just getting worse, and the temperature inside was even hotter than before. Many of the women had brought hand fans to keep from fainting from the heat. The town supplied a number of coolers with plastic water bottles, but they quickly disappeared, leaving only lukewarm water in the Styrofoam containers.

It took a while for all of the attendees to take their seats. When asked later about the mood in the room, Marley said it was hard to describe all the emotions that night. Some faces were bright with optimism that their problems would be resolved. That's what many people expected of their government: to fix problems. Other faces seemed to droop with fear that nothing would be done.

Ed's crowd just looked smug, probably because Folly came from the East Side. They trusted him and figured they could count on him not to spend their money. They also figured they didn't have much to lose. They were older and didn't pay much in taxes anyway.

It surprised Marley to see that some of the crowd was still upbeat. Certainly, the council would fix some of the things; they had to. But Jim had told Marley there were no quick fixes. It would take years to slow down The Warming or fix any of The Changes now that the tipping point had been passed. They had simply waited too long.

Marley sat in the front row again, listening to Joe talk about the probabilities of success. Joe was not encouraged by the reports. The microbes had not yet gotten as much insight or feedback from their scouting efforts as they had hoped. They, of course, had no previous experience in this political realm, and with only limited data, they weren't sure how far SVE would go to get its plan adopted. Doc had said that keeping their monopoly and keeping their coal plant operating was worth a great deal of money to them.

Doc had also expressed hope that SVE might be considering the solar options. Most utilities in the country were pursuing solar and wind for part of their supply. It made sense, economically and operationally. SVE just needed to figure out the best way to make money on it.

Marley was also encouraged when Brianne told him that many of the younger people in town and many Baby Boomers got the big picture. They were ready to change some of their habits to help reduce The Warming. "They just want a plan we can all rally behind. It's just easier to change a bad practice, like smoking, when one's friends are changing at the same time," Brianne said.

Joe said to Marley, "Well, here we are at this critical meeting. I am finding it all rather exciting. I think the phrase in English is, 'It is all coming down to the wire.' I just hope our scouts made it to Folly, and that it is not too late to change his mind. The scouts did say Folly's microbiome was committed to doing whatever it takes to get his attention."

Marley leaned back on his folding chair and stared up at the ceiling. He watched a cluster of moths flying in circles along a linear crack in the ceiling between him and the stage. He wasn't sure if they were trying to come in or go out through the crack. But whatever it was, they all seemed to have the same goal. Then the moths landed on the crack and were lined up in a row. *How did they do that? How do they communicate? How do they all agree on a strategy?*

He then wondered about the people in the room. They were running around in circles as well. He wondered if this diverse group of people could ever agree on a singular goal and get organized like the moths. It would probably take having a common enemy fierce enough to get them to all work together. *Aren't the impacts of The Warming scary enough to get us to work together?*

Marley sat there, waiting and listening to all the sounds in the hall. The sounds merged into a buzz, a high-pitched buzz much like cicadas in August at noon. His mind drifted off. He thought about all the things that had happened over the past week that had brought him here to this meeting tonight. Graduation had been just a week ago—it seemed like a lifetime. He reflected on the dramatic and surreal changes that had happened to his town. Everything in his world had changed. Now, one week later, here he was, trying to rally support to save the town. It was all so bizarre.

But then he reflected on where he was tonight. He was glad to be here with his friends and with people he respected, trying to do something positive. They were good people, and they were doing what they thought was best. He smiled, happy he was part of something bigger than himself.

* * *

Finally, the back door opened, and Marley saw Folly come in, staring directly ahead. The other council members followed. The back of Folly's dark blue shirt was soaked—it looked like the shape of Blue Lake. Folly didn't look at anyone or say anything until he plopped down in his chair at the front of the room.

The whole council looked glum. A few looked angry, and one appeared to be on the edge of tears. They were all scratching their arms and legs because of their rashes. Marley leaned over and spoke into Brianne's ear, "I'm glad I don't have their job."

Folly's face was pasty. He looked out at the crowd. He mopped his brow with his handkerchief and then let out a very loud burp. "Excuse me," he said, embarrassed by the volume of the burp. "My stomach's not agreeing with me tonight. But let's get on with business." He burped again. Joe smiled; his microbial friends in Folly's microbiome had gotten the message and were hard at work trying to figure out how to influence their host.

Marley just sat there and waited as the room quieted down. All that could be heard were the fans and the occasional cough. Then Folly spoke. "The council has decided that it's too expensive and too risky for our little town to abandon our coal plant and try something new, especially during these uncertain times. The power plant provides us with jobs—jobs our people know how to perform. We can depend upon it for all our electricity needs, twenty-four hours a day, seven days a week."

Marley heard moans from all around the room. Folly hit his gavel to quiet people down. "Since we have decided to keep the plant, we should take full advantage of SVE's generous offer to burn the oil from the streets and the methane from the lake—at no cost to us. We will instruct them to begin as soon as they can."

A cheer went up from a handful of old-timers in the back of the room. The easy and cheap way out made sense to them. Their cheers were offset by boos and chants of, "Save our town."

Folly burped again and continued, "Although we appreciate the proposal for building a solar farm, the council has decided that going solar should be left up to SVE. We have a long-term contract with them to provide us with all our energy generation and delivery services. They have met our needs for over a hundred years. Why should we change?"

The murmurs grew louder and angrier. All of Marley's enthusiasm drained from his body, replaced by a fiery anger rising up from his gut to his heart and his head.

"We encourage Betsy and Luke Alexander and the solar panel vendor to talk with SVE in case they decide to add solar to their mix of energy sources. We consumers shouldn't care where our electricity comes from as long as SVE provides it to us reliably."

Marley couldn't believe Folly was serious. He jumped up. "How about the impact to the health of the citizens from burning dirty fossil fuel? That plant just dumps its combustion wastes directly into the air we breathe. Of course we care how our energy is produced."

Folly pounded his gavel and called for order. "This is not a hearing. Any more outbursts like that and you will be removed from the room."

Marley sat back down, but his anger did not fade away. *Boy, that was intimidating. He really is a bully. I'm not going to let that stop me.*

Folly continued, "As far as buying saplings, we don't see any reason to pay for them. New trees will grow naturally. Trees have been doing that for thousands of years without our help."

There was a rumbling, almost an eruption from the corner where Max and his contingent were standing. Marley felt the whole building shake. He glanced over to see how Max was taking this.

"We also don't think it's necessary to add staff. We will allow our town engineer to go to a conference or two this year so he can stay current on issues and solutions related to The Changes."

When Doc heard this decision, his body started to vibrate. The kudzu vines that had invaded his clothes left him and worked their way toward the stage.

"We do appreciate the offer of the Neighborhood Network but believe that should stay in the non-profit sector so it can easily receive donations and help from others."

Marley just shook his head.

"And finally, as far as the rising temperatures, there's nothing we can do about that. The Earth's climate has been changing since the Earth was formed. Man has always found ways to adapt—and so will we." With that, Folly thanked everyone for their efforts, banged the gavel, and adjourned the meeting.

Many of the attendees, like Marley, were in shock. It couldn't be over. The town would have to do more than that. There was barely any acknowledgment of the cause of the problem, and no steps to deal with The Warming. Folly didn't even acknowledge Jim's list of actions or Wanda's plan.

After all the effort Jim had put into this battle, Jim just sat there looking totally rejected as a great crescendo of voices rose from all around the room. As more and more members of the community absorbed what had just happened, they stood up with questions.

Folly slammed down his gavel, again and again, pulverizing the antique black walnut stand. He repeated over and over, "This session has ended. There will be no more debate. All decisions are final."

Shouts to reopen the meeting came from an increasing number of people. They were waving their arms and jumping up and down, trying to get Folly's attention, but to no avail. A black cloud formed inside the grange and rumbled over the audience. Some people later claimed they had seen lightening shooting out of it. But most attendees just mumbled their anger as they flowed out of the old building and onto the streets. The news spread like hot lava, pouring into all the houses of the town. The decisions penetrated everyone's minds like toxic gases.

Folly and the whole council got up and headed toward the exit. Folly headed directly to the men's room. His stomach wasn't agreeing with him—or maybe his gut just wasn't agreeing with his decisions. His microbiome thought he should have "followed his gut" and made different decisions about how best to save the town.

Marley watched as Max got up, grunted, and left. The armadillo growled and scampered out as well. The woodcock, sensing that Folly was the bad guy, spiraled up into the rafters and dive-bombed him, stopping just inches from his bald head. The woodcock hovered for a moment in mid-air, wondering what else he could do, and then made a beeline for the door.

Seeing no realistic future for the Alexanders, their banker came up and handed them an eviction notice. They had lost their farm and any chance to return to normal life. Betsy bit her lip, but Luke, ever the stoic, just stood there, motionless like a mountain.

Jim couldn't even talk—he was so flabbergasted with the outcome. He just stared ahead zombie-like and stumbled toward the door. When he finally caught up with Wanda, he blurted out, "Did the council even understand what we told them? Did they read my action list? Did they read your plan? Do they realize the terrible cost of their decisions?" He was clearly in shock. Wanda had never seen him like this before. She took his arm firmly, and as she guided him out the door, all he could say was, "Stupid! Stupid! Stupid!"

Even Ben and Ed looked at each other with some concerns. Ben said, "It's nice to have the big utility on our side and willing to pay for the fix, but I'm not so sure about their proposal for the lake. We should have looked at it more carefully. I wish the town would have offered incentives to reduce fertilizer use. That would go a long way to help the lake recover."

"You don't get it," Ed chided him. "That wouldn't be in SVE's interest. They want the generation of free methane to continue forever."

"Oh. Yeah. I guess you're right," Ben replied. "Sounds like fishing and swimming may be off the table for a while."

Marley came up to Doc with his lips pressed tightly together, realizing their efforts had been a total failure. Doc seemed to have accepted the fate of the town. All he said was, "We lost." Then Doc really looked at Marley. "Marley, I've never seen you so mad."

Marley was in fact very mad. "But they didn't listen to us at all," he shouted. "It was a total waste of time. Is this democracy?"

"Yes, Marley, this is democracy. It's sloppy and doesn't work well. Sadly, in this case, it has doomed our town unless the council is replaced in the next election. But by then it'll probably be too late."

Both Brianne and Marley felt totally deflated and dejected. They had been spending all of their time over the past five days helping their neighbors build a network of support in response to the challenges the town faced. Their efforts had all made sense until this moment. They had become engaged in the issues, found a reason for working with others, and felt they were playing an important role in the community. Now they felt rejected, like they had wasted their time, like they no longer belonged. They both were thinking, *maybe it's time to move on.*

On leaving the meeting, Marley's gut was rumbling. He realized Joe had failed as well. There must be a lot of fear and maybe even a revolt going on in his biome. He hoped Joe was okay. At this point he missed Joe and wanted to talk with him, maybe even to talk about the future. After all they were still in this together, weren't they? But there was no inner voice to be heard.

As if to seal the deal, Marley noticed drops of oil from the asphalt-shingled roof had started dripping from the crack in the ceiling and onto the floor. The moths were getting coated in oil and dying. Their efforts at getting organized had failed as well. Marley also noticed that the continuous series of drops formed a sort of curtain, a closing curtain perhaps, a curtain between the stage and the audience, between the decision makers and the people, between the past and the future. He wondered if this had been the last performance ever to be held in the old grange hall of Sleepy Valley.

* * *

Marley and Brianne were boiling over with anger. They were as hot as the air around them. They needed a place to go to let off steam and try to understand the repercussions of what had just happened. It was the outcome they had feared.

They headed over to the Blue Lake Diner on the East Side— the only place except for bars that would be open this late. As they drove down the dusty gravel road in Brianne's mother's Jeep, they noticed the neon lights of the diner were clouded by a haze. The haze could have been caused by the methane coming off the lake, the dust from the road, or smoke coming from the diner itself. Or was it just reflecting the confusion they felt descending on their lives? After all, they weren't seeing very clearly through their moist and bloodshot eyes. Nothing seemed clear to either of them.

As they approached the entrance, they walked past several people in a cloud of their own, smoking just outside the front door to the diner. As they entered, the smell of fat frying filled the air. The greasy smoke quickly permeated their lungs and clothes. The haze inside the diner was as thick as the haze outside. Nothing appeared to be real: not the people in the diner, not the decisions made that night, and certainly not their future. *What would happen to them, to the town, to life in Sleepy Valley?*

Looking around, Marley recognized several familiar faces. Sam and Ed Perkins sat with Ben in the corner. But nobody in the diner seemed to have noticed Brianne and Marley, nobody waved, nobody welcomed them. It felt as if they didn't exist or that Sleepy Valley was no longer real—just a fading figment of their imaginations.

They found an empty booth close to the front door, the only source of relatively fresh air. They sank into the cracked, red vinyl cushions as if this could be their final resting place—here in the diner, waiting for the town of Sleepy Valley to self-destruct.

Marley was only half surprised to see Jim and Wanda float in a few moments later. Apparently, they weren't ready to retire for the evening either. They looked like two lost boats floating on a murky sea, in search of a new port or maybe just a new purpose to their lives.

Brianne waved them over and offered them a seat. "Please, come join us. We could use some company."

They sat down without a word, and each ordered something cold to drink. Marley just slumped further into his seat, as if a 50-pound feedbag weighed down his shoulders. No one had the energy to be upbeat. They were each exhausted after a week of anxiety, work, and sleepless nights.

"Thank you both for everything you've done," Jim said as

his whole body sagged and settled into the booth. "You were so on point and rational. I can't believe your testimonies didn't carry the day. It was a behind-closed-doors deal. SVE was much more prepared than we were and offered a package the council couldn't turn down."

"But they didn't listen," Brianne blurted out.

"So there's one thing you learned," Wanda told her. "Public meetings are designed for people to get a chance to have their say in the process, to offer suggestions. Unfortunately, the real discussions often go on in private. I wish we'd had the luxury of working with all the parties—especially SVE—ahead of time to forge a better solution. What we got tonight was a Band-Aid on a symptom or two, an attempt to satisfy the short-term needs of the business community. What we needed was a whole brigade of people testifying, a groundswell of public support to convince the council to invest in the long-term viability of this town."

Marley looked at Wanda. "Well, what happens next? I get the feeling the town is doomed. I was starting to care about Sleepy Valley's future. Now I feel like giving up."

"You may be right about the town," said Wanda. "Then again, if you look on the other side of the coin, this isn't all that unusual. But it's a great lesson. To change anyone's behavior usually requires multiple rounds and collaboration with others."

"That takes a lot of time and energy. I don't know if I have much energy left, and I don't think we have a lot of time," Marley replied.

"You're right," Wanda agreed. "It may be too late. We should have taken action years ago. A lot of damage has already occurred, and it's getting more serious every day. Our only choice may be to move somewhere else." She took a sip of her drink then put down her glass. "This is a classic case where thoughtful leaders could have worked with individuals and businesses to have prevented a lot of what we're seeing."

Jim added, "Another thing you learned is that the council members are politicians—they believe in the art of compromise. That's in stark contrast to scientists. I make decisions based on the data, not on compromise. We have to remember that Folly and his colleagues aren't bad people—they're just very cautious when it comes to anything new, especially governmental action."

Brianne shared the only bright spot she could muster. "It's interesting to me how many good people live in this town—you guys, Doc, Luke, Betsy, and Max, just to name a few. You all seem to care a lot and have created a pretty nice place to live. It's hard to believe any of us would abandon it. I'd really miss you if any of you left."

"You're right, it's been a great place to live," Jim said. "But no longer—the climate is changing, and the town council is not. I'm afraid this is the turning point for Sleepy Valley. Not many people will be able to live in a town that doesn't plan for the future. I'm afraid all of us will be scattered to the winds. We may never see each other again."

Marley wiped his face. His cheeks were stained with sweat and tears. He couldn't remember the last time he had felt so defeated. He slid out of the booth and stood up. "Let's go, Brianne. I need to stop thinking about this and get some sleep. Maybe we'll find some reason for hope tomorrow."

PART THREE

THE CONSEQUENCES

CHAPTER TWENTY

THE FIRST WAVE

B ut hope was nowhere to be found.
Starting the very next day, Marley could feel the town's foundations beginning to crumble all around him. He could hear it in the voices of his customers, he could see it in their eyes. Everybody was scared. Without a plan to reduce The Warming, and no confidence in the council's plan for dealing with The Changes, no one could picture how the town could survive. All hope was lost.

In conversations with his neighbors, they talked openly with him about leaving, their ideas for where to go, and their options for getting new jobs. Many had already begun their search by calling family and friends in other parts of the country. They were all looking for an exit strategy, a way they could escape the chaos descending on Sleepy Valley.

Everyone had heard stories of places that had not been hurt as badly. They grasped at any lead, trying to find someplace where their families could be safe. They were turning their anger with the town council into action. They had given up on saving the town and now were focusing on saving themselves.

Marley noticed an uptick in his online social networks as well. He was getting inquiries from distant friends and relatives, and he started connecting more with people he knew who lived in other areas. It was a game of trying to guess who was better off and where one might want to move. It was depressing, reading messages from friends filled with fear, friends looking for a lifeline to somewhere else.

Marley noticed the first to leave Sleepy Valley were the businesses. Over the next week, businessmen who saw the writing on the wall started the process of shutting down their local enterprises. Marley watched them pack up their inventories, take down their signs, and drive away at night to more responsible and responsive towns, abandoning Sleepy Valley, maybe forever.

Several of the families on Marley's cul-de-sac who feared for the security of their paychecks, put their houses up for sale and followed the businesses. Most of them would go anywhere they had to in order to keep their jobs. Marley's fears grew along with the number of For Sale signs he saw sprouting up all over town. The signs spoke to him of escape and desperation. He felt hopeless, his desire to act locally slowly shutting down.

It should have been a boom time for realtors, but there were no buyers. Nobody was moving to Sleepy Valley. Home and office building values plunged overnight. The once prosperous little town became just another example of an economic meltdown.

The residents may not have been eager to take actions to prevent The Warming before the tipping point had been reached, but they responded in droves to the declining job market and the rapid devaluation of their homes. These events put a great deal of fear into their hearts. They raced to be one of the first to get their homes on the market. It appeared that everyone was trying to escape. Marley saw more and more moving vans of all shapes and sizes lining up along the streets of the town.

As he skated by Colin's house, he saw the whole family loading a van. Marley stopped to help and to talk to his longtime friend, realizing he may never see him again. "Where're you moving to?" Marley asked.

"We're not sure. Someplace cooler, I hope."

"I hope you find something close by."

"We might move in with my grandparents for a while till my folks can find work someplace else. My dad says we've got to get out of this place. It's collapsing. Aren't you guys moving?"

Marley didn't know what to say. "I don't know. Let's keep in touch. You've got my number."

"Sure do. Don't wait too long to leave."

Marley took off again on his board. He was scared. He realized all his friends were scared about the future too. Their families were leaving town, hoping for more stable jobs in other communities. He felt a knot growing in his gut. *Why isn't my family leaving too?*

And it wasn't just friends he was losing. His family dentist and doctor both left the valley, along with many of their compatriots, leaving the valley's medical services grossly understaffed.

His doctor told him, "We've got to go to where the people are. Half my patients have left already, and the rest are considering it. I've got college bills and mortgages to pay. There are also no drugs left in the pharmacy here. How can you help people without any medicine?"

It wasn't long before the hospital shut down due to lack of staff. The schools also announced they would not reopen in the fall. The library closed and the waste treatment plant staff shrank to a single old timer.

The initial wave of human migration away from Sleepy Valley took place largely late at night when the tar on the roads was a little harder due to the slightly cooler conditions. The late-night traffic was all in one direction, except for a few food delivery trucks that managed to bring basic staples into Sleepy Valley.

Over the next two to three weeks, traffic on all the main roads and arteries heading north—toward cooler climates—grew dramatically. The roads were congested for miles. Gas stations ran out of fuel. All the local grocery stores ran low on anything worth eating. Many cars were abandoned, and long lines of people were seen walking along the sides of the roads with bags in hand. To Marley it felt like their town was just a house of cards that was quickly collapsing. He said to his folks, "I can't believe this is happening. I never thought any of these events could happen here. Why didn't we take The Warming seriously?"

"I didn't believe it could happen here either, no matter how many times we saw similar events on TV," said his father. "Now I'm wondering how much longer we can hold on. Fortunately, I do most of my work online, so my job is more secure than most jobs. We won't have to move unless we lose internet connectivity with the rest of the country. My bigger fear is the loss of our savings—a lot of our money is tied up in this house. It would be hard to get up and walk away from it. I had planned on taking out a second mortgage to cover your college costs. That will be harder to do now."

The businessman who was once a shoe salesman and then a solar salesman packed up and left as well. He still thought solar was part of the solution, but he needed a town where the people had the money and desire to invest in the future.

The moving business was one of the very few businesses conducting commercial transactions anywhere in Sleepy Valley. But it soon became a cash-only service. Families anxious to leave readily paid. Then the banks ran out of cash and shut down their ATMs and closed the doors at their branches. Everyone quickly became short on cash. Marley's Neighborhood Network became more and more important as bartering replaced the use of money.

As the occupants abandoned each home and office building, the kudzu moved in to claim the land. Within hours Marley could see vines stretching across lawns and sidewalks, enveloping For Sale signs and reaching up the sides of buildings. Within a week the abandoned buildings were covered. It was a good way of knowing who had left town. Kudzu and other drought-resistant invasive vines covered the remains of the park, the downtown statues, and even those streets and sidewalks where whole neighborhoods had been abandoned by humans.

When the local skateboard shop closed up, Marley got bummed—no more access to spare parts. It had been an important part of his life. Grant and other friends had worked there, and it was one of his favorite places to hang out. He was losing his friends at a time when he needed them the most. "Brianne, all our friends and neighbors are leaving for other towns. It's starting to feel lonely and a bit claustrophobic living here in this shrinking town of ours."

"I know . . . It's getting real," Brianne replied. "My mom has decided not to renew the lease on our townhouse now that it's permeated with oil. She also lost her job, and without Dad around anymore, we have no other income. She says her sister can help us find something if we move in with her, but that's a long ways away."

"Oh no. You can't leave too!" he moaned, grabbing his head with both hands. It felt like it was going to explode.

"I don't think I have many choices," she said, looking at him closely. "There's no money for me to go to college."

Now Marley was devastated. Not Brianne. This downward spiral had just become too painful for him to endure. He was crushed. He couldn't picture a future without her.

Doc told Marley that what started as an *environmental meltdown* had quickly evolved into an *economic meltdown,* and now it had blossomed into a full-fledged *social meltdown.* The neighborhood communities were being broken up and scattered all across the country as people moved off to a range of destinations. What could he do? Most residents left in town were asking themselves the same question. Marley felt like he was having a personal meltdown as well.

* * *

Everyone did not leave Sleepy Valley right away. Many of Marley's Network participants were retired people on fixed incomes, trying to hang in there as long as they could. They told him, "We're going to stay as long as we can get the services and support we need. We'll stay as long as our friends and families remain here in town, and as long as you're here to get us what we need."

But it was clear to Marley that the days of normal life in

Sleepy Valley were over. It was just way too hot, and new challenges were constantly arising. *What's going to happen if I leave? Will the Network fall apart?* He decided he had to make it resilient enough so the people using it could keep it going if he left.

Marley watched as the people who tried to remain in Sleepy Valley, at least for the short term, did their best to adapt to the changing environment. It wasn't easy to do. Anxiety levels were high, and depression was setting in with many of the folks who remained. They worried about everyday life: access to food and medicines, the value of their homes, and what the future would bring. As a result of all the stress, the men and women of the town developed a range of coping mechanisms, in addition to the Network, for bringing light and sunshine into their gloomy existence. They needed to find ways to avoid the pain of their new reality.

Marley began to notice that a few of the more agile men went to Charlies' Bar. Charlie did what he could to meet the needs of his clients. Many of his customers had been coming in for years, and he considered them close, personal friends. Charlie provided them with his homebrew and a welcoming ear to listen to their personal plights. He offered advice when asked and commiserated when needed. He became the support system for many of the remaining residents living on the East Side. But he too knew the end was near—he was almost out of the hops that he needed for his homebrewed beer.

In addition to Charlie, Marley knew Bertha and Gertrude Hall also felt a sense of responsibility for the remaining residents living downtown. They owned and operated the Two Sisters Tea Room—the only dining venue still in business downtown. Marley stopped by every couple of days to see if they needed anything. "Great to see you're still open. Can I pick up anything for you?"

"We still get a few ladies each day, so yes, we need flour and sugar for the scones. And more tea of course," Bertha responded.

"So you're planning to stay open?"

"We sure are. What else would we do? This is our life. We've pledged to our patrons that we're not going anywhere," Gertrude said.

The Tea Room operated in an old Victorian building that reminded everyone of their grandmother's house. The place was full of crocheted doilies, dark mahogany antique furniture, and faded lace curtains. One could smell the history from the dust on the curtains. It spoke of many happy afternoons from times past and it served as a retreat for many ladies from all across town.

Of course the sisters did have to make a few adjustments to their normal operations because of The Changes. All patrons were asked to leave their shoes by the door so they wouldn't track in oil from the streets. The sisters offered free loaner pairs of slippers to all their customers. They also offered iced tea and lemonade in addition to their regular hot teas.

One morning, shortly after the town hall meetings, the sisters were busy scurrying around their kitchen, baking a variety of scones for their customers. The smells were wonderful and permeated every room in their home. Bertha stopped kneading the dough, looked out the window at the empty streets for a minute, and then broke the silence. "Fewer people are bothering to leave their homes to come downtown. I worry about their mental health with all this stress. We need to figure out how to serve them better during these hard times." Then after a pause she added, "You know . . . our mother would have."

After a few moments to digest what her sister was suggesting, Gertrude raised her left eyebrow and said, "Just what are you thinking, Bertha?"

"Mother told me that when she and Auntie ran this tea room during The Great Depression, they took it on as their responsibility to help ease the town's pains. I recall her once speaking about special herbal teas they brewed and special scones they made. They created concoctions for a wide variety of ailments."

"That's right. They acquired special medicinal tinctures from the pharmacist and bought other aromatic herbs from that lady on the edge of town. I hear her daughter still grows herbs. Let's see if Marley can get some of those for us."

Marley was able to get the herbs the sisters needed, and over the next few weeks, business boomed. Anxiety levels across the town lowered a bit. The special tea and scones allowed people to forget about their problems, even if only for a few minutes.

But it didn't last long. It slowly became obvious that the short-term comfort the tea room offered its patrons wouldn't solve their long-term problems. And one by one their patrons moved away. Then disaster occurred. The sisters started to cough and gasp for air—the fumes from the melting asphalt and the power plant had finally gotten to their aging, 80-year-old lungs. Unfortunately, there were no doctors left in town to help them and no medicine available in the stores.

Marley realized that their age and the poor air quality had caught up with them, and these two, normally spry women couldn't recover on their own. He watched with a great deal of sadness as the tea room closed and the sisters retreated to their rooms. Marley never saw them again. The remaining residents were left with only fond memories and now had to learn to cope on their own.

CHAPTER TWENTY-ONE

NATURE'S RESPONSE

W hen the subject came up about leaving town, Max told Marley, "I haven't even thought of leaving. I've got too much to do. I've got beetles to eradicate and a forest to replant. I also want to document all the actions of my forest friends. I want to take the time to watch their responses to The Warming. There's a lot to be learned."

Max's enthusiasm helped keep Marley afloat that summer. Whenever he could, he would stop by and help Max with his work. It was good to have something to do and to have such a positive role model to work with.

Over the long, dry, and very hot summer, Max successfully stemmed the rising tide of the Greater Sapphire Beetles by importing an army of armadillos. Max and Marley watched them scurry about, lipping and lapping and sucking up every last beetle in every last crevice in the park and in town. At first everyone was afraid when the armadillos invaded their yards, but they very quickly realized how important the armadillos were to the future of Sleepy Valley if it was ever to recover.

The heat didn't seem to bother the armadillos, but Max shared with Marley his worries about whether there would be any negative ecological impacts, any unintended consequences, from bringing in so many of these foreign creatures. It was a high-risk strategy, but so was leaving the beetles to invade forest after forest.

Marley thought Max's armadillo plan was brilliant, but he also wondered what would happen to them when their task was done. "Hey, Max," he asked his friend. "What's your plan for the armadillos once they finish eating all the blue beetles? Do they starve or do they start to eat some of our more valuable beetles?"

"That's a good question, one I'm quite concerned about. My plan is to keep track of them all and then move them back down south to their home when the job's done."

Marley was impressed that Max had a resettlement plan but was doubtful that Max could find them all.

When questioned about this, Max said, "I'll lasso every last one of those critters if I have to!"

Marley just laughed, trying to picture the big man on horse-back, rustling up a bunch of wayward armadillos.

The armadillos were helped by Max's woodcock friend. Between futile recon flights searching for a mate, the woodcock would run rapid, aerial surveillance flights and notify the closest armadillo squadron of any new invading horde of beetles. Personally, the woodcock disliked the taste of the beetles, but he was happy to point them out to the armadillos because he was angry at what the beetles had done to his forest home. The interspecies teamwork paid off, and the park slowly recovered from the blue insect invasion.

* * *

Once the beetles were gone and the armadillos were rounded up and returned to Texas, it was time to replant the park. Marley was excited when Max told him he had received a few thousand trees from the Arbor Day Foundation, the state forester, and the U.S. Department of Agriculture.

"It's a start," said Max. "We only need 357,000 more."

When he finally saw the trees, Marley asked, "Do you think these tiny saplings will live in these conditions? It feels way too hot to plant anything in this dry soil."

"Who knows? Trees are tough. Fortunately, these are a variety of hearty, drought-resistant trees that have a decent chance of growing in tough conditions. We've got to give it our best shot. If this is all we get, they've all got to live."

Max sent Buff out to clear sites for planting the trees in the moistest areas of the valley. He instructed the big steer to leave plenty of mulch to protect the tree roots from the heat of the sun. Max then set out to plant the trees all by himself; he had to, there were no scouts left in town to help.

Marley offered to help, but Max turned him down, saying, "Thanks, but there really aren't that many, and I'd rather plant them myself."

Marley and Brianne did check in every couple of days to drop off lunch and see how Max was doing. They realized the tree planting was a labor of love for Max and that it helped him deal with his anger toward the council.

Each morning at daybreak and each evening at dusk, Max could be seen, out planting his trees. He carried a shovel in one hand and hung a bag of saplings over his shoulder. At each site cleared by Buff, Max dug an oversized hole for each little tree. He added natural compost to each hole and was very careful how deep he placed the roots. He then patted the ground like a mother would pat a baby's bottom.

Max sweated away the hours, making sure the trees had every advantage. Like a doting parent, he hovered over them to ensure each one got what it needed. The sweat from his brow dripped off his nose and moistened the ground around each of the saplings.

He prayed for rain and an early fall, realizing that his trees' future depended upon how much moisture they could extract from the ground. He gave each one he planted his blessing, not knowing whether any of them would make it to maturity. He kept focused on his mission by picturing each sapling one day growing to 100 feet tall. He imagined children, generations from now, running around in the forest—his forest, their forest—learning about the great outdoors and falling in love with the park.

Marley marveled at Max's single-minded dedication to the task. Just by watching him planting his trees, Marley learned a great deal about care and commitment. He would never forget how Max was able to eradicate the beetle threat and rebuild a forest from scratch. It was a wonder to behold.

In areas that were not restored, they watched with utter dismay and disappointment as a whole range of invasive plants quickly took over. Large parts of what was once a forest of tall trees became a sea of kudzu and other invasive plants. Max's face became weirdly distorted every time he saw what was happening to the abandoned parts of his park.

Marley felt sorry for his friend and for the park. Many of these forsaken areas just ended up as an impenetrable mishmash of dead trees and vines highly subject to fire. When the wildfires came, they took out large sections of the abandoned park and then spread to the town; houses, trees, and all went up in smoke. The oily roads caught fire, as did oil-filled gullies, streams, and the black river. The fires raged for days since all these waterways were full of oil. The fires chased most of the remaining residents out of town.

* * *

During that summer, as Max cleaned up the beetle problem and replanted the park, he told Marley how he was keeping a detailed journal of everything he saw. "It might prove valuable someday when future scientists and historians try to make sense of what happened here during The Warming."

After that, Marley would stop by to share his observations of what else he saw happening around town.

Max's journal entries were short but telling:

Monday, August 7 – *It's hot. Five degrees above normal. It's so hot that it isn't just human residents who are migrating away from Sleepy Valley. I have been tracking deer, coyotes, rabbits, and beaver migrating out of the valley as well. If one looks carefully, you can also see that even the earthworms, snails, squirrels, and sparrows are leaving.*

Some go solo, some in pairs, and others en masse, much like the Greater Sapphire Beetles when they left their home in the south and moved north to Sleepy Valley.

The armadillos are doing their job. The number of beetles has been dropping dramatically, from a high of thousands per day to just a handful today. This armadillo vigilante plan might just work.

Tuesday, August 8 – *The temperature continues to climb. Anything and everything that can move is migrating. Most of the migration occurs at night since the melting asphalt roads are way too hot to cross when the sun is high. Wildlife tends to migrate upstream or north, depending on the availability of forests, hedgerows, or other migratory pathways. Jim says the migration is far easier in those towns that built interconnected greenways. In Sleepy Valley, where we do not have a green infrastructure network, there has been an increase in roadkill as many species have to cross roads to get out of town. It's amazing how many animals were living in the park. It's sad to think how many have died. The good news is that I only saw three Greater Sapphire Beetles today.*

Wednesday, August 9 – *Everything is so dry it's like kindling. Three small fires were found and put out by Buff. We're hoping the whole valley doesn't go up in flames. Migration northward continues. We've seen lots of animals coming into town from the south and many heading north. Migration is tougher for the mosses, fungi, and plants. They wait for a particularly strong, southerly wind and then release all their seeds, sending millions of their spores into a future they hope will be better than the present. One can see these big, puffy, yellow, green, and red clouds of spores erupting all around the valley. The spores are on their way north and making everyone sneeze in the process. No beetles seen today!*

Thursday, August 10 – *It's unbearably hot today. Nothing is out during the day. Most plants have withered away. The only animals that loiter here are the ones that invaded from the south. A whole host of invasive plants, like toxic giant hogweed and Chinese yams, are also colonizing our valley, crowding out the native species. The insects that are* moving in probably consider Sleepy Valley a smorgasbord of delights, relative to their old roasted homes down south. We will see how long they stay here before the rising temperatures drive them even further north. No beetles today. That's two days in a row!

Friday, August 11 – Hottest day of the week. I have been watching the buzzards adapt to the changing conditions. They are acting strange and avoiding the thermals. The buzzards do seem to be having a heyday with all the roadkill on the highways. At first they were hesitant to eat the oil-soaked carrion, but then they realized that squirrels and pigeons covered in oil were often nicely baked on the inside, a real delicacy. But as the bulk of the animal population moves north, so do the buzzards. I hear from other rangers that this is causing a dangerous overcrowding of buzzards in the northern regions of the country. The skies are darkened with the large black birds. They report that this congestion of the airways is already resulting in a series of horrific vulture wars which fill the skies day and night with piercing screams and falling carcasses.

Saturday, August 12 – The beetles are gone. The infestation is over. I will keep the armadillos here for a few more days to ensure there are no beetles left and then drive them back home. Nights are starting to cool down just a bit, so it's time to start planting the trees. I planted 50 saplings today, so I am hoping for a bit of rain.

CHAPTER TWENTY-TWO

THE SECOND WAVE

None of Marley's colleagues from the town council meetings left right away. Instead, they stayed around to see what more they could do to help the town survive. Marley and Brianne continued to help organize, manage, and expand the Neighborhood Network. The network grew and was able to support the people who remained in town with at least the basic necessities. Marley also used it to engage all the members in an effort to slow The Warming. He kept highlighting items from Jim's "Ten Steps for a Cooler Climate." He kept nudging the remaining residents to do their bit, step-by-step, to slow down further warming. But it was a discouraging time. There was little hope the town would make it for much longer. Most people were planning to leave.

One day Brianne's mom told her, "I'm going to pack up during August and move in with your aunt on September 1st. You're welcome to come. There's a bedroom for you. But it's your call."

Brianne told Marley that she was really torn. She loved her mother and little brother, but she was ready to move on with her life.

Marley's dad sat him down one evening and said, "I'm losing quite a bit of business because the connectivity is so poor. If this keeps up, we'll have to move. We won't be able to sell the house, so you and I will board up all the windows with the hope that we can move back or at least sell it one day."

Marley just sat there, trying to absorb all the bad news. He didn't know what to say or do.

His dad continued, "I'm going to hold out for at least another month before moving. My biggest concern is that the whole town might go up in smoke or that, with our house empty, desperate people might scavenge all the copper tubing and whatever else they could sell. If you want to go to college, we'll do our best to support you. Just realize that all of our savings are in the house."

That sounded to Marley like there wasn't much money for school. He was on his own, too.

* * *

Mixed in with all this bad news were several exciting opportunities that popped up for Marley's friends.

Max of course was busy all summer, herding armadillos and planting trees. But it wasn't long before he was recognized for his work—his beetle eradication reputation had spread far and wide. One day when they stopped by, Max showed Brianne and Marley a letter offering him a coveted position with the National Park Service. They wanted to hire him to combat the Greater Sapphire Beetle pandemic nationwide. "I'm flattered, but I don't want to abandon the park and the valley—it's my home."

Marley understood that perspective very well; he felt exactly the same way. Brianne pointed out, "Yes, but most of your wildlife family and friends are gone, and they're not coming back anytime soon."

The deciding factor was that Max couldn't let go of his intense disappointment in the town council. He decided he could no longer work with them; therefore, he accepted the offer and agreed to show up for work on September 1. He was honored to accept this new opportunity and did feel a deep calling to save forests everywhere.

Max was sad he would have to say goodbye to his friends.

The whole group of them had gotten close during the council meetings.

"We're going to miss you," Brianne told him. "Thanks for all you've done here. You really turned me on to the outdoors. I remember my first encounter with a fox. I'll never forget when he came up to us. It was like he was your friend."

"It's amazing how you stopped the beetles. You certainly taught me the importance of taking the time to stop, watch, and learn from nature," Marley added.

Max thanked them and said, "Let me be an example for you. No one loves this valley more than I do, but I'm leaving because I think I can do more good in this new job. I think you both should go find a town where you can make changes, and also go to college to learn even more. You guys would make first-rate foresters."

As soon as Max had finished planting the trees that summer, he turned the park over to his bovine partner. Buff knew his job was to keep the roads open and to create large firebreaks in order to reduce the likelihood and spread of wildfires. Buff could be seen every day, working as a one-steer battalion, up before breakfast, dragging trees to the mill. With time he built a broad firebreak between the unattended, fire-prone parts of the park and the replanted areas.

To help keep the invasive plants under control, Buff trained himself to only eat non-native, invasive plants. When word got out, he became the role model for a new generation of natural food advocates, naturalists, and sustainability wonks. It turned out that a diet of invasive plants not only kept the invasive plants in check but was also the fastest way to build muscle tone. Many adherents claimed that eating invasive plants helped shy people, making them a little more aggressive in new surroundings.

* * *

Although ignored by the council, Jim Quartz kept working, tracking all The Changes in the valley. He had a daily blog going to his colleagues around the world. Marley and Max often commented on it, adding their perspectives as well.

It was closely followed, and it wasn't long before Jim too was recognized nationally and internationally. All sorts of groups praised him for the universal relevance of his "Ten Steps for a Cooler Climate" list. Jim was ecstatic when he received an offer to join the Global Stabilization Center to help direct international efforts to slow the rate of warming. They wanted him to promote his list globally. He ran into Wanda's office, literally jumping with joy. "Wanda, I'm going to have a second chance to slow The Warming."

"It's a great choice on their part," Wanda said. "You can share your experience dealing with a conservative town council to the international body."

"Yes, now that it's clear what could happen to a town, more people should want to take action. It's going to be necessary to get everyone engaged in the fight. It's a fight against a common enemy." Jim knew this was a second chance for him, and he wasn't going to blow it this time. Again, he had that feeling down deep in his gut that he was born for this fight. His first step, of course, was to ask Wanda to join him. He had to have her by his side. Jim leaned over and put both of his hands on her desk. "Will you come with me?"

A big smile came over Wanda's face as she looked at him, "What do you mean?"

"I need you. The cause needs you. I failed in Sleepy Valley because I didn't know how to deliver the message. You did. If only we'd had time to implement your plan. Now we do. You could build the global coalition that will be necessary to win the day. Will you take on this new job as my partner? Your skills will be critical in convincing all the people of the world to get involved, to save civilization."

Wanda sat back in her chair, looking quite relieved and quite honored. She was excited but wasn't quite sure what he meant or what he was offering. What did he mean by partner? But despite the uncertainty, she reached across the desk and put her hands on his. "Of course I will. We make a great team."

Jim was overjoyed. Normally not an expressive person, he was so excited that he grabbed both her hands, pulled her to her feet, and spun her around the observatory in something like a polka. Wanda wondered whether this dramatic gesture was the result of his excitement about the new job, a new stage in their relationship, or if he had just been breathing too much of the contaminated air.

To celebrate, they took Marley and Brianne out to lunch to discuss their plans.

"Wow. I don't know what to say. That's a terrific opportunity. You guys are bigwigs now," Marley said.

"We're sure going to miss you. I hope there's some way we can stay in touch," Brianne added.

"Oh, I'm sure we'll be in touch," Jim assured them both.

* * *

Over the summer, Doc disappeared from sight. Every time Marley tried to reach out to him, Doc would say, "Can't talk now Marley, too busy."

"But, Doc, what're you up to?"

"I'm writing. I need to be totally focused. No distractions. I'll call you when I'm finished."

So Marley gave up and waited, hoping to hear from his old teacher and hoping he was being productive.

During this period of time, Doc took his notes from the town council meetings and merged them with Marley's first-person accounts of The Changes. Slowly and carefully, he turned the notes into a book. While he was writing, he never left the house. Everybody thought he had left town, gone on vacation, or died. His house completely disappeared from view, and even the path to his mailbox closed in. It was like an empty lot, devoid of life. It looked like an impenetrable jungle.

But one day he emerged, fighting his way out through the kudzu with a chainsaw. By the time he reached the mailbox, the neighbors who had not left town yet had gathered in the street to welcome him back. "It's a miracle," they exclaimed. They all acted as if he were born again.

Even Doc enjoyed the celebration. He called Marley and asked him to review the manuscript and then sent it off to a big-time, New York publishing house. Then he waited.

One day he walked out to the mailbox, pulled off several vines, and opened the little metal door. It creaked. He pulled out a thick envelope and saw it was from the publisher. He squeezed it. "Hmm . . ." He stood right there at the mailbox and opened it. He read the first paragraph and then reread it several times. Yes, the manuscript had been selected for publication. A smile came across Doc's face. Maybe it was worth the effort after all.

Marley was happy for Doc when the book was released to great fanfare. Mistaking it for a work of fiction, all the critics panned The Big Melt when it first came out. They said it was unbelievable that any group of local politicians would not have taken more action.

However, when grass-root activists realized the book spoke to them, and it correctly sized up the nature of their own recalcitrant town councils, sales took off. It became the go-to reference for "what not to do" for small towns all around the globe. The book was translated into 152 different languages. Truth be known, it was rarely actually read. It was mainly used as a prop to wave in front of town council meetings while shouting, "We don't want to be another Sleepy Valley!"

Doc became famous. He smiled when he realized how wrong the critics had been. "I'm just happy the book's being used to help save the Earth," he told Marley.

His daily trips to the mailbox started to pay off. He even engaged his neighbors in neighborly chats. They didn't seem to care about the looks of his front lawn anymore, now that most of them had stopped cutting their lawns as well.

With the proceeds from the book, he was able to acquire a new dog that proved to be a wonderful muse. Although the dog did accompany him to the mailbox each day, Doc never let this new dog off the leash to play in the yard. He was too afraid the dog might get lost or get strangled by the kudzu.

As the town disintegrated, there were fewer reasons to stay and less and less to do. Doc moved to the Northwest to a writer's colony high in the Cascades that had always prided itself on being self-sufficient. Before he left, he told Marley, "I'm going to miss our random chats by the mailbox. Keep asking questions." He had no regrets, and would relish his memories of the good old days.

Doc spent the rest of his life, at least as long as the new dog was alive, writing one best seller after another—all based around a couple of young adults named Marley and Brianne.

CHAPTER TWENTY-THREE

THE HOLD-OUTS

Despite the collapse of the town, Betsy and Luke Alexander somehow persevered longer than most of the other local farmers. They negotiated an extension on their foreclosure by borrowing money from a different, out-of-state bank. They then put a full-court press on SVE. They were determined to win the battle to become solar farmer pioneers.

Marley never mentioned Joe and the microbial connection to his aunt or uncle but told them, "Keep in close physical contact with the people at SVE—it's an important way to break down barriers. Try it."

So they did. Luke stopped by and visited the utility reps almost every day. Every time he'd say, "Hi. Just came across a few more articles about solar energy. Thought you might enjoy them." He never left without shaking hands and slapping backs.

Betsy took Marley's advice to heart as well. She baked home-made apple pies and took them over to the SVE offices whenever she had the chance. "Just being neighborly," she would say when she came by.

As a result of these intimate exchanges, Joe's network paved the way for a closer, more collegial relationship between the Alexanders and the people at the utility company. The SVE team looked forward to seeing them both.

One day Marley stopped by and found Betsy and Luke celebrating. "SVE has decided to move into the solar business," Betsy said. "We've just signed an option to let them develop a solar farm on our land."

"That's awesome. You did it!"

"Go tell your mother that we get to stay on the farm."

When the dilapidated, coal-fired plant outside of town finally collapsed, SVE did build the solar farm on 300 acres of land they leased from the Alexanders. The contract left 50 acres to Betsy and Luke for more conventional farming.

Surprisingly, the SVE contract never said that the land used for solar farming couldn't also be used for other types of farming. The Alexanders bought thousands of pigs and let them forage beneath the solar panels. The pigs were delighted. They loved the shade; they slept under the panels during the hot days and rooted in the soil during the night. They also liked to scratch their dry, hairy backs on the metal struts. This brilliant, multi-use strategy helped make the Alexanders' livestock operations profitable.

SVE wasn't sure what to think about the pig invasion of their solar plant. "What if a four-hundred-pound boar with dry, itchy skin dislodges a solar panel? Or an inquisitive, pregnant sow gets electrocuted by the high voltage lines running across the site?" one of the engineers asked.

SVE engineers and risk assessors convened dozens of meetings on the subject and even involved their lawyers to read the fine print. They soon realized there was nothing they could do to stop the pig-farming operations and no actual harm was being done. An enterprising young engineer took advantage of the public relations opportunity and became famous, publishing multiple articles on "The Innovative Solar Pig Farm of Sleepy Valley."

Much to their parents' chagrin, the Alexander boys grew up to have no interest in innovative solar pig farming. They told Marley one day on the phone, "Nobody's living here in the valley anymore. All of our friends are gone. There are no sports teams. No girls. It's boring."

Betsy and Luke were distraught at the thought that they would be the last of the Alexanders to farm in the valley. They eventually sold the farm, including the pigs, to the utility company and moved north.

* * *

During the summer of The Changes, Marley and the other remaining residents of Sleepy Valley watched as SVE tried to implement their proposals to clean up the oil and methane. The utility company's efforts failed. It turned out that the oil from the asphalt shingles and roads was indeed too difficult to harvest and too dirty to burn without producing an enormous amount of pollution.

In addition to the oil recovery fiasco, the SVE engineers never figured out how to collect the methane bubbling off the lake. The winds were just too strong to keep a covered collection facility in place. The engineers had not taken into account the changing wind and weather patterns.

SVE was bought out by a larger utility that quickly lost interest in the clean-up proposal. They shut down all the local operations except the solar farm, which they operated remotely. No one was left to blame.

Marley told Brianne, "The SVE proposal was just too good to be true. What're we going to do now? We need another town council meeting."

"Is the council even still here? I bet they've left town too."

When Marley's asked his dad, he was told, "The town has lost its entire tax base. There's nothing left to spend on projects of *any* size. I'm afraid we've lost our opportunity to save the town."

Folly became known as "the man who destroyed Sleepy Valley." His poor leadership and his actions—or rather lack of action—chased away all the businesses and the citizens.

Initially, these developments weren't all bad in Old Ed's eyes; he had always wanted the town to revert back to the way it had been in his youth. But he soon realized you could never bring back the good old days—especially when you've messed up the climate.

Ed Perkins didn't move, but he didn't make it through the year either. The heat finally did him in—as was the case with all of the old-timers—and he had a stroke. The pavilion was never used again.

* * *

Throughout the long hot summer following the council's decisions, Sam Perkins watched as his friends tried to respond to The Changes. They all struggled, looking for ways to make a buck, at least enough money to live through this "downturn." They all believed, with varying levels of confidence, that business would come back; it would "just be a matter of time" before people returned and the state and federal relief funds arrived.

Sam also wanted to capitalize on The Changes, so he took an inventory of his assets and tried to create a plan for what he could do to make money. After all, he saw himself as a survivor. "I'm smarter than the other guys. I should be able to find some contract work."

He quickly realized that his greatest asset–maybe his only asset—was the Humvee. "The Humvee's one of the few vehicles in town that can get around easily," he told his dad. "It's rugged enough to bounce off cars, trees, and mailboxes with no real damage to me or the Hummer. I'm going to start a pick-up-and-delivery business, much like what Marley's doing. I hear he's having trouble keeping up with the demand."

To help get the word out, Sam called his sister, who was always on the computer. "Emily, can you announce through your social media network that your very capable big brother is open for business as Sam Perkins, LLC?"

"Sure," she replied. "But you'll need a tagline of some sort to let people know what you're offering."

"I have no idea what to say. You're the creative genius in this family."

"How about something like: Take you where you want. Bring you what you need."

"That's perfect. It says it all. Get the word out there any way you can. I'm ready to make some easy money."

Sam did get plenty of business, but he started to consider Marley as a threat to the growth of his firm. Marley, after all, was undercutting Sam's rates by working for tips. This made Sam mad, so whenever he had the chance, he tried to run Marley and his skateboard off the road.

* * *

The real competition kicked in by mid-summer when online companies started delivering items with drones. Sam kept seeing them all over town, delivering items he could have delivered. "I'll shoot any alien drone out of the sky that comes into my neighborhood," he threatened.

To back up this threat, he purchased two, 12-gauge shotguns at a local gun show. He carried them fully loaded in gun racks mounted in the back window of his Humvee. He was also sending a clear message to everyone that he was the toughest and craziest man on the street, and he didn't want any competition.

Shortly after that, when he was driving down the dusty road to make a pastry delivery to the Blue Lake Diner, Sam heard the whiny sound of a drone flying overhead. He slammed on the brakes and skidded to a stop just in front of the diner. Looking up, he saw a blue-and-white commercial drone descending to the cellar door. His face turned red. "This is war!" he shouted.

Any logic that ever visited his brain immediately escaped through his ears, along with a good bit of steam. The drone was delivering a package of chai tea mix from Chai Wallahs of Maine. But all he could see was competition—big-business drones infringing on his territory. This made him so mad that he took out his shiny, new Smith and Wesson shotgun and blasted the drone out of the sky.

When the dust settled, everything was quiet, and there was nothing left of the drone. Tea leaves and spices sprinkled down on the pavilion. The spicy aroma lingered for weeks. This singular event catapulted Sam into the realm of legends. Overnight, he became a local hero around the East Side.

On the West Side the reaction to the drone incident was far different. The authorities, supported by the owner of the drone, put out a warrant for Sam's arrest. They wanted to create a deterrent to anyone who might consider damaging their delivery system in the future. But the warrant did no good. The rapidly shrinking town wasn't collecting enough revenues to pay the police, so the police had stopped responding to calls and most had stopped coming to work. Sleepy Valley was returning to the wild frontier—the days before law and order—and Sam, the vigilante, was going to take full advantage of it.

Doc, Brianne, and Marley's mom each cautioned Marley, "Stay clear of that crazy man."

Marley shrugged. "I've been avoiding bullies for years, and Sam's no different from the rest."

"But he has guns, a big, polluting truck, and no common sense," Brianne told him. "He also drinks a lot and thinks you're the competition. Please stay clear of him."

Marley agreed. "I have no interest in competing with Sam. I'm probably going to leave Sleepy Valley pretty soon anyhow. Maybe he can help meet the needs of the townspeople when we leave."

With no repercussions from the first shooting, Sam decided to do the same thing if he ever saw another drone in his neighborhood. He figured it was open season on them. Sure enough, the next time he was making a delivery to the diner, he saw that another blue-and-white drone had already landed by the basement doors. He just smiled and went to get his gun.

This time when Sam shot he wasn't as careful. Some of the buckshot broke the basement door window and ignited the basement air—air rich in methane that had migrated up a sewer line from the lake. When the methane exploded, it took out the whole diner.

From that time on, most people realized Sam was a threat. They avoided him at all costs. It wasn't too long before he was standing in the unemployment line with nearly all the other remaining residents of the valley. The downward economic spiral had affected them all.

With time Sleepy Valley and the myriad of other non-responsive towns across the world lost their population, their income sources, and even the interest of the big marketing firms. Fewer and fewer drones came to the valley, and eventually, all commerce stopped. Civilization had abandoned the valley. It became an increasingly hard place to live for anyone trying to hang on.

CHAPTER TWENTY-FOUR

TIME TO LEAVE

With all their friends leaving town, Brianne and Marley realized it was time for each of them to make a decision about the next steps in their lives.

As usual whenever they were at a loss for good answers, they sought out Doc. It was a good thing they knew where he lived, because his side of the street was one, big kudzu jungle. They found him, as always, on his way to the mailbox.

Marley had to jump up and down just to get a glimpse of Doc over the kudzu-covered fence. "Hey, Doc. You got a few minutes? We're really thrashing about what to do next."

"Sure. Come through the gate. What's up?"

Brianne kicked off the big question. "It's just that we don't know if we should stay here in Sleepy Valley or move somewhere else. We like it here, but it feels like the town's dying. Everyone we know is leaving."

"Well, that's certainly the question on everyone's mind. You have to decide what you really want to do with your lives. Then pick a place to live that will help you do that. Doesn't that sound easy? It never is. Why don't you tell me what each of you wants to do in your life?"

Marley fidgeted a bit and commented, "That's just it, I don't know. I do know that I want to build things. I love working with my hands, fixing up my skateboard, stuff like that. But the world's falling apart and I want to help save it. Unfortunately, I don't have any skills. I'm at a loss as to how I can help."

Brianne added, "I feel the same way about all the chaos going on. I really want to help people survive in these challenging days. But I don't know what that means in terms of taking any real action. I also loved working with Jim and Wanda last summer. I just wish I had some talents to pursue."

Doc seemed quite taken aback by their statements. He looked at them quite seriously. "I strongly disagree with both of you. I think you both have great skills. You can quickly analyze a situation and argue a point logically and in public. That takes a lot of guts and talent. Furthermore, you now have the experience of rallying people to a cause, fighting in a civic debate, and organizing others. That's valuable, no matter where you end up. Don't sell yourselves short. Society needs people like you—people who care and aren't afraid to get involved."

"Yeah, sure, but we lost the fight," Marley responded a bit testily, still deflated about the town council's decisions.

"I don't see it that way," Doc said, stomping his feet to keep the kudzu from crawling up his pant legs. "You may have lost a skirmish, but this is the fight of the century, and you have now been tested in the arena. It's time to take what you learned and go to the next round. Don't ever expect to win something as important and complicated as this in a single contest."

"That may be true," Brianne said. "But I don't see the second round happening anytime soon here in Sleepy Valley. The last I heard from the council is they're dead set against changing their minds."

"You're right. If you stayed you would have to change the council's or SVE's mindset. That would take some work, and in fact I think they've both checked out. Your second option is to find a place where you can learn more skills, be more effective, and succeed. And we have to succeed, of that I'm sure."

Brianne looked at him and asked, "Why do you think we'll eventually succeed?"

Doc replied, "Because we have to. The cost of doing nothing is increasing every day. Furthermore, I believe that, with the passing of each day, more and more people are waking up and realizing that The Warming is our greatest enemy and that we have to deal with it.

"Take your father as an example, Marley. He's pretty conservative, but he gets it now. He never did before. It wasn't even on his radar. He thought the economy was the only thing that was important. He overlooked the importance to the community of a heathy environment and a healthy workforce. Just listen to him now. He's ready to act and even invest in the future."

Marley smiled. "Yeah. It's like he just opened his eyes to the problem and realizes he has to do something. I hope that's happening to people all around the world."

"I think it is, and communities all across the world need leaders. They need *someone like you* to help them understand the need to act now. The Earth needs ten thousand people like you two—maybe ten million—people who are engaged in this awakening. So if you want my advice, go find a place that helps you achieve your goals. And stay active. I'm counting on you."

Marley smiled. *There goes Doc, putting pressure on me again.* He had to chuckle.

"You might also look at Wanda's strategy for collaborating with others. She had a great plan but didn't have the chance to implement it. But remember, you cannot give up on this one." Doc turned to go inside. Under his breath he mumbled, "Something pressing."

Brianne and Marley looked at one another and laughed for the first time that day, realizing this was typical Doc behavior. They waved to him and took off to think about and absorb his comments.

* * *

Marley and Brianne continued to talk a lot about their conversation with Doc and about their lives and their futures. They were so thankful they had each other to process all the things that were happening to them, their families, and the town. It was a little daunting to think they might be going off in different directions. Marley also spent a lot of time in his basement, continuing to tinker on his skateboard. He had a dream of designing the skateboard of the future. He also took apart and reassembled the drones he had collected, trying to fully understand how they worked. He found the drones fascinating. Brianne often sat there watching him work as they discussed the future. They both continued to think about leaving town.

Marley also thought about Brianne a lot. They had grown close. He had decided he didn't want to leave town without her. He wasn't really sure what that meant, but he knew that wherever they ended up, the most important thing in his mind was to be together. He just hoped she felt the same way about him.

But how should he broach the subject with her? He didn't want to ruin their tight friendship by being too bold. Fortunately, they had both been accepted to and committed to colleges in the same town up north, but he wasn't sure that was relevant any longer, as everything was collapsing around them. Could they even afford to go now? Were the schools even going to open in the fall? They hadn't heard.

He also appreciated that the challenges faced by the town had caused them both to become engaged in something greater than themselves. Now he wanted to go to a place where his efforts might pay off. This understanding helped lift his spirits. He felt it was time to spread his wings and use his newfound skills to fight The Warming in a town more inclined to take action.

Marley brought up the subject at the end of a long, hot day of helping their neighbors. They were exhausted and wished they had a swimming hole nearby to jump into. One with water in it. Since that wasn't possible, they stopped by the outdoor hose at Brianne's house and had their fill to drink. Brianne then turned the hose on Marley and drenched him from head to toe. It felt good. He laughed and returned the favor. It was the first time they had felt cool all day.

As he wiped the water from his face, he said, "Brianne, we

have to talk. There's got to be more to life than staying here in Sleepy Valley."

She put the hose away and said, "Yeah. I always imagined myself going to college. Jim has encouraged me to study science. But that seems a little less realistic now. Mom doesn't even have a job."

Marley replied, "I agree you should pursue that interest. You love understanding things. I bet with Jim's help you could get a loan or a part-time job."

"How about you?" Brianne asked.

"I want to get a job building things or studying something that will be useful in this struggle for survival. It's time to decide."

"Yeah, it's time to leave. Mom's leaving at the end of the month. She thinks I should go with her and get a job. But she did say she'd do what she could if I decided to go to school."

"So you've got a deadline. Besides, college starts in a few weeks too. We better check to see if they're still going to open."

"Yeah, I'd love to go someplace where I can study and work. I'm sure going to miss this place and the people. I'm going to miss running around Sleepy Valley with you, too."

"Yeah, I've been thinking about that a lot. Let's both go to school in the same town, and then we could work together to organize people to fight The Warming. We make a great team."

Brianne smiled, but he noticed it was one of her hesitant smiles, as if she didn't think it was going to be that easy. Or maybe because she was looking for something more certain. He didn't know what to do or say and the silence was awkward.

All of a sudden a familiar voice spoke up in Marley's ear, "Kiss her, you fool!"

Marley, a little shocked at himself, leaned over and kissed her. She pulled away for a moment, looked into his eyes, smiled, and kissed him back. A hundred trillion voices cheered. They held each other for a long time without speaking.

Over the next few weeks, they spent all of their time together, calling the colleges and local organizations in the college town to see if they needed any help. Yes, the schools were still going to open. Fortunate. the streets had not melted yet since the town was farther no . They agreed they would try to make it through college and i at didn't pan out, they would at least be living in a more pro ive town where they could get more involved.

Once they made that ion, they went around and told their friends of their plans. immediately called his meteorology contacts at the school re Brianne was going. Then he called Brianne. "Hey, I just ed that a scholarship position has just opened up. Someone d it down because they're staying put to help their family h these hard times. It's yours if you want it."

"Wow. Thanks so much." Brianne

As it turned out, Jim's friend's wife ow lucky she was. the local city sustainability office. Jim s pened to work for told her all about Marley's and Brianne's h her as well. He with the Sleepy Valley Neighborhood Ne ing experience tioned the "Ten Steps for a Cooler Climate le also mentioned for Saving Sleepy Valley." nda's "Plan

The local sustainability officer was so intrig they both could come in right away and help o he said they were creating two new part-time advocac said work with local communities. Jim was elated, a to Marley and Brianne then felt like they had mad e choices.

"Jim, how can we ever thank you?" Marley asked.

"Well, you'll be learning as much as I will in my n and I think we'll be collaborating a lot over the next year of Wanda's efforts will be coordinating local sustainab efforts all around the globe. She'll need your feedback on wha working."

Marley and Brianne told their parents and made plans for leaving. In such a dark time in their lives, it felt so good to be moving on to something they were both excited about and to be moving on together. They felt they had learned a lot from their friends and their experience in Sleepy Valley, and they were excited about continuing the fight.

At the end of the summer, their famili planned a send-off
party up at the observatory. After saying oodbye to Doc, Max,
Wanda, Jim, the Alexanders, and th parents, Marley and
Brianne stepped up onto the deck o arley's newly modified
skateboard. Brianne put her arms a d him, and they leaned
forward together, accelerating dov l to speeds they had never
achieved before on this concrete tch of road. Everyone held
their breath as they watched th o.
halfway down the slope, the

After reaching critical ve l off the ground, with the help
board and passengers slowl y flew high above the town and
of a few pirated drone pa k, the effervescing lake, and their
saw what remained of t ey floor below them. They smiled,
homes, all laid out on ' caught the edges of the super ther-
waved warm goodby ed town. They rode it to the base of
mal high above the , turning north, set sail for cooler and
the stratosphere a
more proactive

CHAPTER TWENTY-FIVE

TWENTY YEARS LATER

O ne day, twenty years after the summer of The Changes, Marley was stooped over his workbench, tinkering with a new idea, when a message came across his communications implant. "What! That's impossible." He stood up straight and let his hands fall to his sides. He was surprised—in fact, shocked—to hear that the global monitoring network had found evidence of human life, living totally off the grid, back in his hometown of Sleepy Valley.

He scratched his head. *How could anyone live in any of the outlying areas? They were abandoned years ago due to their unlivable conditions.* Marley quickly messaged back that he would volunteer to go find out who was still living there; nobody knew that town better than he did.

When his trip was authorized moments later, he bounded around his shop, telling everybody about this discovery and his plans to revisit the town of his youth. That evening over a robot-created dinner, he told Brianne of his plans, hoping she would join him.

"How can that be?" she asked. "Who could still be living under those harsh conditions?"

"I don't know, but I've got to go back and check out our old neighborhood. It must be some crazy survivalist, a mutant, or an outlaw." He was so excited that he immediately started to plan the trip, trying to think of all the new hazards he would face in such an isolated location.

Marley was now the head of Marley Jones Skyboards, LLC, which produced zero-carbon vehicles. He also volunteered with his adopted town, trying to keep consumption in balance with what the Earth in their sector could produce. Living sustainably on a hotter planet was a much bigger problem than anyone had realized back before The Changes.

People no longer took clean air, water, food, and other natural resources for granted. They now understood the difference between needs and wants. It had been a hard adjustment for those who grew up in "the age of plenty."

Marley and Brianne lived together on the 34th Level, East Branch, 742nd Unit of the Great Banyan Tree Ark. Their living unit was above ground and in the shade of the UV protector/water collection canopy. The Ark provided all the water and nutrition needed for their mid-sized city.

In the Ark, offices, academic and research facilities, nano-mining operations, waste recycling, and manufacturing plants were all below ground in vast mycelia-like networks. Most people lived above ground in apartments selected by lottery which had ended most socio-economic tribalism and biases. Few people ever ventured away from the Ark to travel to outlying areas due to the unbearable heat, the pollution, and lack of essential services. It was too risky.

Automobiles had disappeared. They were so wasteful of Earth's limited resources, so polluting, and so 20th century. Now everyone was riding *personal mobility units,* including skyboards and bikeboards they were a lot more fun. Marley had been far ahead of the curve in designing and building his drone-skateboard, cross-over vehicles. He had continued to refine them over the intervening years, and now his firm was mass marketing them at such a low cost that everyone could afford one.

In his position Marley had the freedom to take a few days off, and he was excited about having the opportunity to visit Sleepy

Valley. Brianne, on the other hand, couldn't get away from her job making and marketing CarbonFitBits. He understood. He was proud of her work, it was important. She designed and created these arm straps so everyone could monitor the amount of carbon generated from each of their activities. Most people readily adjusted their behaviors once they realized how much carbon they were still using. "I'd love to go, but I can't get away," she told Marley. "I'm way too busy. Take good visuals and be careful. You never know what you'll find out there in those wilderness recovery zones."

It was a big deal to be able to visit one's original hometown. People rarely did. Marley was smiling as he suited up in an orange, protective suit for the trip. He then jumped on his latest model skyboard, exited through the secure, vapor-lock doors, and headed south in the direction of Sleepy Valley. As he accelerated up into the yellow skies above the Ark, Marley let out a primal yell; it felt like the good old days.

Marley knew that Sleepy Valley and thousands of other towns had been left alone so nature could clean up the mess humans had caused. It was projected to be a slow process, at least by human standards. He was looking forward to seeing how life had recovered since he had left the valley.

As the town came into view, Marley quickly recognized the hill and valley, the river and lake. But everything else had changed. It had metamorphosed from a busy and populated town into an empty valley with surface features reflective of past human settlement. Flying over the remains of his old town made him feel a little queasy and brought up images from his old history books of Easter Island, Persepolis, and the Aztec empire— other civilizations, abandoned after the destruction of the local environment.

Marley caught a thermal and flew slowly over the land, looking for signs of life. *What were the global monitors referring to when they reported signs of human activity?* He saw the area replanted by Max and the healthy new trees reaching for the skies. He also noticed that invasive flora had engulfed many of the ravines in the moister parts of town.

The flat, dry, windswept farmland had reverted to desert-like conditions and was covered with sand dunes. Much of the man-made parts of the valley had collapsed and been erased. Even the observatory was in ruins and covered with kudzu. It was sad to see that large parts of the park and town had burned. The only remaining billboard was a faded, sand-blasted, and graffi-ti-covered picture of Mr. Folly greeting people to Sleepy Valley: "Welcome back to the good old days."

Marley was perplexed—there was no evidence of recent human activity. Just an eerie stillness that had settled on the land. But he didn't want to leave without figuring out what the reports were referring to. Then, as he took one last flight over the East Side, he saw subtle movements down by the lake. At first he thought it was some large, mutant, drab-green, snapping turtle inching its way toward the lake. There had been numer-ous sightings of mutants all around the globe. They were nature's attempt to find new lifeforms better suited for the warmer climate.

Marley zoomed in close to get a better look. As he watched it crawl, he realized it was not a lifeform but a badly weath-ered, vintage Humvee, still moving after all these years. A big grin came across his face. *Of course.* As Marley brought his sky-board to a smooth stop by the side of the lake, a wizened old Sam Perkins stretched his long neck and bald head out the window and growled, "Get the hell out of my way."

Taken aback at the rude greeting from his old nemesis, Marley looked at him for a moment and then asked, "How are you, Sam? It's been a long time."

"Yep. It sure has been, but not long enough. You newcomers sure made a mess of this town. I'm glad you left." Sam retracted his head back inside the protective shell of the Hummer.

Ignoring the illogic of Sam's thinking, Marley went on with his questions, "So what are you up to these days? I see you've kept the old Hummer operating. That's amazing. How have you been able to live here by yourself all these years?"

Slowly, stretching his neck back out the window, Sam snapped, "Well, if you must know, it's become unbearable. In fact you arrived on my last day on the old homestead."

Surprised by the serendipity of the timing of his visit, Marley asked, "So where are you off to?"

"It's none of your damn business," Sam growled. Then after a few moments, he admitted, "I don't mind saying that I'm going back to the good old days."

Marley squinted at him. "Your father always talked about the good old days. But I don't get it. Where are you going?"

"To the place where we all came from eons ago. Back to the days when our ancestors were amphibious."

"What are you talking about?"

"I'm moving back into the lake."

Marley couldn't believe what he was hearing.

Sam continued, "I've had to adapt. When there were no more diesel service stations around, I converted the Hummer to run on methane—there's plenty of that. I've also had to figure out how to get clean air to breathe. Look at the sides of the Hummer. See the gills I've added?"

Marley was intrigued. He walked around the converted vehicle. Sure enough, the Hummer did seem to have sprouted gills. Marley smiled. Being a tinkerer himself, he could appreciate what Sam had done. "How do they work?"

Sam sat up in his seat and spoke with pride. "The gills extract air from the lake water and separate the methane, leaving fairly clean air. The Humvee uses the methane to run the engine, and I breathe what's left. It's good air—better than what we're breathing standing here." Sam coughed.

"Sounds to me like you're evolving, Sam, along with the Hummer, into some new species. What are you planning to eat?"

"The Hummer has a digester to convert algae to food. The lake's still full of algae. I'm all set, forever. I certainly won't need to depend on anyone else.

"Well, time's up. I'm out of here. So long, SkyBoy." With that, Sam retracted his head and rolled up the window, sealing himself within his new world. The Humvee inched toward the lake. Within minutes it had submerged beneath the foam. Marley stood there, mesmerized, as he watched Sam disappear, shell and all. He looked around. All was quiet. Nothing stirred. He realized he was now all by himself. A permanent sleep had finally settled on what was once the town of Sleepy Valley.

∗ ∗ ∗

When Marley returned from his mission, he sat down with Brianne in their flat and described what he had seen. He knew that she would want to hear the news from home. "You won't believe how much Sleepy Valley's changed. Everything's fallen down and is buried by kudzu. The park looks completely different, and there're no people especially now that Sam's submerged himself beneath the foam of the lake. It's hard to recognize." He waved his arms as he described flying over the town and mimicked his surprise at discovering the Hummer.

"Do you think we could go back there to live someday? It's been a dream of mine ever since we left," Brianne said.

"No way. It'll take a hundred years to recover. And then only if the climate reverts back to the way it was. That's not going to happen. It's just not the nice green community we remember."

"Wow. That sure puts our life here into perspective."

"Yeah, life has changed. We're much better off living here under the current harsh climate," Marley said, sitting back in his chair and reflecting on the trip. "The town of Sleepy Valley, as we knew it, is gone. Just like thousands of other small towns all around the globe. I keep thinking of all the people who didn't leave their towns, who didn't survive."

Brianne grimaced. "We were lucky to find a town where we were taken in and supported."

Marley got up to get them both a cold drink, and when he returned he commented, "The Big Melt could have gone either way. Instead of a wake-up call, it could have been the end for all of us. I just wish we could find some way to cool the planet down to the way it was and make the whole country productive and habitable again."

"We just have to keep working at reducing our use of carbon. It's not that easy to reverse a climate trend once it passes a tipping point. But we're making progress," Brianne assured him.

Marley agreed. "You're right, Brianne . . . I just miss the freedom we had as kids when we could run around *outside* whenever we had free time."

"Me too," Brianne agreed. "I wish we had gotten involved in the fight earlier. Just think if we could have stopped The Warming before it reached the tipping point."

"Yeah, I know. I keep wishing we had. But like everyone else, we were numb to the news. It took a catastrophe to motivate us."

"Our losing efforts in Sleepy Valley certainly inspired us to get more involved once we moved here," Brianne said. "I can still feel the excitement of those early days of getting the message out and organizing people to take action. It was the first time we found something to be passionate about."

"We were also lucky to be surrounded by great people—both in Sleepy Valley and here," Marley added. "Working with Doc, Jim, Wanda, Max, and Joe was great. They played big roles in getting us and everyone else to act."

"Yeah, it was an amazing group of people." Brianne then looked quizzically at Marley. "You included someone named Joe. Who was that? I've never heard you mention him before."

"Ahhhhhh . . ." Marley took a minute to respond. How could he have let his great secret slip out after protecting it all this time? But then again, was any of it real?

It's been years since I've heard from Joe. In fact, it's all a bit hazy now, that whole business with microbes talking to me and me alone. It's crazy. I have no proof that Joe ever existed. Was it just an adolescent thing, an inner voice that helped me learn to find my own voice? He wasn't so sure anymore—he had never been sure—but Brianne was looking at him, waiting for an answer.

All of a sudden Marley's skin started to itch, his gut started to rumble, he burped, and of course it all became quite clear again. "Joe? Oh, yes. He was one of the key guys behind the scenes. You never had the chance to meet him. He was the one who convinced us of the importance of getting *everyone* to work together. We owe him and all his colleagues a lot. We couldn't have done it without them."

Brianne looked at Marley again, obviously wondering why she had never heard of Joe before. Marley simply smiled.

THE END

AFTERWORD

T he topics raised in this book are large and complex. As a result, many people don't think their actions will make any difference. Let me assure you there is nothing farther from the truth. People all around the world are taking actions and creating new technologies and services that will have a significant impact on slowing the warming. Just remember Margaret Mead's quote *"Never doubt that a small group of thoughtful, committed citizens can change the world; indeed, it's the only thing that ever has."*

I encourage all of you to make your own list of actions and champion them to your family and friends, the businesses where you work, and to your elected officials. If you need more ideas than were presented here in this story, pick up a copy of Paul Hawken's book, Drawdown. There are many ways each of us can make a difference.

TEN STEPS FOR A COOLER CLIMATE

1. Reduce energy usage: insulate, drive less, use hybrids & electric vehicles, unplug

2. Switch electricity supplier to 100% solar or wind

3. Buy only the most sustainable products to incentivize businesses to make more of them

4. Plant native trees and shrubs to clean our air & water and cool things down

5. Support local and national environmental non-profits

6. Reduce meat consumption and food waste

7. Encourage businesses and governments to support solar and wind energy development

8. Encourage energy-efficiency upgrades in all buildings and vehicles

9. Support the expansion of interconnected green infrastructure networks

10. Implement a national "carbon cap and dividend" policy or a "carbon tax" to pay for the real and hidden costs to society of using dirty fuels

DISCUSSION GUIDE

1. What was real and what was surreal in this book?

2. Who were your favorite characters? Why?

3. What challenges did Marley and Brianne face and how did they respond to each of them?

4. Why did Marley seek out help in addressing the challenges? Why did he pick the people he did to help him answer his questions? Who would you go to in order to answer questions on this topic?

5. Why do you think there were different views about what the town should do? Which ones made sense to you?

6. Why was Marley so reluctant to get involved in the political process? What changed his mind?

7. Why didn't the members of the council listen to the citizens? What would you have done? Why?

8. What was the turning point for Marley and Brianne when they decided to leave the town? What would you have done? Why?

9. Do you think fiction can inspire us to act? Did this book inspire you? How?

10. Is climate change a First World or Third World problem, or both? Why?

11. Okay, the climate's changing. What do we do now?

ABOUT THE AUTHOR

The outdoors has always played a major role in Ned Tillman's life. As an earth and environmental scientist, he has traveled and worked in many countries and explored a wide range of habitats. He has served on health, scientific, education, sustainability, and environmental boards and advisory panels. As a result of these experiences, he has gained a broad perspective on the challenges that we face today on a planet with a rapidly changing climate.

Ned gives talks and writes books to inspire all of us to become more engaged in solving our climate challenges and preserving the wonders of our current climate for generations to come.

Ned Tillman is the author of two award-winning books, *The Chesapeake Watershed* and *Saving the Places We Love.*